Praise for the nove...

"*Little Secrets* is both twisty and ... ...ecrets simmering in a dying town. Snoekstra writes an original tale that is mysterious and dark but also touching and true."
—Janelle Brown, *New York Times* bestselling author of *Watch Me Disappear*

"A smart and compulsive psychological thriller with an original, engaging, and ultimately surprising protagonist. I couldn't put it down!"
—Graeme Simsion, *New York Times* bestselling author of *The Rosie Project*, on *Little Secrets*

"Twisty, slippery, and full of surprises, this web of lies will ensnare you and keep you riveted until you've turned the final page."
—Lisa Unger, *New York Times* bestselling author of *Ink and Bone*, on *Little Secrets*

"Snoekstra's excellent debut stands out in the crowded psychological suspense field with smart, subtle red herrings and plenty of dark and violent secrets."
—*Library Journal*, starred review, on *Only Daughter*

"Truly distinctive and tautly told, *Only Daughter* welcomes a thrilling new voice in crime fiction."
—Mary Kubica, *New York Times* bestselling author of *The Good Girl*

"Unreliable narrator thrillers are practically a subgenre of their own, and there are two unreliable narrators here as well as a wickedly twisted and fast-paced plot that leaves numerous questions unanswered… Readers who enjoy a creepy thriller that will keep them guessing will be unable to put this down."
—*Booklist*, starred review, on *Only Daughter*

"A must-read for fans of Lisa Gardner and Gilly Macmillan, and is sure to be enjoyed by most mystery lovers."
—*BookPage* on *Only Daughter*

"A suspenseful, multi-layered puzzle, and the characters are complex and emotionally damaged, making this dark and twisted tale a veritable page-turner."
—*RT Book Reviews* on *Only Daughter*

Also by Anna Snoekstra

Little Secrets
Only Daughter

THE
SPITE
GAME

ANNA SNOEKSTRA

▸ mira

ISBN-13: 978-0-7783-6996-7

The Spite Game

Copyright © 2018 by Anna Elizabeth Snoekstra

For questions and comments about the quality of this book, please contact us at
CustomerService@Harlequin.com.

BookClubbish.com

Printed in U.S.A.

For Joan Robyn Bruce.

THE
SPITE
GAME

PROLOGUE

2018

I know what you'll want. My confession. Plain and simple, just the facts. That isn't how this is going to work. If you want me to confess, then you'll have to listen to the whole thing. My story. I need you to understand what has led me here to this small concrete interview room, waiting for you to come and take my statement. This isn't where I thought I'd end up.

First, I want to tell you about what I was like before any of it started, back when I was just a normal seventeen-year-old girl. If such a thing is even possible. I'm going to tell you about that regular Sunday night at home with my mum and my sister.

I think of it as regular, because the details have blurred with time. They have lost their sharpness in contrast to all that came after. At the time though, there were things that stood out from the mundane. Like my mother's eyes. She had done a double shift at the hospital, and they were redder than usual. Being a nurse she was used to death, we knew that, so it must have been something particularly bad for her to cry by herself in the car before coming inside.

My sister, Beatrice, made her a cup of tea. I put on the radio and we told her we would make dinner. Standing in our small kitchen, Bea sautéed the garlic and I deseeded a red chili. It was a hot night, really hot. That was irregular too. It was early

March 2008. The heat had usually blown out of Melbourne by March, our shorts and summer dresses long packed away. But the heat had lingered that year. I wasn't wearing shoes and the cracked kitchen tiles were rough under the soles of my bare feet. We had the windows open, letting the sizzling smell of the curry we were making spill out into the street.

We ate dinner and Mum cheered up. I remember wondering how she did that. How she managed to draw a line between home and work, how she could hold someone's hand as they screamed in pain and then come home and eat curry and laugh.

After dinner, we watched the news. Mum in her armchair, Bea and I sharing the couch. She had her bare feet up on my lap, and every so often I'd push them off, but they'd always find their way back there. I wasn't really watching the news anchor on the television drone on about the Global Financial Crisis. I was thinking back over the day. It was only a few weeks into year twelve then. Everyone had come back from the summer with stories of holiday romances and new tans. Not me. Already, at school I was like a shadow. Always watching, listening, but never quite part of anything. There were three girls in particular that I watched, and I often spent my evenings wondering what they were doing.

Later, in our bedroom, Bea fell asleep before I did. She was two years older than me, but ever since she'd been diagnosed with epilepsy, I was always checking on her. Lying in the dark, I listened to the sound of next door's television. We lived in a terrace house in the inner city suburb of Clifton Hill. The walls were like paper and you could hear everything. That was normal; I was used to the constant hum of noise. Rolling onto my side to turn off the reading light, I stared at the reassuring line of Bea's body under the sheet and easily fell asleep.

When I woke, it was very quiet. The neighbor's television was off. I couldn't see Bea anymore. There was something in the way. Tilting my face on my pillow, I looked up at a shadow of a man. He was standing over my single bed. The streetlight shone through the open window, lighting up his face. He was staring down at me, a baseball bat in his hand. We locked eyes for a moment before I began to scream.

You won't want to hear all this. It's getting late. You might have someone to go home to, a husband or a wife maybe. You'll just want to cut straight to the facts. You'll want to know where she is. The missing woman. Melissa Moore. Mel. You'll want to know where she has gone and whether I had something to do with it. Of course I did. We both know that already. That's why I'm here.

Part 1

LACK OF EMPATHY

2008

1

It began in the change room. The bodies of sweaty adolescent girls, the steam of the showers and the intensity of emotions gave the room a living pulse. The bad thing inside me took root there. Like mold, it grew in that hot, moist place.

The change room always stank of sweat and strawberry body spray. I slipped my T-shirt over my head, and then slid my sport top off from underneath. Ignoring the squeaks of rubber soles against the wet floors and the cackles and chides of the girls around me, I tried to tune my ears into the conversation going on in the corner. I only caught snippets.

"…so filthy."

"…bet her bush was poking out the sides and…"

"…pervert…really, Mel…"

I sneaked a glance. Cass and Saanvi leaned against the wall, decked out in their oversize Doc Marten boots, undersized flannel dresses and thick black stockings. Mel reclined in the corner in just her boots, bra and underwear, braiding a piece of her hair.

Other girls begun disbanding.

"See you later!"

"See you in English."

"Bye."

I could hear them clearly now. Cass's soft voice: "She kept

trying to demonstrate how to do a jump serve right in front of my face."

"That's disgusting."

"Come on, it's almost showtime." Saanvi threw Mel her dress. She tucked the braid behind her ear and pulled it on.

They whispered something I couldn't hear, and laughed, their eyes darting around the change room. I look around too. Almost everyone had gone. The only girl left aside from us was Miranda. She fumbled with something in her bag, her wide back to us. Really, she was just waiting to get changed. There was no way she would risk exposing the rolls of fat on her stomach if anyone else was there, not after what happened last time.

Throwing my PE clothes into my backpack, I walked out of the change room before they noticed me. In high school, eavesdropping was a cardinal sin. Out on the oval, the sun glinted off the wet grass. It must have rained. Summer was long gone; it had been three months since I'd woken to the man standing over my bed. He had run off when I screamed, back through the living room window. The frame had been rotted ever since we moved in, and like most of the other windows in our house, the lock didn't work. Mum had been on at the landlords for years to fix those locks. It was the last straw. We were moving in a couple weeks. At home, most of my clothes were packed into boxes.

Not that it mattered. I wore the same thin gray hooded jacket every day. I'd pull the sleeves down over my hands and constantly fiddle with the drawstrings. I washed my hair every day and didn't think to use any product, so I always looked a bit fluffy, like a newborn chicken. Skirts or shorts were out of the equation because I still hadn't quite mastered shaving my legs. Somehow I would always both nick myself and miss bits, so my calves were a mix of tiny cuts around the ankles and sparse, furry patches down the back.

What I want to explain to you is that Mel, Cass and Saanvi

were in a different league to me. It wasn't a popularity thing. They weren't the queen bees of the school or anything like that, although compared to me they may as well have been. No, it wasn't popularity that I craved. There was something luminescent about the three of them. They were the sort of teenage girls who knew their power and potential. I had no idea what I was doing and was painfully aware of it. Just watching them—and daydreaming of the kind of girl I could be if I was their friend—that was as close as I ever thought I'd get.

I'd paused, only for a moment, to smell the wet grass and zip up my hoodie, when a hand gripped my arm.

"If anyone comes in, you stop them, okay, Ava?" Saanvi was beside me, talking in a loud whisper. I could smell something sugary on her hot breath.

"What?" This was the first time she'd ever spoken to me.

"Don't let anyone in!" she hissed, then, "Idiot!" as she turned back into the change room.

I hovered in the doorway. A few stragglers skittered toward the gym, but no one even looked up. A tiny smile tugged at my lips. She knew my name, which meant Mel and Cass probably did too. Maybe I wasn't as invisible as I always felt. She'd called me an idiot, but somehow that didn't bother me. I'd prefer to be an idiot than no one.

It was silent behind me, and my view was obscured by a row of lockers. I had no idea what I'd do if anyone tried to get past me, or what they were doing that was so secret that no one could see. I took a quiet step back to look behind the lockers. Inside the change room, Mel, Cass and Saanvi were hiding in one of the showers, all squashed together and covering their mouths with their hands to stop from laughing. Miranda was still in her spot in the farthest corner; she couldn't see them from there. She thought everyone had left. Her top came off over her head, revealing her pale doughy torso.

She looked up, as though she could feel that someone was

watching her. I ducked back out of view to the doorway, worried she might catch me looking.

Still, no one was around. No one to challenge me or try to squeeze past. I was going to be late to math class. I didn't really want to be a part of whatever they were about to do, but also I didn't want them thinking that I was too much of a scaredy-cat to stick it out. The indecision made me freeze, hovering with one foot forward.

The idea of going back in and stopping it didn't even occur to me.

A scream echoed its way toward me. It was followed by a chorus of shrieking laughter. I couldn't help turning back again, although a big part of me really didn't want to see. Cass and Saanvi were throwing wet-looking gray lumps at Miranda, who was desperately trying to cover her body. Mel had her hand over her mouth in shock, but underneath her hand I could see a smile.

One of the lumps splattered a few meters away from me. It was a piece of mashed-up Chiko Roll, the meat and bits of carrot shiny with oil.

"Oink! Oink! Oink!" chanted Saanvi and Cass.

"Stop it, guys!" Mel protested, a laugh in her voice.

The three girls ran toward me. Mel grabbed my arm.

"Come on!"

I took one look back at Miranda, cowering and smeared with mashed-up meat, before I was pulled away with them.

Cass and Saanvi exploded with laughter as we ran toward the main school.

"That was so mean!" said Mel.

"Fuck off," Saanvi said, "you loved it!"

We stopped at the doors to catch our breath.

"You won't tell, will you?" Cass fixed her big eyes on me.

"Of course she won't!" Mel let go of my arm and grinned at me.

I shook my head.

"Nah, I won't say anything."

"Better not." Saanvi flung her bag over her shoulder and the three of them walked away.

"See ya!" Mel called back, looking over her shoulder at me.

I knew what I had to do, but I waited for there to be a few meters between us. Then, I jogged back toward the gym. My stomach was knotting with guilt.

When I reached the entrance to the girl's change room, I hesitated. My face was hot from running, and my ears cold. Slowly, I stepped inside, already fidgeting with the drawstring of my hoodie. With the fresh air in my nostrils, the stink of stale sweat and meat was revolting.

For a second I thought that maybe she'd gone. But no. One of the showers was running, and, just faintly, I could hear the sound of crying. I stood in the middle of the change room, frozen. Should I knock, ask if she was okay? Or would that just humiliate her more? The image popped in my head again, of her naked flesh smeared with oily meat and chunks of vegetables. I turned and walked back out toward my math class. I told myself it was the nicest thing to do, but deep down I knew that wasn't it. I knew that I wasn't giving her privacy because I pitied her.

Deep down, I was disgusted by her weakness. Deep down, I didn't even care, and that scared me.

2

"Do you want a glass of water or anything?"

The cop from the front desk is standing in the doorway of the interview room, staring at me. Behind him, it's bright. I can see the bustling station, police in uniform bent over desks or answering phones, detectives in suits walking swiftly, their backs stiff with self-importance. Not like in here, with its dull fluorescent lights and one small window.

When he'd led me through that office, one of the police-women had looked up from her paperwork. She'd given me what seemed to be a reassuring smile. I'd gaped at her. It took a second to click. She'd clocked my small frame. My thick-lashed eyes. She thought I was a victim. It was almost funny.

"I'm okay. Do you know how long the detective will be?"

He shrugs. "Hard to say. Today has been nonstop."

Is this a ploy? I don't understand. Have you sent him in here to sound me out? Or maybe he's offering me water in the hope of getting my DNA off the glass? I've seen them doing things like that before in cop shows. I thought it was just an overused trope by lazy disenchanted screenwriters, but now I wonder if it's something that really happens.

"Sure you don't want anything? I'm sure I could scrounge up a tea bag from somewhere. There's coffee too, if you're game."

The guy is probably only a year or so older than me. He's being pleasant enough, but I want him to go. I don't want to play these games. It doesn't have to be complicated. I want to talk. I want to explain it all, to make you understand. I've been weak before. That time in the change room with Miranda, I was spineless. Not being liked seemed as though it would be the worst thing in the world.

For once in my life I want to do the right thing.

"I'm fine," I tell the cop, and he shrugs again.

I could still run. I could push past him, say I got mixed up. Made a mistake. That I don't know anything about Mel. That I have no idea where she is. I could give in to that weakness one last time.

"Well, thanks for your patience," he's saying now.

All I can do is look past him at the light as he gives me one last lukewarm smile and pulls the door closed. The light and sounds of the station are snuffed out. I'm alone again in the gloom.

Twisting in my chair, I stare up at the window. The sky is a pale blue. I watch the gray clouds inch across it. Time feels meaningless in here.

I'm in the right place. I'm sure of it. As hard as this is going to be it's got to be easier than the last few weeks have been. I haven't been able to eat. I've had nightmares every night. My skin is turning gray. I look pinched.

Still, I should have said something when I left this morning. That's my only regret. I'd said I was going to a meeting with the contractors. That it might run late. I didn't want to lie; I've told more lies than truths in the last ten years and I wanted today to be the end of all that. But I couldn't say that I was coming here. If I had, I would have had to explain why. What happened. I only have it in me to tell this story once.

I'd started to feel carsick by the time we got there. We'd been driving through solid bushland for more than an hour before we reached those big ugly gates from the brochure. Lakeside Estate was written in block letters on the wall next to them.

"Beautiful," I said.

"It is," my mum said.

"She's being sarcastic," Bea told her.

"I can tell."

The wall went farther than I could see. All the way around the estate and back to here. Locking us in. My mum pressed the intercom and told them our surname. Only the sound of static replied to her. She keyed in a code and there was a loud buzz. We drove inside.

I don't know what I had been expecting, but it sure wasn't this. I'd realized then why my mum had gotten the house so cheap. The gated community wasn't even complete yet. As we drove up the hill she told us that the company had gone bankrupt, which had put a halt on the building. She said it would be finished; they just didn't know when.

Even though the sun was out, it was cold outside. It bounced off the concrete, making us all squint. The hollow convenience store looked as though it was the first to be built; it stood beside the skeletons of a primary school and community center. We drove past a deep brown basin. I guessed that was meant to be the lake. A group of crows scavenged at the overturned soil.

"Paradise," I said.

"Not helpful," said my mum.

I looked back in time to see the gates shut and lock behind us.

As we got farther up the hill, the houses started to look more completed. There must have been at least a few other people living here, but I didn't see anyone. There weren't even any other cars around.

Inside, our new house was empty. Just freshly painted white walls and cream carpet that smelled of plastic. I followed Bea up the stairs.

"My room!" she called. I walked hesitantly past it to the next door. Opening the door, I could see my new room was a small white box. Claustrophobic, even without furniture. The sun shone through the blinds, casting strange black shadows across the room, like bars.

"Girls, come and help me with the boxes!" my mum yelled from downstairs.

Later, while my mum cooked dinner, Bea and I tried to put together her bed. It felt strange to have separate rooms.

"Are you going to miss me at night?" I asked.

"Yeah, sure," she said, struggling to turn an Allen key. "You know, finally I have a place I can bring boys back to and now we are in the middle of nowhere!"

"What boys?" She'd broken up with her boyfriend six months ago.

"I dunno," she said, "just hypothetical boys."

"I'm sure you can find some sexy locals."

"Yeah, right."

"Where does this bit go?" I held up a long piece of wood.

She sighed and put the Allen key down. "I have no idea."

I looked up at the window. "Hey, look," I said, "there are lights on."

She stood up and leaned against the window frame, out into the estate.

"I'll just sleep on the mattress tonight. I can't be bothered to finish this right now."

I got up to stand next to her. Three of the houses glowed in the blackness. I rested my head on her shoulder.

"It'll be fine," I said.

"You're the little sister. I'm meant to say that to you."

"Go on, then."

She put her arm around me and I breathed in her comforting Beatrice smell, but she didn't say anything.

3

At 5:30 a.m., my alarm went off. I lay there, staring into the abyss of black in front of me. My body started to fall through the mattress and I shook myself awake again. Every part of me was begging to go back to sleep.

Outside, the air smelled light and wet. It was still dark. Closing the door quietly behind me I walked down through the estate, treading lightly, trying not to make a sound. They hadn't even put in the streetlamps yet. The black was thick and rich around me. In this darkness, anything could happen. Someone could be watching me from just a few meters away and I wouldn't have known it. I knew I had to stop thinking like that. This was a safe place—that's why we were here.

I walked for a full ten minutes before I could even see the gates. They were open by just an inch; you wouldn't notice from a distance. Someone had escaped. Or someone had gotten in.

Waiting on the side of the road at the bus stop, I resisted the urge to look behind me at the trees. It was too dark to see much, but I knew that the woods there were deep and impenetrable. Rows and rows of thin white trunks. I'd seen so many horror films about people being murdered in woods like that. Of running forever but always being caught eventually. I kept my back to it.

Staring at my feet, I felt like a sitting duck out there in the

dark. I prayed that no cars would come by. We'd learned about
Ivan Milat at school, the way he picked up hitchhikers from the
side of the road and the next people knew of them was when
their bones were tripped over in the bush. By the time the bus
arrived, I was shaking. My fingers were numb and pink.

The bus driver nodded hello as I boarded. There was only
one other passenger, a man in a crumpled suit asleep in the back
row. The heater hummed softly. I took off my coat and leaned
against the window, letting the heat and vibrations of the bus
calm me. My mum had wanted me to change schools; she said
it was too far to travel every day. I would have considered it,
if it hadn't been for what had happened in the change room. If
Mel and Cass and Saanvi hadn't started saying hi to me in the
corridor. I was so close.

I should have felt triumphant for making it onto the bus, but
my mind was too tired to even think in the warm, dark silence.
The wheels revolved, pulling me back to where I belonged.

The bush turned to suburbs as the sun rose. When we
reached the city, the bus was full.

"Have you ever heard of dream hypnosis?"

"Nah, what's that?"

"I'll show you."

The sound of snickering and then the warmth of breath on
my ear. I knew who it was. Theodore. I always found him annoying and kind of smug. He was always loud in class, even
though he had nothing funny to say. He thought he was better looking than he really was, and was always finding an excuse to display his pierced nipple just so he could pull up his
T-shirt and show everyone his unimpressive abs. I was fairly
sure Mel had a crush on him though, she always laughed at
everything he said.

"You are a big, sexy monkey." A tiny flick of his spit hit
my ear. "When you wake up you will strip off your clothes."

"You wish," I said, forcing my sleep-sticky eyes open. Theodore pulled away.

"You're so mean, Theo," Mel said, slapping his shoulder playfully.

Science class. I always sat at the workbench behind Mel and Theodore's. Usually they didn't talk to me.

"Why so tired?" Theodore eyed me. "Up partying all night?"

"We moved house." I rubbed my eyes and attempted to look like I wasn't thrilled to have a reason to speak to them. "It's, like, two hours away."

"Why'd you do that?" asked Mel.

They were both looking at me, not even bothering to pretend they were doing the experiment, whatever it was. I didn't want to tell them about the break-in. Instead I dropped my gaze like I often did back then when too many people were looking at me, and talked toward their chests.

"We've been renting for ages, and they were selling these houses really cheap. My mum thought it was a good opportunity." I rolled my eyes. "I didn't want to go to some redneck school out in Doreen though."

Mel smiled at me, one eyebrow slightly raised, then turned back to her bench.

I half tried to figure out what the class had been about, but the fatigue was turning to dizziness so I just stared dumbly ahead. My mum kept telling me I needed to focus; it was year twelve so my marks actually mattered. The idea of life after high school seemed incomprehensibly distant. I had more important things to worry about.

At lunch, Ashleigh and Ling always talked incessantly about university. Ashleigh was passionate about statistics and Ling was committed to genetic engineering. They were both 100 percent certain that this was what their lives would be.

The only thing I was certain about was having no idea at all what I was doing.

"I don't know. I mean, do people who are hiring really look at your transcripts? I think the more cred the uni has the better you look, even if you only pass," Ashleigh was saying.

"As if you'd only pass anywhere though!" Ling assured her.

"Good point. But I want to do a course that offers the specific units that I want to focus on."

It went on and on like that. We sat where we did every day at lunch: on the pavement against the wall to the library, rather than on the oval like most of the other groups did. I leaned my back against the bricks and stared out at where Mel, Cass and Saanvi sat. Mel in the middle, Saanvi leaning on her shoulder looking at her phone. Cass was lying on Mel's legs, drawing something on her thigh. I watched as Mel giggled at the feeling of it. There was something about them that seemed so free.

I knew I should feel bad about how much I was wishing to be over with them rather than where I was. The truth was that I was already feeling a shift with Ashleigh and Ling. It wasn't like it used to be. I'd been friends with them both since year seven. In that first week of high school, sitting with them had felt natural. It's strange how that happened, how you have that first week to find your tribe and then that's where you're stuck for the next six years.

We didn't bother much with clothes, were good at schoolwork and too embarrassed to even talk to boys. As far as the social strata went, we were barely in the equation. We were cooler than the kids with chronic acne who played cards in the back of the library, but not by much.

But now things felt different. Ashleigh and Ling had started spending more time together just the two of them and I didn't even care. Ever since what had happened with Miranda, I'd been changing. I'd gone to a secondhand shop and spent hours replacing my wardrobe. I bought some tight black jeans and got rid of my faded blue ones. I found some T-shirts with pictures of bands I'd never even heard of, which must have meant they were cool. The absolute prize were the black Doc Martens that I found, the leather so cracked that they were no longer waterproof. Altogether, I looked different, more like them. Although I hadn't abandoned the hoodie and my hair was still fluffy, inside I felt ready. I wanted to see the true potential of my life, to have fun and get drunk and kiss boys and skip school. I wanted to see what I was capable of. I was just waiting for my in.

When I finally got home I collapsed into bed. It felt like the longest day I'd ever lived. Outside, the sun was already starting to set. Part of me wanted to go and open the window. The plastic smell in my room was even worse than yesterday. But I was too tired. The idea of even sitting seemed impossible.

"How was school?" Bea called through the wall.

I groaned in response. I heard Bea slide off her bed and come out of her room and into mine. She lay down with her stomach across my legs, and propped her head up on her hand.

"Did you talk to them today?" she asked.

I smiled.

"That's a yes," she said. "I swear, you should just go sit down with them. They obviously think you're cool."

"It's not that easy," I said. "I try to talk to them all the time but they aren't interested."

Bea just rolled her eyes. She had never had trouble in high school. She started unlacing my Doc Martens.

"What do your little nerdy friends think of these?"

"They didn't mention them," I said, stretching out my toes as she pulled each shoe off.

Bea scooted up so she was lying next to me, sharing my pillow.

"It's really boring here, Ava."

"I know."

"No, you don't. It's so quiet, and the other people who live here are really strange. I saw an old lady check her mail in her underwear earlier. It was the most excitement I've had all day. At least you have someplace to go."

"Yeah, school!"

"I'd take school right now."

Bea had decided to take a gap year to figure out what she wanted to do with her life. I don't think she'd planned on spending it in Doreen. I watched her profile as she stared at the ceiling, a crease between her eyebrows. The sinking sun made her skin glow. She was so pretty. I hoped I looked like her.

"I need to get a job, but there's nothing here."

"Are you pissed at Mum?" I asked. When our mother had told us about this place she'd called it a "thriving community."

"A bit," she said. Then she turned to me and smiled. "I think she feels guilty. Guess what she said?"

"What?"

"Now that we have so much more space she said maybe we could get a dog."

"A beagle?"

"No way! A Staffy."

"Nah, a poodle. One of those giant black awkward-looking ones."

"What about a Boston terrier? They're so cute!"

"Or a mix of them! What are they called?"

"I think it's called a Bossi-Poo," Bea said, totally straight-faced.

"No!"

"Yeah, I think so."

I rolled on my back and started to laugh. All the tiredness and the seriousness of the day dissolving into giggles. "A Bossi-Poo?"

"Yeah, that's what they're called," she said, but she was smiling too.

"You're a bossy poo," I said.

"You are!" she squealed, and started sniggering too, and it was just like when she was nine and I was seven and *poo* was the dirtiest word we knew.

4

This probably won't be what you expected. Teenage girls, crushes, pet puppies. They're probably not the things you usually hear about in this room. I'm going to get to the point, I promise.

It's cold in here, and I can hear rain against the high square window. Outside, the sky is beginning to darken. It's faded from pale blue to gray. I wonder if you're out there already, looking at me through the glass. Are you looking at the wool jacket I have pulled tight around me, wondering if it's an imitation or real deal designer? It's real. Although, you probably aren't the kind of person to notice that sort of thing.

I imagine you with a beer gut, a crumpled suit, nice at first but harsh when you need to be. If that's the case you're more likely outside, looking at my car. You'd be inspecting the expensive finish, the plush leather seats, trying to figure out how someone like me could be involved in all of this.

Or is it the waiting that is the whole point? You want me to fall apart.

If that's the case, you don't need to wait. This is what I'm here to tell you: I fell apart a long time ago.

My media class was in the same corridor as Mel's drama class. We had PE together right after. The bell had already rung but I was having trouble moving quickly. It was day two of my long commute to school and I felt even worse than I had yesterday. Even putting my books back in my backpack felt like too much of an effort.

There was barely anyone in the corridor when I left. Just a guy leaning against a locker trying to chat up a girl as she pushed her books inside. I couldn't hear what they were saying, just the rumble of the bass of his voice and her vapid giggles. When I walked passed the drama room I looked in. I always looked in. Just to see if Mel had already left or not. I knew I was late, so I didn't expect to see her in there that day, but I looked inside anyway. Habit. As I walked past I saw a flash of something that seemed so wrong I kept walking before I realized what I'd just seen.

Taking a step back I looked again into the small window in the classroom door. Mel was standing at one of the desks. The drama teacher, Mr. Bitto, was standing behind her. Something wasn't right. He was too close to her, whispering something in her ear, but it wasn't just that. It was the look on her face. She looked scared.

Then I saw his hand. It slowly snaked around her body and gripped onto her left breast.

My instinct was to hesitate, do nothing, just watch, but then I thought of what had happened with Miranda. I had the power to stop this. I pushed the door open.

"We're going to be late for PE, Mel," I said.

Mr. Bitto jumped away from her. Mel looked between him and me, and then grabbed her bag and ran past me out the door.

I couldn't move. All I could do was stare at Mr. Bitto. I'd always liked him. He had fine features and a soft voice. He always seemed so nice. Like a teacher who remembered what it was like to be young. I stayed in the doorway, staring at him, wanting him to explain it.

"Off you go, then. Don't be late," he said, like nothing had happened, but his face was all sweaty.

I was fuming all through PE. I kicked the soccer ball harder than I ever had and it felt good. In the change room, I waited until everyone had left, then I went to talk to them. They'd been hovering in the corner all through the match, not even bothering to pretend to play. I had seen them looking over at me a few times.

"Are you okay?" I asked Mel.

She was sitting in the corner of the bench, her arms around her knees. Cass and Saanvi were standing in front of her, like a shield.

"Yeah," she said, not looking at me, "thanks."

"I just can't believe it."

Mel didn't look up as Saanvi and Cass folded back in around her. It was time for me to go. I'd said the wrong thing. How stupid to think that this might make us friends. I grabbed my bag and walked out the door, but stopped just around the corner, listening to see if they said anything about me.

"I knew he was a perv!" Saanvi exploded. "He's too nice to everyone."

"So gross," said Cass's soft voice. "Makes my skin crawl."

"How do you think I feel?" Mel's voice was so quiet I could barely hear it.

"So what are we going to do?" Cass said.

Mel's voice rose slightly. "What can I do? If I go to the principal, it will become a huge big deal, everyone will find out. They'll call my parents."

And I guess that meant the case was closed. There were a few moments of silence, just the squeak of shoes as they got changed. I was about to make a run for it; if they found me listening in it would be awful. Then I heard Mel's voice again.

"I feel so stupid."

"Shut up, Mel. Don't do that," Saanvi said.

"No. It's just—" her voice cracked, like she might cry "—he

kept saying how talented I was and I believed him. He's the whole reason I decided I wanted to be an actor."

Everyone was already scattered out on the oval for lunch, sitting on backpacks or jackets because the grass was wet. The clouds were a menacing gray; it would probably rain again soon. I pulled my hood over my hair, which was getting even fluffier from the damp air, and walked slowly toward our spot by the library. My thoughts were swimming. The anger I'd felt earlier had changed, turned into something coiling and sharp inside me. It wasn't fair. Nothing was going to happen. Mr. Bitto was going to get away with it. Maybe I was naive, but up until then I'd always believed that justice prevailed. If some-one did something wrong, I took it for granted that they'd be punished. It didn't seem right that the only way for Mr. Bitto to get in trouble for being a creep would cause Mel more pain. I didn't get why what he'd done was now her responsibility.

It all went around and around in my head, until something else, the shadow that had been lurking in the back of my mind became clear.

It'd been months since the man had broken into our house, but I still believed the police would find him. In some ways I was just waiting for it, sure that everything would go back to the way it was as soon as he was apprehended. That I'd feel safe again.

It didn't matter that my mum had told me he must have been off his head on drugs and didn't know what he was doing, and Bea had said we should just try to let it go. Still, I'd been sure. The cops had come, they'd written notes, they'd let us know as soon as they had any new information. We hadn't heard from them. It wasn't till that very moment that I realized we never would.

Something wrong had happened, and no one even seemed to expect it to be put right except me.

"Hey!" Ling grinned at me when I dropped my bag down next to her and Ashleigh. "Guess what?"

I didn't answer, just sat down on the cement, my head still whirring.

"You okay, Ava?" Ashleigh asked. "You look kind of pale."

I looked up at them, wanting to explain.

Ling leaned forward and put her hand on my arm. "Did something bad happen?"

"Bad things happen all the time—" I don't know why I sounded so angry "—and no one does anything about them."

I didn't have to look up to know that Ling and Ashleigh were exchanging a look.

"The cops do. Detectives and journalists too," Ashleigh said.

"Yeah, and aid workers. Plus not-for-profit organizations and charities."

They didn't get it. I looked up, opening my mouth to snap at them again. They looked back at me with real concern and worry. Maybe they hadn't even been exchanging a look, maybe they really did care about what I was saying.

"I guess." I didn't want to talk about it anymore. "What were you saying before? What are you excited about?"

"Oh yeah." Ling pulled something out of her bag. "I printed off the list of stalls that are going to be at the careers expo tomorrow. I thought it would be fun to make a timetable, so we don't miss anything. My sister said it can be really overwhelming."

I told them to go and get started in the library and I'd catch up with them, but I didn't go. I sat by myself by the wall instead, staring at the spot that Mel, Cass and Saanvi usually sat in on the oval. They weren't there either. They were probably skipping. I wondered if Mel was somewhere, crying right now. She'd been rude to me in the change room, but I knew it was only because she was upset.

Soon it was pouring down rain. The people on the oval

leaped up, some squealing, some laughing, and rushed toward the school buildings. I stayed were I was, the roof of the library shielding me from the downpour. Looking toward the car park, I saw Mr. Bitto. He ran from his car, his jacket over his head, slipping a few times before he made it to cover. He looked ridiculous. This man wasn't scary; he wasn't some big and powerful monster. It kept raining all through lunch, but I stayed where I was, staring out at the empty school yard. It made the classrooms look dark for the rest of the day, and pelted the bus windows on my long commute home.

I got drenched as I walked up the hill of Lakeside. A guy around my age that lived in the house across from us was looking at me through his kitchen window. It must have looked weird that I wasn't rushing out of the downpour. I ignored him. I didn't care. My head was buzzing. Mr. Bitto was going to pay for what he'd done. I may have been just a girl, a nobody, but he was just a creep with a hard-on for his students. If I could figure out a way, I could make this right. I spent all night thinking up a plan.

I watched Mel on the bus the next morning. We were all on our way to the careers expo. She sat in the back with Saanvi and Cass and some guys. She was laughing along, but I knew she was still upset. I was sitting right near the front with Ling and Ashleigh. They were discussing their priorities for the day. I tried not to listen. Instead, I stared at the back of Mr. Bitto's head. He was leaning forward and talking to the driver in his gentle voice. I could see through his hair very slightly. His pale scalp was shiny.

Finally, the bus pulled into the Exhibition Center. It was starting to drizzle again outside. There were a few days until spring, but winter wasn't giving up. I pulled my hood up as we filed noisily from the bus.

"Come on, Ava," Ling said, looking back as I dawdled.

"I'll catch up with you guys," I told them.

"Okay." Ashleigh smiled at me and they rushed on ahead, timetables and notebooks in hand.

I walked slowly, watching Mel, Saanvi and Cass. They had linked arms, become a wall of skinny thighs and shiny hair. Watching them walk together like that made my resolve start to shake. I felt queasy, and my mouth still tasted weird from another shockingly early morning, even though I brushed my teeth. I wondered if I would ever get used to it.

I scampered to keep up as they entered the building, taking one last long breath of chilly air. The ceiling inside was high and the side wall was solid glass, all fogged up so you could barely see the little droplets sliding down the outside. Inside, it was loud with all the vendors. Beauty schools, Sports Colleges, the local paper. Tables decked with pamphlets. The people behind them smiling too wide. Miranda had already been pounced on by the straight-backed guy in camo at the Army table. I ignored it all and kept up my following.

The three of them looked so complete, even from behind. I wondered if they'd picked each other on the first day of high school because they looked so similar. Same long legs and dark hair. Mel was the leader of the group. No matter what, she was always in the middle. She was always the focus. Saanvi was snarky and loud, but she always listened to what Mel said. Cass was quieter. She always stared out the window in class. But with the other two she seemed to come to life.

They ignored the vendors too and went straight into the girl's bathroom.

I stopped walking. My plan was crazy. They might laugh at me. I could just go back and join Ashleigh and Ling. I slowly took my hoodie off. My hands were shaking. I didn't have to do it. Then, I forced myself to think about how I would feel tonight. When I walked back up the hill in Lakeside Estate imagining what might have happened, wishing I hadn't chickened out. The feeling of it was devastating enough to propel me forward.

The toilet door squeaked as it swung open. Mel and Cass were sitting up next to the sinks and Saanvi was leaning against the wall. They all looked up at me.

"Hi," I said.

"Hi," mimicked Saanvi, raising an eyebrow.

I looked down at the cracked tiles. It stank in there. "I've been thinking about what happened yesterday," I started.

"Just forget it! It's none of your business." Mel's expression was fierce. I hadn't expected her to get mad.

"I know."

"So do you need to pee, or what?" asked Saanvi.

This wasn't going the way I'd hoped.

"No. Listen. I've got a plan about how we can get him back. A way where no one will know it was us."

"Yeah?" said Saanvi, looking me up and down. She thought I was about to say something lame.

"We get him on video. With a student. We'll shoot it so you can see his face but not hers. But they'll know from the uniform."

I grabbed the school sports shirt out of my bag and showed it to them. It was the one we all had to wear for PE, with the big school logo on the back.

"Then what?" asked Mel.

"Put it online."

They all stared at me. I was sure for a moment they were going to tell me to get out, tell me I was an idiot.

Then Cass clapped her hand over her mouth and started laughing.

"That's awesome!"

"Really?" I asked.

Saanvi looked at Mel, who smiled at her.

"I didn't realize you had that kind of balls." For once Saanvi looked impressed.

I felt tingly all over. I'd done it. We were going to be friends now for sure.

"Would you really do that for me?" Mel stared at me intently.

For a moment I didn't understand what she meant. But of course, it was obvious. There was no way she was going near Mr. Bitto. Cass and Saanvi wouldn't want to do it either. They all assumed I would be the one. The one to be in the video. It had been my idea after all.

"Sure," I said, the tingles turning cold.

It was my price of admission. If I wanted to be one of them, I'd have to pay for it. I should have known that from the beginning.

"You're so cool, Ava," Cass said, as she pulled some hair product out of her bag and started slicking it through my hair.

"This is just for him," Saanvi said, smearing foundation over my face. "No one will see your face. Now pout."

She smudged red gloss on my lips. Mel sat back, watching.

"Are you sure you're okay to do this?" she said, when the girls had finished and I had changed into the gym shirt. There was something in her tone that made it seem like a test, as if she wasn't really asking.

"Yep."

"Good." She jumped down from the sink and surveyed me. Then, she reached over and undid the top two buttons of my school shirt.

"You're so sexy now." She smiled. "Look."

I turned to look in the mirror. I was unrecognizable. The fluff was gone, my hair coiled in shiny tendrils. The makeup made my face look different, my eyes and lips popping. I wasn't sure if I liked what I saw.

"What a babe," cooed Cass.

"Pedo won't know what hit him," said Saanvi.

★ ★ ★

We waited until the presentations. Everyone was to be at the main stage at one o'clock sharp. We decided that under the stage was the place to do it. He'd feel like it was safe there.

When it hit ten past, I crept out into the corridor. The vendor tables were empty now. I kept my head down as I walked. Watching my feet pressing down into the dirty carpet. Every part of me was twisted up, but still I kept going. There was a drive in me, willing me to go through with it. Not just because of Mel. Because of Miranda, because of that strange feeling of not caring that someone was hurting. I wanted to test it, see how far I could go. To see exactly what I was capable of.

Mr. Bitto was standing inside the auditorium right near the door at the back. On the stage, a man was brushing a student's hair with the hand of a skeleton. Everyone was laughing.

"Mr. Bitto," I whispered.

He turned to look at me, then his eyes bulged slightly.

"Find a seat, Ava," he said.

"I need to talk to you."

"Now's not the time."

I looked around, desperate.

"I can talk to one of the other teachers instead. I'm sure they'd be interested in what I have to say."

His eyes flicked around the auditorium. He was panicking. I turned on my heel and walked out the door before him. I stepped down the stairs and heard his footsteps behind me. For a moment I felt a rush of power. This was too easy. Maybe it wouldn't be so bad.

It was dark under the stage. The lights only came from the small window in the door behind me. You could hear the presenter's talk echoing down here and the thumps and shuffles as he moved around on the stage above. It smelled dusty. I wove around the big stage lights and the microphone stands, and then sat on a stack of thick blue exercise mats with my back to the door.

"What is it?" came the soft voice behind me. It didn't sound as gentle as usual. I didn't answer, not yet. I needed him to stand in front of me. So they could see his face from the window in the door.

"I thought you had something to say to me?"

"No. I want to show you."

I heard him sigh and then his footsteps as he walked toward me. Cold sweat prickled my skin.

"Yes?" He was in front of me now. Staring at me. I couldn't look him in the eye.

"I saw what you did to Mel."

"I didn't do anything!" His voice rose slightly and he looked around as if worried someone might hear it. He was so pathetic, yet so ready to put his own gross pleasure first, no matter who it damaged. The world was a dangerous place, I knew that now. People were capable of just about anything. There was no hiding from it.

"No." I choked the words out. "That's not it. I liked what I saw."

He gaped at me. Then, slowly his eyes changed. He looked around again and then back at me in a different way. I reached up, and undid another button of my shirt. He stared at my hand. You could see my bra now. I thought I might vomit.

He was on me in seconds. Kissing my neck. Breathing so loud. Squeezing down on my boob so hard it hurt.

The presenter above was wrapping up his speech: *There are so many reasons to choose a career in medicine.*

Mr. Bitto's mouth closed over mine. He pushed his tongue into my mouth, forcing my jaw to open as far as it could go.

Not only does it open countless doors to so many different possible trajectories…

I never thought my first kiss would be like this.

...but it also creates the potential to make a lasting difference to the world, to help others every day and get paid for it!

His hand slid up my thigh.

"Stop it." I tried to push him off, but he didn't move. His hand slid up farther. I gripped his wrist with my fingers and rammed him away. But it made no difference. I closed my mouth but his tongue just licked over my lips.

"Stop!" I screamed and kicked out at him. He pulled away, panting. His lips wet with my spit.

When the others came into the bathroom, my face was red and blotchy. I was rubbing at my skin as hard as I could with wet toilet paper. Sodden lumps already filled the sink. They were marbled red, beige and black from the makeup. It was so heavy and itchy on my skin. I needed to get it all off.

"That was amazing!"

"You rocked!"

"I can't believe you actually did it!"

Their voices blurred together. I kept going, trying to get the last of the mascara off. It had turned into gray smudges under my eyes. It hadn't been worth it. Nothing could have been worth that. I felt a hand on my arm. It was Mel's.

"Thank you," she said. "Really."

She meant it. I could tell by the way she was looking at me, with real admiration.

I shrugged. "No big deal."

5

When we got on the bus I looked just like I had when I'd gotten off that morning. Mel, Saanvi and Cass helped me get the rest of the makeup off and make my hair look the way it had. I had my hoodie back on. No one would know I was the girl in the video.

I walked right by Ashleigh and Ling on my way to the back of the bus. I didn't even look at them. As I sat down I could feel their eyes on me, but I ignored them. They'd always been better friends with each other than with me anyway. They would get over it.

We huddled into the corner.

I looked up as Mr. Bitto boarded. He smiled at me. Then, his eyes flicked around and his smile fell. Mel, Cass and Saanvi were all staring at him too. Finally, we were united.

"Almost done," said Cass. She had set up a fake email address and from it had made a fake Facebook and YouTube account.

Theodore turned around. "What are you guys doing?"

"Fuck off, Theo," Saanvi snapped.

"Just give us one minute and I'll send it to you," Mel said softly.

"Whatever." He turned back around.

"This is going to be so good," whispered Saanvi.

It went down the bus like a wave. You could tell which row it reached when the voices turned hushed, when heads turned to stare at Mr. Bitto. He was the only one who didn't notice. He kept chatting away with the bus driver in his mild, low voice. I saw the exact moment when Ashleigh got it. The first thing she did was lean forward and show it to Mrs. Clarke, whose eyebrows shot up as her hand went over her mouth.

When the bus pulled into school, everyone was silent except for Mr. Bitto, who was still chatting to the driver. He hadn't noticed. There was a police car waiting.

Through the window, I watched the policeman talking to the pale-faced principal. I tried to tell myself I'd done the right thing. But now, watching Mr. Bitto get off the bus and walk toward the police car, a panicked smile on his face, I wasn't so sure. Right or wrong, I'd surely destroyed the man's life. I tried to swallow the feeling away. He'd deserved everything he got. What I'd done had been justified.

There were only six months left till graduation and this would be the worst thing I'd ever do at high school, and that really wasn't too bad. That's how I rationalized it. I think I might have even told myself that it could be the worst thing I'd do, ever.

I wonder if you'll find that funny? Considering where I am right now, you might consider it ironic. Will you also find it funny how sure I was that my plan had worked? That now that I'd proven myself, I was one of them? How I was envisioning our futures already: marathon phone calls, roommates at uni, drinks every weekend, bridesmaids at each other's weddings. I had no idea what they were going to do to me.

But then again, I guess we're not here to laugh, are we? I am here to confess, and you to hear my confession.

Part 2

PATHOLOGICAL LYING

2011

6

Theodore started his day by smoking a cigarette in bed. Maybe he'd seen it in a movie. Or he could have read about one of his favorite authors, Bukowski or maybe Salinger, doing it.

He held the smoke in his mouth, then let it rise above him to the low ceiling. If there was a girl sleeping next to him, which there often was, he'd rub a hand over her naked back or fondle one of her breasts as he smoked. No matter how hungover he seemed, he'd make sure to get up in time for college breakfast, though he'd rarely ask the girl to accompany him. He'd pull on a pair of track pants, no underwear and yesterday's T-shirt. He'd taken out his piercing by then, and it had left one of his nipples slightly larger and pinker than the other.

Unlike most of the other residents of the college dorms, he had his own room and bathroom. It was his third year and he was, supposedly, a residential adviser. It was him that first year students were meant to go to if they were feeling homesick, or if they'd locked themselves out of their rooms in the middle of the night. Even though his room was on the ground floor, he always left his curtains ajar and sometimes even the window open.

If he had an early class he wouldn't bother with a shower, especially if that class was philosophy. He seemed to be under the impression that the sharp odor of his unwashed body was alluring. You would think that Theodore's undergraduate degree was in philosophy given the way he incessantly spoke of the constant revelations and epiphanies it supplied him with. It wasn't. Philosophy was his elective. He was really studying science, with a major in applied chemistry.

As he walked to his first class, he'd wink at the people he passed, sometimes pulling a hand through his hair if he wanted to seem particularly charming. He walked with a slight swagger, an air of unhurried ease, as he made his way toward the main university buildings.

In his science classes, this nonchalance would disappear. His hair would go behind his ears and stay there as he bent over his textbooks and took notes.

In the evenings, while the college dinner was being prepared, he would sometimes call his mum. I'd sit around the corner and listen. He mustn't have realized how much his voice carried.

"But everyone else is getting supported," he'd whine.

"Yeah, sure, teaching me to stand on my own two feet means making me wait tables instead of studying. I'm falling behind—is that what you want for me?"

"Well, should I still bring around my laundry on Sunday, or don't you have time for that anymore either?"

He would end the call annoyed, and light another cigarette.

7

"I'm going to be late for class!" I yelled through the door.

Bea was in the shower. She'd been in there for ages. If I didn't get in the bathroom soon I'd miss my lift with Nancy, the woman who lived with her elderly great-aunt down the street. Three times a week she went into the city, and if I was at her house before eight she'd drive me in with her.

More than anything, I was dying to use the toilet. I jumped and fidgeted, ran up and down the stairs, squeezing my pelvic muscles. If I stopped moving, I was sure I'd wee myself.

"Come on!" I called, but she didn't answer. It was too late anyway, I'd never make it.

I opened our front door and ran to the corner of the street. Nancy was there, leaning against her car waiting for me.

"Morning!" I yelled.

She looked up at me, raised her arms in question.

"Class got canceled!" I called.

She smiled at me, as if to say *lucky you*, and turned to get in her car.

I half ran back toward my house. If she was still in the shower, I could sit up on the kitchen sink. Or I could pee in a bowl or something, then tip it in the yard. If only we had a backyard, then I could squat behind a tree.

"Why are you walking like that?"

The guy who lived with his brother across the road was staring at me through his open kitchen window, again.

I'd seen him a few times over the years, but I'd barely ever spoken to him. It was during the one and only night that Mel, Cass and Saanvi slept over at my house. He said hi to me a few weeks after that, but I was so miserable I'd just ignored him.

"No reason," I said.

"Okay." He shrugged and turned away.

The truth was the panic was starting to set in. I was absolutely busting and there was no way I was going to do it in the sink.

"Hey!" I yelled, crossing my legs in front of me. "Do you mind if I use your toilet?"

He came back to the window and looked me up and down. "You really need to go, don't you?"

"Yeah! Obviously, or I wouldn't be asking you."

He stared at me, smirking, as I began jiggling on the spot.

"Don't be an asshole," I said.

He laughed. "Fine. Come in."

I ran to the door, but he didn't open it. I knocked, and heard slow footsteps. He opened the door and looked at me with fake confusion.

"Can I help you?"

"For fuck's sake!" I pushed past him and ran up to the toilet. It was in the exact same spot in his house as mine. I banged the door shut behind me, pushed my foot against it and pulled my pajama pants down. The flow started before my bum even made contact with his toilet seat. The relief was exquisite. I closed my eyes.

"Wow, I've never heard a chick piss that hard."

He was on the other side of the door.

"Fuck off!" I screamed, my voice high and pitchy, making me cringe even more than I already was.

I heard him laughing as he walked away.

When I was done, I stormed back down the stairs.

"I'm making a coffee—do you want one?"

"No! What the fuck is wrong with you?" I yelled.

"Evan! What did you do now?"

I turned around. The other guy, who was in his early thirties and I was pretty sure was Evan's brother, was standing in the doorway to the living room.

Evan didn't reply, just looked at me.

"See ya," I said, and half ran through the door and back to my own house before they could see my blush. That would only make the whole thing even more hideously embarrassing.

As I closed the front door I could still hear the shower. Walking slowly up the stairs, I could already feel it. Something was wrong. Bea never had showers that long.

I tapped on the door.

"Bea?" I said. No answer.

"Bea? Are you okay?" I said louder. She might not be able to hear me over the water. Maybe she was washing her hair or something.

I went back into my room and sat on the bed. The sound of the shower running filled up the whole quiet house. I made myself count to a hundred, sure that when I did the water would be turned off. It didn't.

Going back to the door, I knocked again. An image appeared in my head. Bea, lying in the tub, blood pooling around her, the water creeping up over her nose and mouth.

"Bea!" I screamed. No answer.

I took a step back and tried to kick the door. It shuddered, but didn't budge. Mum would be on shift. I could call the hospital reception and get them to go find her, but that could take a while.

"Bea!"

I put my ear to the door. Behind the sound of the water, I heard a quiet moan.

I ran back down the stairs over to Evan's house, banged on the door. It swung open.

"Need to go number two now?" His face fell as he took in mine.

"I need you to come kick my bathroom door in!"

"Aiden!" he yelled.

The older brother came around behind him, but Evan didn't wait for him. He followed me as I turned and jogged back inside.

"She's epileptic," I told him, as we raced up the stairs.

"I don't know if I'm strong enough," he said, and I eyed his spindly arms. He was probably right. He tried anyway, running backward and throwing himself into the door.

"Ouch!" he yelled, rubbing his shoulder.

Our dog, Chucky, started barking from the noise, snuffling at Aiden's heels as he took the stairs two at a time.

"Is it Beatrice?" Aiden said.

"Yeah," I told him. I didn't know they knew each other.

"I'll do it. Move."

Both Evan and I stepped backward into Bea's room.

"Beatrice," Aiden yelled, "we're coming in."

Instead of charging at the door like Evan had, he kicked it near the hinges. On his second kick, the wood split with a loud crack. He kicked it again, and the door opened a few inches, enough to see Bea's naked flesh through the gap. I stepped forward.

"Don't look!" I snapped.

"Sorry," he said, and both of them instantly turned around.

I pushed the door wide enough so I could squeeze through sideways. Bea was lying half in and half out of the shower, which was still streaming over her thighs. There was water all over the tiles and I half walked, half slipped toward her. Her eyes were open, and she looked at me as I crouched down next to her. There was vomit down her cheek and in her hair.

"Bea," I said, "you okay?"

"Yeah," she whispered so quietly I could barely hear her.

"Should we call an ambulance?" Aiden called.

"Not yet!" I called back.

"Who is that?" she murmured.

I brushed her wet hair off her face. "Those guys from across the street."

"Oh God," she said.

"Well, if you insist on locking the door when you're about to have a seizure, then what do you expect?"

She closed her eyes and almost smiled.

"Did you hit your head?" I asked.

"Nah, shoulder."

"How bad?" I stood up and turned the taps off.

"Not broken."

"Is she okay?" Aiden called out.

"Make them go," she whispered.

I grabbed a towel and put it over her, then went back to the door and put my head through the gap.

"Thanks," I said to them. "You don't need to stay."

"Are you sure?" Evan asked, looking genuinely concerned.

"Yep," I said, then softer, "She's fine—honestly, you guys are just going to embarrass her."

Evan looked to Aiden, who reluctantly shrugged.

"We'll be in for the next hour. Come over if we can do anything. Really."

I nodded. "I will."

Evan gave me an unsure half smile, and then followed his brother down the stairs. The front door banged shut behind them. I turned back around.

"What do you think? Do you want to go to the hospital?"

"No, just call Mum."

"Okay."

"Get the puke off my face first though."

"Yeah, I was planning on it."

She laughed, a hollow sound, and I smiled back at her as I grabbed a facecloth off the rack. It was already wet from the steam.

"Did they see?" she asked, as I wiped the vomit away.

"Nah." I wrapped the towel around her properly, and started pulling her onto her knees. When I got her there I hugged her tight.

"Your pajamas are getting soaked," she said.

"Don't care."

After a few seconds, she started to cry. "I hate this," she whispered into my ear.

I held her close, tears streaming down my own face. "Me too," I said. "That was so scary."

When I got Bea into bed, I called Mum, who said she'd come straight home. I went into my sister's room and lay on the bed next to her. I'd wrapped a towel around her hair, but her pillow was still wet.

"Don't go to sleep until Mum checks you," I said, "just in case."

"I know."

I held her hand. "Do you feel a bit better?"

"Yeah. Sorry I made you miss class."

"Doesn't matter," I said, swallowing away the guilt. There was no class.

She took a long deep breath.

"You know what this means, right?"

"What?" I said, although I had a feeling I knew what she was going to say.

"No driving for six months."

"Shit."

Epileptic people aren't meant to drive after they have a seizure. It's a stupid rule in my opinion, but still. It's the law.

"I'm going to have to quit my job," she said.

"No."

"Yes. That was the whole reason I got the car—there's actually no way of getting there by public transport. I could walk I guess, but it would take me three hours each way."

"Well, quit then," I said. "You hate that job anyway. Your boss is a dickhead."

"Yeah, but I'm still paying off the car."

I shrugged. "Get Mum to pay you back some of the rent money you've been giving her."

"I can't do that," she said. "She's already used it on the mortgage. Plus I'm twenty-two, Ava, it's embarrassing."

"I'm twenty."

"Yeah, but you're at uni. Mum wants you to focus on that."

I stared at the ceiling. I wanted to help her make this better, but I also didn't want to reveal just how much of my life was actually a lie.

"I'll go part-time, get a job so I can help pay off the car."

"I don't want you to do that."

"Bea," I said, and waited until she looked at me, "let's talk about this later."

She closed her eyes, and then nodded.

8

I told Bea I'd spend the next day with her. Watching bad soap operas about accidental incest and illegitimate children like we had after her seizure, Chucky sleeping on my feet, a bowl of snacks between us. She said no and, secretly, I was glad. It felt so good to do nothing with Bea, just to be with her and feel like a real person with a real life. But that wasn't me. By the end of the day I'd been itching with it. Knowing that Theodore was out there, doing something, and I wasn't there to see it.

The whole thing had started innocently enough. Facebook, Twitter, Instagram, Tumblr. I had been forced to delete them all during high school, when my pages began to be filled with words like *psycho*, *freak*, *shithead*, *die*. But a few months after graduation the lure had been too strong. I just wanted to see. To look. To see what their lives were like, while I was still grappling with the pieces of my own.

As much as I tried not to be, I was still so focused on them. On what had happened. I wanted to move on. I didn't want to think about that horrible wretched night and all that came after, but it felt like not thinking about it took all my energy. I didn't have space to do anything else, to carve out a life for myself, to really live. No matter what, I still felt stuck in those last few months of high school. The idea that they could have kept going, become different people, seemed impossible. I couldn't imagine it, but I didn't really have to try. It only took a few clicks, and there they were.

Mel was in Europe. Cass barely posted. Saanvi just uploaded pictures of her architecture assignments, punctuated by photographs of coffees and comments on how stressed she was. But Theodore posted daily. I could see his whole life. His whole pretentious, blessed life. Photographs from parties, plastic cup in his hand, arm stretched around a girl's shoulders. Or sitting and smoking with some boys, staring furrow-browed into the camera with his practiced almost-smirk. He went on weekends away to the coast. Lay on beach towels, filmed himself singing along in the back of cars. He got countless pictures of funny cats in paper hats for his birthday, and a new friend almost daily. He looked so happy.

I'm not stupid. Everyone knows social media is all lies. People show what they want you to see. I knew that he couldn't really be that happy. But he was. I saw that soon enough in the flesh. It was easy—he always posted about where he was. It was like an invitation. I don't know what I was expecting to find the first time I followed him to the bar he'd posted about. I guess maybe I'd thought that when I saw him I'd see a shadow there, some reserve in his manner that showed that high school had changed him too. But there wasn't; that was clear straightaway. For him, the past didn't matter. He didn't care about what he'd done. It was all about his potential, his golden bright future.

I know I'm a lot of things, a liar for one. But I do believe in fairness. Theodore had screwed up my future, so it was only fair I did the same to him.

An eye for an eye. That's the idea, right?

As Nancy drove us toward the city the morning after Bea's seizure, I filled her in on what happened.

"Now she thinks she's going to have to stop working for a while. It's really unfair."

"How awful," she said. "Poor darl."

I shrugged. "I'm going part-time at uni. Get a job."

"Really?"

"Otherwise I would feel really selfish."

"But being at university isn't selfish. Just means you'll get a good job. What are you doing again, honey?"

"Nursing," I told her. That's what I'd been telling everyone else.

"Nothing selfish about that," she said.

We drove in silence for a while. That was something I liked about Nancy. She didn't try to make conversation all the time. I stared out the windscreen, looking at the dappled sunshine through the leaves. I liked this part of the drive the best. When the car zoomed down the road, shrouded by snow gums towering above. It felt totally uninhabited. You wouldn't know in ten minutes the car would hit the freeway and you'd be sitting bumper-to-bumper in smog for the whole rest of the way.

Nancy tapped her fake nails on the steering wheel.

"I have an idea for you."

"Yeah?"

"I was thinking of getting a nurse to call in at my place sometimes. Cil's getting bad at being on her own all the time—not that she'd admit it. Maybe if you could be there, on two weekdays say, and maybe a Saturday? Just read to her and, you know, make sure she takes her pills, makes it to the loo, doesn't burn the house down. She's still in remission, but she's getting better every day."

"Remission for what?"

"She had breast cancer. It was early stages, and I made sure she did everything right for it."

I swallowed. "Doesn't she need a real nurse for that?"

"Oh, you'd be fine, hon. Honestly. You must know the basics by now."

I hesitated.

"No pressure. I just thought if it was someone from the community she'd be less likely to slam the door in their face. You know how she gets."

I did know how she got. I'd seen Nancy's great-aunt dancing in the yard one night, totally naked, singing loudly and out of tune to "You're So Vain." But still, money was money.

"Okay," I said, "I can give it a try."

She turned to smile at me, then shifted her eyes back to the road. "You're a real sweetheart you know, Ava. An angel."

Nancy dropped me on Collins Street before she swung down into the underground car park beneath the bank offices where she worked. Pulling up my hood, I walked down toward Swanston Street, the main drag, where all the trams went up to University of Melbourne. I always liked this part of the city. It still had the hustle and bustle, the women in heels and the men with briefcases, but it felt cleaner up here. It was where all the fancy clothing brands had their stores: Chanel, Givenchy, Armani. "The Paris end," was what it was called, but I quickly put that out of my head. It made me think of Mel.

Once I reached Swanston Street I was met by the grease and grime I was used to. Kebab stores, the lingering smell of last night's vomit, the yells of someone off their meds wandering in front of trams. All of these were normal. What was different were the tents that had been set up in City Square, the area usually reserved for the gaudy Christmas tree that came out once a year, or the occasional market. There were a few police lingering around too. I ignored it all and clambered onto my tram. If I hurried, I'd still make it in time for Theodore's morning cigarette.

I wasn't watching Theodore because I was in love with him—I need to make that clear. It was almost the opposite. I found him repellent. Watching him smoke that cigarette, I wasn't consumed by the desire to be the girl in bed with him. No, my desire was to take that cigarette out of his mouth and stub it out on his eyeball. But I won't say that. It doesn't matter what I wanted to do, only what I really did.

I'd stuck around for a few college parties. I was the right age, I blended in well enough and I was hoping Theodore would get drunk enough to let something slip. Something about how he was really making his money. But I was too afraid he'd recognize me to do it often.

You see, I wasn't the only liar. He'd told his mum he was waiting tables, but I'd never seen him with an apron on. He had cash though. A lot of it. His wallet made the back pocket of his jeans bulge. I knew he was doing something, but I couldn't figure out what it was. It was in the way he'd whisper into the phone sometimes, the way he closed the blinds when he was in the chemistry lab alone, the way other guys would catch his eye and he'd immediately get up and follow them to the bathroom.

At first I thought maybe they were having sex, but sometimes he'd be in there for less than thirty seconds. Even for a guy like him, surely that wasn't enough.

I walked behind him and his friends as they left the college dining hall after breakfast.

"But it's a fact, man," Theodore was saying. "There's no such thing as race."

"That's so ridiculous." The guy next to him seemed irritated. I wondered how long this argument had been going on.

"It's true. Race is not a biological reality. It's a myth!"

"Okay, sure. But you can't say that it means there's no such thing as racism."

"It follows though, right? If there's no race, how can there be racism?"

"You know, man, that's kind of offensive."

"Fuck, don't be so PC."

"I'm not."

They came to stop outside Theo's building, and I kept walking slowly past them, staring down into my phone.

"I'm just stating a fact," the guy went on. "If you say this shit people are going to get offended."

"I don't think you get it. Anyway, there are no facts, only interpretations," Theodore replied. "Or do you think Nietzsche isn't PC enough either?"

He said bye to them smugly—I guess he thought he'd won that one—and went into his building. I stayed where I was, leaning against the wall, staring at the blank screen of my phone. For a moment I had no idea what I was doing there, hanging around a place I didn't belong and giving all my attention to such a jerk. It felt pointless. I should have been with Bea. But I reminded myself that she was why I needed to be here. I wanted to live an honest life, to really focus on her, to be there for her. But first I had to finish what I'd started. If I was going to stop doing this, I had to do it right. I had to humiliate Theodore like he had done to me. I'd put so much time into it, spent so many hours watching and listening. If I was going to stop, first I had to do something. Something that would really leave a mark. I just hadn't figured out what.

Still, I couldn't shake the frustration. I stayed where I was, leaning against the wall outside the building, rather than going around the back and peering in through his window. There had been a girl in his bed this morning, one of the recurring visitors. I'd heard her crying to him one morning that he didn't want to date her because she had no thigh gap, not because he didn't believe in labels like he kept saying.

I put my phone in my pocket and stretched my arms up above my head. Out of the corner of my eye, I saw him. Theodore, sprinting out of his building. He pushed his way through the heavy wooden door of the next building, and it slammed against the wall loudly. I followed, trying to walk quickly without running.

Inside the building, I could hear his footsteps echoing on the cement stairs above me.

"Move!" he yelled at someone on the next landing. As I reached it I saw it was a wounded-looking first year staring up after him.

I'd seen Theodore smug, I'd seen him irritated, I'd seen him joyful and bored and angry, but I'd never seen him panicked. The footsteps stopped. He'd run down the third floor. I rushed now, running myself, until I got to the carpeted corridor. I looked back and forth, having no idea where he had gone. A door opened to my right, and a girl in a pink dressing gown smiled sleepily at me, a toothbrush in her hand. Then I heard it, faintly, coming from the laundry room.

"I'm sorry!" It was the voice of the girl who'd been in his room this morning.

I approached slowly, trying not to let my tread make any sound.

"I just wanted to wash my clothes," she was saying. "You spilled your beer all over my dress last night, remember? I didn't think you'd care."

"Well, I do mind, you fat bitch."

"But it's only laundry detergent! Why does it matter?"

"At least you didn't put the fucking water on yet."

I risked a peek around the door. The girl was standing next to the washing machine, wearing Theodore's T-shirt and shorts. He was trying to scoop the laundry powder out of the machine and back into its little sachet. I stood there, staring. I'd seen those sachets in his room; I'd thought of it as being sort of weird that he bought the single-use packets rather than a full box. I'd even noticed a bunch of them in a plastic bag after he'd come out of the chemistry labs alone one time. I thought he'd just gone to the shops.

"What?" the girl said, glaring at me with tearstained cheeks.

I ducked away before he could turn around and see my face, see my smile.

9

When I walked through my front door that afternoon, I could hear a man's voice. Reaching the top of the stairs, I saw Aiden standing at the bathroom door. Bea was with him, and she was laughing. Not her real laugh. A light, soft giggle, her hand over her mouth as though she didn't want him to see inside.

"Hey," I said.

"Hi! Look what Aiden's done." She pointed toward the bathroom door. It was almost back to normal, except the color of paint he'd put on to hide the repair was a slightly brighter white than the rest of the door.

"Least I could do," he said to me, although he was still looking at Bea. "I was the one that broke it."

I wanted to say how stupid that was, but I held my tongue. He picked up his toolbox and the tin of paint.

"See you both soon, then," he said, and nodded to me as he passed.

"Huh?"

"Bye!" Bea said, grinning at the back of his head as he walked down the stairs.

I watched him walk out the door, then turned to Bea, eyebrows raised.

"I invited them over for dinner."

"What? Fuck, do I have to come out of my room?"

"Yes," she snapped, the grin instantly disappearing. "We have to say thanks."

"Is Mum going to be here?"

"No, she's working."

"Well, I'm not cooking."

"I didn't expect you to!" she said, the grin coming back as she went down toward the kitchen.

"He's not hot!" I called after her. "Plus he's like ten years older than you."

"He's a babe!" she called back. "And Evan's not too bad either."

"What?" I leaned over the railing to look at her. "You know, he listened to me pee through the door yesterday. It was so weird."

"Well, he's coming over too. In an hour. Be ready!"

I sat in my room in a huff for a bit, but ended up going down to help Bea cook in the end. I still felt so fizzy with exhilaration. Finally, things were going right. I was going to get Theodore. Tomorrow I was going to sneak into his room and I was going to steal one of those sachets of whatever drug he was making. I was going to prove what a bad person he really was. Spending an awkward evening making polite conversation wasn't my idea of a celebration, but Bea looked happy.

It was rare that both of us were happy at the same time. More often than not, neither one of us was happy. But that night we were both distracted, both thinking of men but in very different ways.

"Crap, crap, crap," she said, as she chopped up the tomato. "How can pasta take this long?"

I shrugged, adding a bit more salt to the boiling water. "You're the one that wanted to do the sauce from scratch. We have that bottle of it in the cupboard. Anyway, I'm sure they won't be right on time."

On cue, the doorbell rang. I emptied the bag of pasta into the water and went to get it.

"Hello again," I said as I opened the door.

"Thanks again for having us," Aiden said, passing me a bottle of red wine. Evan stood next to him, his hands in his pockets.

"Wow," I said, "I didn't realize we were having such a fancy evening."

I stood back to let them in, noticing that Aiden had changed his shirt since he'd left.

"Hello," Aiden said as he entered the kitchen. He went to give Bea a kiss on the cheek, which she misjudged as a hug, and he ended up kissing her hair.

I caught Evan's eye. We both smirked.

"Sit down," I said. "I don't think we'll be eating for a while."

"Actually, it's not too far off."

I looked from Bea to the frying pan, which was now filled with red sauce. I opened my mouth to laugh—she'd sneaked in the premade stuff while I wasn't looking—but her expression made me shut it again.

"Everyone in for a glass of this?" I said.

"Oh." Bea looked at the bottle. "I shouldn't, because of. You know. Still not feeling quite right. But you guys enjoy!"

"I'm so sorry. I shouldn't have brought it," Aiden said, turning pale. "That was really insensitive of me."

"It's fine," she said, "honestly."

"I'm not really a wine drinker anyway to be honest," he said. "Just thought, you know, since you're cooking."

"Well, I'll have one," I said, taking out a glass.

"Me too," Evan said.

I poured it into two water tumblers; we weren't really winos either. It smelled great through, spicy and rich.

"Cheers," I said to Evan and we both took sips as we leaned against the table.

"So how are you feeling now?" Evan asked Bea once he'd swallowed, sitting down and spreading himself out in the seat.

"Fine," she answered, "just a bit wobbly. Honestly though, thank you both so much. Really."

"Don't thank me. I didn't do anything. Apart from banging up my shoulder and proving what a weakling I am."

"You should see Bea's shoulder," I said, setting the table in front of them.

"Is it bad?" Aiden asked, sitting down awkwardly next to Evan.

"Show them," I said.

"It's not that bad." Bea looked embarrassed.

"Bea, they've seen your naked bum. Don't be ashamed to show them your shoulder!"

"What?" She whirled around. "You said they didn't!"

"Fuck," I said.

"Only for a second." Aiden was coloring now. "Honestly, it was a blur."

"Well, I for one saw your entire unblurred arse, and I have to say your sister is right—you have nothing to be embarrassed about. It's a very fine buttocks."

"Evan!" Aiden kicked his brother under the table.

The kitchen was totally silent for a second.

Then, I couldn't help it. A snort of laughter escaped me. Bea looked at our faces, then started cackling too, although her cheeks were still flushed. She put the pasta in the middle of the table and sat down.

"Fine," she said, and slipped down her sleeve to reveal the mottled blue-and-black skin of her shoulder.

"Wow, that's a good one!" Evan said.

"That must be really painful," Aiden said.

"Could have been worse."

I sipped my wine and ate my food and realized, at some point, that I was actually having fun.

Although I didn't see either of them move their chair, Aiden and Bea seemed to be somehow shifting closer and closer together as the evening went on. I stood up to take the bowls up to the sink and Evan followed me. He rinsed and I stacked the dishwasher.

"Yours is still working?" he said. "Ours died almost as soon as we moved in."

"You probably did something to it."

Another of those girlie giggles came from Bea, and Evan caught my eye. He cocked his head toward the door and I nodded reluctantly.

"Me and Ava are going to go for a stroll."

Bea looked at me over her shoulder. "Are you sure?"

"Yep."

"I think she'd prefer even my company over watching you guys try to flirt."

Aiden moved away from Bea like a shot.

"True," I laughed. I was starting to warm to Evan and his weird sense of humor. "See you guys in a bit."

I grabbed my coat from the hook and opened the door, but Evan was loitering.

"The wine," he mouthed at me.

I nodded, and went back into the kitchen. "Yoink," I said, grabbing it from the table. Aiden looked at me disapprovingly, which I thought was a bit rich. He was the one that had brought it.

The sun had set during dinner, and the air had turned chilly, like rain was coming. I pulled my jacket collar closer to my neck as Evan closed the door behind us and we walked out onto the road. I had gotten used to the quiet out there. How it heightened everything, the crunch of our feet on the asphalt, the faintest of winds, my breath and his.

In the darkness, the four occupied houses seemed to glow. Sometimes it felt like we'd been forgotten by life out here. The streetlights near the bottom of the estate had never ended up being installed at all. No one had bothered since there were no occupants down there. Even though it felt like the top of the hill was under a dim spotlight compared to the rest, I didn't mind it. The darkness made the stars so much clearer.

Evan and I walked slowly and aimlessly, passing the wine bottle between us and talking quietly. We both looked straight ahead, but every so often I stole a glance at him. The cold light made his eyes look like they glittered when he smiled, which was often.

Eventually, he asked me about Bea's condition, and I liked that he stopped smiling then. I ended up telling him about how worried she was about money, and what Nancy had offered that morning in the car.

"She says she's going to pay me the rates of a qualified nurse, so it's a pretty great deal," I said. He passed the wine bottle to me; I took a sip and gave it back to him.

"Are you sure that's what you want to do? I hear that old bat screaming blue murder some days."

"Really?"

"Yeah. But if she's Nancy's aunt, she can't be all bad."

"Great-aunt, but yeah, Nancy's the best."

"You know, I'd sometimes camp out in that house—" he pointed to one of the houses without glass in the windows down the street "—and I think she saw me one morning. I woke up and there was a torch shining in and I was sure I was going to get in so much trouble. But the next day, she'd left all these snacks there. It was just when I'd decided that all of humanity was shit too, so it was good timing."

I almost blurted out the truth, but managed to hold it in. Instead I asked him why he would camp out there. I'd wanted to know that for a while.

"After fights with my old man," he told me, "I used to enjoy storming out of the house. But it's not like there's anywhere around here to storm to."

I stopped walking and he turned to look at me.

"Your old man? As in, Aiden?"

"Yeah."

I looked away, not wanting to gape. "I thought he was your brother."

"Nah, but don't worry. Lots of people think that."

I couldn't get my head around it. "But wait, how old are you? I thought you were my age?"

"I'm nineteen," he said.

"But Aiden can't be much over thirty." I started attempting the math in my head.

"Don't try to work it out," he said, serious now. "It's gross. They were just kids playing at being adults. My mum's parents were really religious, so they made her keep me."

He passed me the wine, and we continued walking. I wondered whether Bea already knew Aiden was Evan's dad.

"What do you think that guy's deal is?" He looked toward the lit-up windows of the house across from Nancy's, changing the subject ungracefully. I knew a man lived alone there, surrounded by family portraits.

"I heard he murdered his whole family and buried them under the house," I said. He looked at me and my stomach twisted and puckered. I had revealed myself already. But Evan only whistled low through his teeth.

"Do you want to hear a story?" he said.

"Sure."

He sat down on the front lawn of one of the empty houses, and I sat next to him, swigging from the bottle again, my stomach starting to loosen.

"So this friend of mine, she was on the last train to Frankston. She got on the carriage at Richmond, and it was basically empty. There were these two big guys near the door, and a middle-aged couple down the other end. So she went and sat across from the middle-aged couple, as you would, right?"

"Yeah, sure," I said.

"So it's really late, and the couple are dressed nicely, like they've just gone out on a date. The woman is leaning on the guy's shoulder, and his arms are around her, but she just keeps staring at my friend in this really weird way."

"Where was she going?"

"Who?"

"Your friend?"

"I don't know. Home. Anyway, so my friend smiles at the lady but the lady doesn't smile back. She keeps looking away, and then looking back, but the lady is still staring at her in the real creepy way."

"Weird," I said.

"Shut up—you're ruining the flow."

"Don't tell me to shut up. How old are you?" But I smiled and leaned back on my elbows.

"So eventually my friend is like 'What?' But the lady doesn't reply, so she goes 'Can I help you with something?' and the husband looks at her and is like 'Sorry, my wife has drunk too much,' and the lady just keeps on staring. Then the train stops at the next stop, and one of the big guys grabs my friend and pushes her out with him onto the platform."

"Fuck."

"Yeah. And she's all screaming and stuff, and the man tells her he's actually a cop. He says that the husband murdered his wife on the train half an hour ago."

He took the wine from my hand and swigged it, grinning at my open mouth.

"Wait, so hang on," I said, "the woman was dead? That's why she was staring?"

"Yep."

"That's horrible!"

He nodded.

"But wait, so he killed his wife on the train? Wouldn't there have been blood everywhere."

"I don't know."

"But didn't your friend find out? Surely she'd be a witness or something?"

He cocked his head. "It didn't really happen to my friend. Just makes the story sound better."

"What?"

He grinned. "It probably isn't even true. It's just an urban legend. It's a good story though, right?"

I shook my head. "That's one of the most fucked-up things I've ever heard."

"Really?"

I thought for a second. "Actually, probably not."

So I told him the story about the man who had dressed up as a clown and murdered little boys, which he'd heard before, and the twin sisters who'd killed their mum together, which he hadn't. I expected him to ask me how I knew all these stories of murderers and psychopaths, but he didn't. He just told me some of his own in return.

"This is so morbid," I said eventually.

"Yeah, Bea and Aiden would hate it."

"Do you think it's weird to be kind of interested by this stuff?"

I expected him to say yes, that we were both being creepy and inappropriate, but he didn't.

"Not at all. I mean, people actually do this stuff. Real humans, like you and me. It's fascinating to think about what gets them to that point, don't you think? Where you're ready to do something so evil to another person?"

"I guess." I leaned back on the grass, staring up at the moon in the clear sky. It looked a little too big, too low, like we were in a painting and the artist hadn't gotten the proportions quite right.

I wondered if he'd consider what I'd been doing to Theodore as an evil thing. Following him around, looking in through his window. But no, it was Theodore who was in the wrong here, not me.

"We've almost finished it," he said, showing me the near-empty bottle of wine.

"Yeah," I said, "we should probably get back."

"Yeah," he agreed, getting to his feet. "Let's see if they've gotten to the holding-hands stage yet."

Walking backward toward my house, he smiled at me.

"What?" I asked.

He shrugged. "Nothing." But he was still smiling.

10

It can be overwhelming when a chapter in your life ends. The last day of school or the day you quit your job. Even when it's something you don't exactly enjoy, it's still sad when a stage of your life has ended—done and dusted, kaput. I felt sad that morning. But it was the best kind of sadness, the most exquisite, the most rare. It's not often, at least for me, that things end in victory.

I took the tram down Swanston Street toward University of Melbourne. Squashed in near the door, hot air pushing through the vents, wet parkas squeaking against wet parkas, backpacks smacking into shoulders, sweating from the body heat, I wasn't frustrated. I got off with all the other students, and almost felt like one of them. Usually, it was the opposite. I would feel so conspicuous, so obviously not where I was supposed to be. But in that moment, I felt like I imagined they did every day. That my whole future was ahead of me, that anything was possible.

I waited for Theodore to pass by to his applied chemistry class, but he didn't. That was when I started to worry, though only a little. I thought perhaps he was still in bed having hungover sex. I'd seen it before. So I made my way to his dorm room window. It was closed. Pressing my forehead against it to look inside, I saw that his bed was empty, just tangled white sheets. Squinting, I looked toward the bookshelf, where the box of laundry sachets had sat, all this time, in between a chemistry textbook and *The Catcher in the Rye*. But there was nothing but an empty space.

I got on the tram back down Swanston Street. Someone whacked into me with their backpack and I pushed them back.

"Hey!" they said.

I snarled at them, "sorry."

They gave me space then, all the way to Collins Street. I rubbed my arm; it had really hurt. The guy would have felt it connecting with someone, but he hadn't even turned to check. That's the thing about people. They don't care if they hurt you. They'll only notice if you hurt them back.

When I got off I wasn't sure where to go. I didn't know where Theodore's parents lived, if that's where he was, and I didn't want to go home. I'd jinxed it. After everything that had happened, I should have known by then that once I thought I'd won it really meant I'd lost. I could just imagine the look on Mel's face if she could see me now. *Fuck, Ava*, she'd say, *what the hell is wrong with you?*

I sat down on a bench and stared toward the campsite in City Square. It had grown since yesterday. There were probably close to a hundred people there, and lots more tents and small structures. People were sitting around, listening to someone speak, but from where I was, the voice was clipped and lifted away by the passing trams. Every so often the crowd would call "yeah!" in unison.

There was a large banner that had We Are The 99% written across it in black block letters. It sounded familiar, but I couldn't really remember what it was all about. I had just decided to go and get the bus home when I noticed him. Theodore. Like he'd been conjured from my own wanting. He was sitting with his legs crossed in the crowd, no shoes, watching. He wasn't nodding along with the rest of the crowd, but fiddling with his phone in his lap.

★ ★ ★

By the time I got off the bus I had a new plan. It wasn't as straightforward or as easy, though the chance of success was probably higher. But I would need help.

The rain had made the surfaces of Lakeside look shiny. The gates twinkled before me, the roof of the convenience store glimmered and I could see inside to its empty white shelves. The barren hole of the lake had a good inch of brown water in it.

I reached Evan's house, and was relieved to see him sitting in the kitchen through the window.

"Hey, neighbor," I said.

His face snapped up, startled, but he smiled when he saw me. "Do you make a habit of peeking in people's windows?"

I laughed. "Is Aiden here?"

"Nah."

"Good, can I come in?"

He grinned.

Evan made me a cup of tea. He had the heater on, and his kitchen was warm and smelled mildly of burned dust.

"What are you working on?" I asked, looking over at the thick book open on the table.

"I'm retaking my VCEs," he said, his back to me as he poured the hot water into the mugs, steam rising around him. "Totally failed them. You don't want to know my score."

"Trust me—you don't want to know mine either."

He turned to look at me. "Can't be that bad if you got into nursing."

I considered telling him then. Telling him everything. But he turned back around to grab the box of tea bags and I didn't say anything.

He put the mug of tea in front of me and a carton of milk in the middle of the table. He'd tied the string of the tea bag around the top of the handle. I'd never seen anyone do it that way before.

"So were you at uni today?"

"Yeah."

"Did you put your forms in to go part-time?"

"I've been thinking about it," I said, twiddling the paper square at the end of the string around my finger. "I think I'm going to just defer the next semester."

"Pity," he said.

"Yeah."

On the long bus ride here, I'd planned this conversation, but now that I was here in his kitchen, having tea, my request felt bizarre. He'd laugh at me. Or worse, he'd see what was really inside me. I took a sip from my mug, and the liquid was unexpectedly hot. I coughed, and it sounded loud against the quiet rasp of the heater.

"You okay?"

"Yep," I said, rubbing a sleeve over my mouth. "Okay, I have a favor to ask you."

"I see. So you're not just here for my A-grade tea-making skills?"

"I don't know about that," I said. "Why do you tie the string on? It's so crazy strong now."

"It's so it doesn't get into the tea, and then you don't have to stick your fingers in to get it out and burn yourself."

"Yeah, but I did anyway."

"I thought you wanted a favor? You're meant to be buttering me up," he teased.

"That sounds weird." I leaned back in my chair to look at him. "It's a big one."

"As long it doesn't involve bashing in a door I think I'll be okay. I didn't exactly prove my manliness last time."

"No door bashing."

"Good."

"Okay, so there's this guy at uni," I said, not quite sure how much to say.

His face fell. "Okay."

"No, I mean, not like that," I said. God, I felt like such an idiot. I was sure my face was reddening, but I continued, "This guy is an absolute piece of shit. I think he's dealing drugs and I want to, you know, expose him."

"Huh," he said, "okay, that's not what I was expecting. What kind of drugs?"

"Not sure."

He took a sip of his tea, watching me over the mug.

"It's just," I went on, "I thought if you went and bought some from him and I like, took a photo, or something like that, then we could send it to the Dean. Get him in deep trouble. Expelled maybe."

He put his mug down and looked at me properly. He seemed shocked. I guess that wasn't what he thought I'd say.

"Okay, wow, that is a big favor," he said, "and while I'm honored I'm the person you think is the most convincing to be in this drug bust of yours, I need to ask. Why do you care if he's dealing?"

"I don't think he's just dealing them. I think he's making them."

"Still," he said, "I didn't think you were such a concerned citizen. Are you protecting the youth of today? Who cares if this guy is dealing? It's not really your business."

I took a breath. If I wanted him to do it I had to tell him something. "It's not really about the drugs. It's about, I dunno, payback."

"Oh okay, so this guy cheated on you or something?"

"No," I said, trying to find a way to explain it, "we went to high school together. It was him and this group of girls. They played this trick on me at a party. It was bad. He's just, I don't know… He's just the biggest asshole in the world and he made

my life hell but he just keeps on going around being a dickhead
and getting away with it and I don't think it's right."

His eyebrows rose. "Wow."

I stared at my tea, wishing I hadn't come. I had said too
much, just blurted it all out and now I was exposed. He was
seeing it. Seeing the nasty repellent thing inside that I was trying so hard to hide.

When I looked back up at him, I was expecting him to be
staring at me, but he wasn't. He was looking at the table. He
didn't seem to be freaked out or disgusted. Instead, he just
looked really sad. But then he looked up and the sparkle came
back to his eyes.

"Okay, so when do you want to do this thing?"

11

We caught the bus in together the next day. We could have delayed until the end of the week and gotten a lift with Nancy, but I couldn't wait. The excitement was different from the day before. There was no exquisite sadness, no feelings of letting go and moving on. With Evan I only felt hot, jangling anticipation.

"So the neighbors are starting to worry. No one has seen the whole family for a week, right? At the beginning of the week the lights are all on but, one by one, the rooms are turning black."

"Creepy," he says.

"Yeah. So they break in and of course—"

"Everyone's dead."

"Yep, except—"

"The dog?"

"No, the dad. He killed his whole family."

"That old trick. With what?"

"I don't know—a gun I think. Just *pow, pow, pow.* Yep, so he goes missing for ten years."

"Holy shit."

"Yeah. They think it's a lost cause. But then they put his face on some American crime show, *America's Most Wanted* I think. They, like, age his face to show what he'd look like now and the next day they get this weird call from this lady. The night before she'd been sitting there watching it with her husband

and kids, and she looks from the picture to her husband and they look absolutely identical."

"Ha, that's awesome. You know, I think they made a movie about that."

"Really?"

"Yeah, just a couple of years ago. I think it had the guy from *Gossip Girl* in it."

"Have you seen it?"

"Nah. Do you want to watch it sometime?"

I looked at him, my heart in my throat. "Yeah, sure. We can try to squeeze between your father and my sister on the couch."

"Gross," he said, looking at me carefully.

"Yeah," I said, the fear dissolving. "If they got married, what would that make us?"

"Oh God, don't think about it."

"Would I be your aunt?"

He turned to look out the window. It had steamed up and you couldn't see outside. I worried that maybe I'd offended him, but then I heard the wet squeak of his finger on the glass. He was writing "Auntie Ava" and then drew a sad face underneath. I smiled and turned away.

Part of me had worried that the camp would be gone by the time we arrived. It was the opposite. It had gotten even bigger; the small square was now jammed with people. The tourists sitting at the overpriced coffee shop on the corner were taking photos of them.

"Nervous?" he asked, as we approached.

"Yeah. Really fucking nervous."

"Hey, don't say that—you'll freak me out. I'm the one who has to do this."

I wanted to tell him how much it meant to me. That if we fucked this up, I didn't know what I was going to do. But instead I pointed out Theodore. He was sitting up on one of the black steps to the side talking to a girl.

"He's not what I imagined," Evan said.

"What did you imagine?"

"I don't know."

He took a breath. "I guess we should just do it now, then."

"Are you sure?"

"Yeah." He looked at me, his eyes all crinkled like he really was afraid. But then he smiled and looked normal again. "Make sure you get my best angle."

Then he did it. He just strode right on over and tapped Theodore on the shoulder. I'd watched him for so long, he'd seemed untouchable. It had been like sitting in a cinema, the sounds and vision surrounding you, immersing you like you were really there. But Evan just walked on through the screen like it was nothing.

Theodore turned to him. I felt sick. My skin was cold and hot and prickly all at once. My throat tightened so abruptly I made a retching sound.

"You alright?" a guy said, coming up to me.

"Yep."

Evan was talking, using his hands too much. Theodore wasn't saying anything, just taking him in with his arms crossed over his chest.

"Are you sure? You kind of look like you might faint."

I turned to the guy, ready to snap at him to go away, but he was looking at me with real concern. He had glasses on, and he sort of looked like a dad.

"Really, I'm okay. But thank you."

"Good," he said. Then, "This is all pretty amazing, isn't it?"

Theodore was talking now, shaking his head. Evan's palms went up, and I could read his lips. *C'mon, man.* I opened the camera on my phone screen, my finger so clammy I could barely do it.

"It's so great when people actually stand up and say enough is enough, don't you think?"

I turned to the guy, and he smiled at me, waiting for an answer.

"Yeah, it's great."

"And so peaceful, that's the most important thing. I mean, maybe I'm stuck in the seventies, but I honestly think it's the only way to make a change."

"Yep."

I turned back to Evan and Theodore, but they were gone. No!

I started walking forward, eyes sweeping across the people sitting cross-legged on the ground, the placards, the tents. I couldn't see them. They were gone, totally gone. I wanted to cry. That stupid man! I should have just told him to go away.

I tried to take a breath, to think. They couldn't just disappear. I closed my eyes, breathed in, then out, then whirled around again. There. There they were. Coming out of a tent. Evan's hand in his pocket. He caught my eye and gave a minute shrug. Then strode toward me.

"I'm sorry," he whispered. "He wouldn't do it out here in the open. But I got it."

"Really?" I wanted to kiss him.

"Yep, a hundred bucks."

"I'll pay you back."

"He was so strange about it," he said. "He wouldn't give it to me at first. Kept saying that he didn't actually sell it direct. I was trying to figure what it actually was, you know? I asked him if it was good stuff and he looked at me like I was some creep and said he'd never used it. Said *it's not like I have to*, or something like that."

"Hey, mate!"

We both looked up. Theodore was there, walking toward

us. He was looking at me. Straight at me, an unreadable expression on his face.

"One more thing," he said, stopping a few meters short of us.

Evan stepped toward him. Theodore looked at me again, then turned so his back was to me. Fuck. He knew. I could just hear what he said.

"Don't use it all at once, alright? I forgot to say. There's enough for like five in there."

Theodore turned to look at me again, then walked back over to his friends. If it were a cartoon, my mouth would be hanging open, hitting the floor with shock. He didn't remember. He didn't even recognize me.

12

The baggy was green and white. It had pictures of bubbles around the brand name, and the top was folded and stuck down with a piece of clear tape. It was made from that thin, plastic waterproof paper, and was about half the size of my hand.

"We've got to try it," I said, eventually, as we walked up the hill.

"Really?" Evan asked.

We'd gotten the bus back in silence. There was too much going on in my head, all too muddled and twisted to say out loud.

"Yeah. If we're going to know what to do. Take it to the police or just to the Dean, we need to know what it actually is."

He looked at me. "I'm up for it. Sounds fun! Like a Lucky Dip."

"What do you think it is?"

"Honestly? I'd say it's that ADD drug—what's it called?"

"Can't remember. Why would it be that?"

"Apparently heaps of students use it to study. It just makes you really focused and awake."

"Oh," I said, slightly disappointed. I'd been imagining something more damning. Cocaine maybe, or speed.

"But apparently it's fun just to take too, makes you talk a mile a minute."

"When should we do it?"

"Why not now?"

"What if it really is just washing-up powder?" I asked. "Will we die?"

"I doubt it. I think it'd just make us feel sick."

"That'd be pretty funny," I said, and even I could hear how fake my voice sounded.

Honestly, I was scared. Not because it was an epically dumb thing to do. No, I was scared of what I might do, what I might say if I started talking a mile a minute like he'd said. I was afraid of what I might tell him.

In the end we decided do it at Evan's house, after dinner. Not his real house, it was too possible that Aiden would come home and catch us acting strangely. No, we'd go to the half-built house that he sometimes slept in midway down the hill.

I had dinner with Bea, half listened to her talking about Aiden. She was smitten, she'd decided. He was the one. When I told her I was going to go hang out with Evan she grinned at me.

"If you marry him and I marry Aiden, then that means you'll be my daughter in-law."

So she did know about Aiden.

"That's just weird," I said. "Plus, it's really not like that."

"Yeah, right."

I was surprised sometimes at how little Bea understood me. She thought she knew me better than anyone, that was clear, but really she had absolutely no idea. I often wondered how she would react if she did know. If I sat her down one day and told her all my truths. I don't know what she'd say, but I know her eyes would be different when she looked at me.

The living room to Evan's hideout house was identical to my own in layout. The carpet hadn't been put down, so the floor was unsanded pine floorboards, which were incredibly dirty.

I guess it was the lack of glass in the window; everything was grimy with old dust. It smelled of rot.

Evan was already there. He'd opened up his sleeping bag and put it on the floor like a picnic mat. He was sipping on a can of beer, and he offered me another, but I shook my head. He'd filled a jug with water and brought a little portable stereo, which was now quietly playing the sounds of a woman's soaring voice.

"Is this Florence and the Machine?" I asked.

"Yeah, you don't like it?" he asked. "I thought this would be your kind of thing."

I wasn't completely sure if he was making fun of me or being serious, so I kept looking around the room.

"Is that a candle?" I asked.

"You're very perceptive," he said. "Why don't you sit down." I didn't.

"Why do you have a candle?"

It was a thick cream-colored one, like a church candle.

"What? You think I'm trying to get you high and then seduce you?"

I glared at him. "Maybe."

He glared back, incredulous. "It's about to get dark, you idiot. It's not like the lights work here."

I looked up. There wasn't even a light bulb in the socket.

"Oh," I said, and sat down feeling completely ridiculous. "Sorry."

"So you brought it, right?"

"Yep."

I took the packet from my pocket and showed him. He got his lighter out and began flicking it next to the candlewick. "I'm kind of excited about this. We can do drugs and still feel holier-than-thou."

I put the edge of my fingernail underneath the sticky tape and pulled it off, then opened the packet carefully. Gingerly, I put my nose toward it and sniffed, expecting a sharp chemical smell, but the scent was barely there.

"Doesn't smell like laundry powder," I said. "Doesn't really smell like anything."

"How should we do this?" he asked.

"I don't know. We could eat it? Like sherbet."

"Why don't we snort it? That seems more realistic."

He stood up, and I followed him into the kitchen. Even though it was the same shape as mine, it was even less recognizable than the living room. There were no skirting boards, and holes in the wall that I hoped were for wiring, not mice. There were empty caverns where the fridge and the dishwasher were meant to go and they were filled with dried-up leaves, perhaps caught from drafts that had swept through the glassless windows over the years. The countertops were finished though, with the same shiny fake marble as ours. Evan tipped out some of the powder onto it.

"Not all of it!" I said.

"I'm not. Geez, you'd be no fun to party with."

"Shut up."

He took his wallet out of his back pocket, and withdrew his driving license. Carefully, he separated the powder into two and then attempted to create two thin lines. I took his wallet and looked inside.

"I wish you had a fifty. That would seem way more glam."

"Spent all my dough on this stuff!" he said.

"Oh yeah." I withdrew a five. "I really will pay you back. I'm starting next week at Nancy's."

"No stress," he said. "Are you ready?"

My heart pulsed. "This is sort of exciting!"

My fears of exposure were starting to dissipate. Instead, I wondered if it was going to be like in the movies. Whether, in just a few minutes, we'd be dancing around the estate with huge pupils. I wondered if everything would seem beautiful and nice and maybe I actually would want to have sex with Evan.

"Ladies first."

I carefully rolled the five into a tube. If the kitchen hadn't been so dark and grimy, I might have felt like a rock star.

"Whatever you do, don't sneeze," he said.

"Shut up."

I'd never done this before, but I'd seen it in the movies enough times to know what to do. I put the tube just inside my left nostril, put a finger over the right one, then sniffed. The powder shot up my nose and down the back of my throat, burning the whole way. I spun on the spot and started coughing. The taste was unbearable; it was choking me. I heard a *tsk* sound and turned to see Evan hand me a can of beer.

I took it from him and chugged, letting the cold liquid wash down the claggy acidic feeling.

"You didn't even do the whole line," he said.

"Yeah, well you can have the rest of mine if you like. That was horrible."

I passed him the note, then sniffed again and rubbed my nose. It still felt like it was burning.

"Your turn," I said. "That better not have been fucking detergent."

He leaned down and put the note to his nose. I couldn't really see what he was doing, only the back of his head, but I heard the loud snorting noise. He looked at me, and smiled triumphantly, but his eyes looked all shiny and he held out his hand for his beer.

"Nasty, right?"

"Yeah," he said, his voice sounding weak. He was holding in a cough, I could tell.

"Can you feel anything?" I asked as we went and sat down on the sleeping bag in the living room.

"Maybe a bit," he said. "You?"

"Yeah, maybe," I said, hugging my knees. Really I was just feeling tired.

He took a sip of his beer and then passed it to me. "So that guy," he started, "he really did seem like a prick."

"Yeah, he is."

He was looking at me carefully, like he was debating on whether to say something.

"What? Spit it out," I said. I was feeling a little bit nauseous, although I wasn't sure if I was just imagining it.

"I was bullied too, you know," he said. "These guys at school. They would say this awful stuff about my mum, and kept calling my dad a pedo, even though that doesn't even make sense since they were the same age when he got her pregnant."

"That sucks," I said.

"Yeah, it was shit. They were always tripping me up and threatening to bash me after school and stuff. Anyway, what I mean is. I get it."

"I wasn't bullied," I said. "That's not what happened."

"Oh," he said. Then, "Really?"

"Yeah, it wasn't like that. They were my friends, really."

"The people who played the trick on you?"

"Yeah. I mean I hated them. I still hate them—they ruined my life. But it wasn't a bullying thing."

"Do you want to tell me?" he asked, and without even thinking I shook my head. I was feeling dizzy by then. Light-headed.

"One day?" he asked.

"Yeah," I said, then sank down so my head was on the floor. "Are you feeling anything yet?"

"Nah," he said.

I closed my eyes. The light from the candle was spinning around too fast.

"I don't think it's working," I said.

"You're slurring," he said, the words running together.

"So are you."

I'm not sure exactly what happened then. I remember wanting to tell him the room was spinning, but I'm not sure if I actually managed to say it out loud. I think I remember his hands touching my hair softly. It'd felt nice. I think I might have moved closer to him, to get the warmth from his body, but I'm only guessing.

What I do remember was waking up. It was almost pitch-black. Just the faintest glow of the streetlight accentuating the edges of things. I felt like I had swallowed sand. My mouth and throat were painfully dry. I tried to move my tongue, but I couldn't. It was glued to the bottom of my mouth. I rolled over, and my stomach cramped with the movement. Reaching out, I felt something next to me. I ran my hand over it. It was warm, its surface a rough material.

Evan groaned and my breath caught in my throat. I'd forgotten he was there. I was touching his leg.

"You okay?" I said, but it sounded weird. I could barely remember where we were, or why on earth we were there. It was then that I noticed how freezing cold I was. I was shaking all over.

I remembered the candle, and wondered when it had gone out. Rubbing my hand back up his leg, I found his jean pocket, the lighter a hard rectangle inside it. It took me a while to get it out. My fingers were clumsy. Finally, when I did, I squeezed down to light it. After three attempts, it worked. I leaned toward the candle, but it was gone. It had melted all the way to nothing, so it was just a hard white puddle, the silver disk that held the wick in place had risen to the top. My thumb quivered, and the lighter went out. I grabbed the jug of water and started drinking. The sandy feeling was still there, but the water released my tongue.

Switching the lighter again, I held it toward Evan's face. His eyes were open, and he was looking at me. He was still sitting where he had been, propped up against the wall. He'd had more than me, I remembered, plus the beers.

"Are you okay?" I asked.

"Some water?" he croaked.

I passed him the jug, and he drank directly from it as I had. In the flickering shadow from the lighter I could see his Adam's apple flinch with each swallow. Finally, he put the jug down and rubbed a hand over his mouth.

"That fucking prick," he said.

I just stared at him, my head still woozy and slow.

"That was Rohypnol, or something like it. The dickhead is making roofies."

13

We were okay, I'm sure you'll be glad to know. Well, I was okay, clearly, since I'm sitting here right now. But Evan was fine too. I sent a letter to the Dean of the school with all the information I had, plus what was left of the powder. The more I thought about it, the more it felt like that wasn't enough. So I called the police and left an anonymous message explaining what Theodore was doing, and telling them where he hid his stash.

The City Square campsite was on the news the next day. The police raided it. I wonder if you were one of them? I remember watching the news, my limbs still heavy and slow, and seeing the video of the cops coming to clear the people away in a long black line. I saw him, only for a flash, but I was sure it was him. The nice man with glasses who kept trying to talk to me that day. There was blood on his face. Really, I was looking for Theodore, but if he'd stuck it out until then, I didn't see him.

By the time I was well enough to go and check, Theodore's room was empty. All his stuff was gone. I don't know if the police got to him, or if he was just expelled. All I was sure of was that it had worked. I had ruined him, just like I had set out to do. He would never know it was me that had done it, but it didn't matter.

For the first time in years, I felt good. I'd like to be able to tell you that it was only because I had done something good, put a stop to the horrible thing Theodore had been doing. But that wasn't all it was. I had righted a wrong, put a piece of myself back together. The feeling was addictive.

Part 3

IMPULSIVITY

2008

14

None of this is the point though, is it? You won't want to hear about how I took down another entitled asshole who didn't even see women as people. They are a dime a dozen, right? No, you'll only want to know what I did, and why I did it. My crime and my motive. My mind has taken me down a tangent. Maybe because I like that story better than the other. I like the story where I'm the hero, where good and bad are clearly defined and I'm on the right side for once. What happened next wasn't so simple. But really, there is no point telling you about that yet. There's no point in you hearing about my revenge, if I haven't told you the cause. I do have a cause, trust me. It may have been a long time ago now, but it is not something I'll ever forget.

The trip out to Lakeside felt so different when it was with them. We'd come straight from school. Saanvi was behind the wheel of her mother's Volkswagen, Mel in the front next to her, Cass and me in the back. We were blasting Janis Joplin, and screaming along with her ragged, soaring voice.

The windows were down and our hair whipped in the wind. With them, everything was fun. Everything that had seemed mundane before became an adventure. It had been over a month since we had destroyed Mr. Bitto, but it was the best time of my life.

"I can't wait for you guys to meet Bea," I yelled over the verse, leaning forward from the back.

"I want to meet Chucky!" squealed Cass next to me.

My mum had made good on her promise of a dog. We'd gone to the lost dogs home, and walked past cages of dogs with sad eyes. When we saw Chucky, we couldn't keep walking. The plan had been to get a puppy. Chucky was a grandpa. He was at least seven years old, brown and white, with short legs and scraggly hair. We had no idea what breed of dog he was, but he had the biggest smile I'd ever seen. We couldn't leave him behind.

"Turn left here," I yelled.

"What?"

"Left!"

Saanvi spun the wheel, her tires squeaking as she took the corner. She turned the music down a bit, saying, "Fuck, this really is hillbilly country."

"Yeah, it must take you forever to get to school," Mel said.

"I kind of like it." Cass looked around. "It's so pretty out here. And peaceful. I like the idea of living out in nature."

I looked at her, smiling.

"What?" she said. I'd noticed Cass was always worried she'd said something dumb.

"Just wait," I told her, and to Saanvi, "Go right here."

We turned the last corner.

"Whoa," said Mel, as the gray mass of Lakeside appeared in front of us. Saanvi stopped at the gates.

"Yep," I said.

Driving up the hill, I was glad when Mel turned the music off. It felt obnoxious in the silence. They all turned to look at the empty lake. I saw the cavern of mud through their eyes, the foraging crows.

"Is there anyone else living here?" Mel asked.

"Yeah, a few others. There's a man that lives down that road.

I saw him getting in his car once. My mum told me that there's two women living in that house there." We drove past a concrete house identical to all the others. "She thinks it's an old lady and her daughter. And Bea says there are two guys right near us, brothers I think, but I haven't seen them yet. We're this one here on the left."

Saanvi pulled in behind Mum's station wagon. No one said anything. I can still remember the noxious taste that appeared in the back of my throat whenever I thought I'd displeased them. I looked at each of their faces, knowing they were judging me, knowing I shouldn't have brought them there.

Then, a bark, and Chucky ran to meet the car.

"Aww!" Cass unclipped her seat belt and got out of the car, kneeling down on the road to pat him. He jumped up onto her knees and she squealed as he licked her face.

15

It's harder than I thought to remember back to this time. Not the bad bits, I've always known they would be difficult. That's why I've never said a word about what happened to anyone. No, it's the nice memories that are painful to think of. I was so naive, so ready to give those girls everything: my loyalty, my trust, my devoted friendship. I was ready to spill every secret I ever had, to follow them to the ends of the earth. I guess the last bit turned out to be true, in some ways.

This room is getting stuffy. I've breathed the same air for too long. I can hear the electric hum of the fluorescent light. When I first arrived it was barely audible, but now it sounds loud. My head is beginning to throb, and my back aches from sitting down for so long in this hard plastic chair. I want to reposition myself, stretch out my limbs, let my muscles pop and my bones crackle, but I don't. I stay still, muscles clenched and ready. It's only my mind that is moving, almost too fast for me to keep up with, as I work out what I will tell you.

I want to say it felt natural to finally be friends with Mel, Cass and Saanvi, but that's another lie. I'd thought that with them I could be my true self, but I couldn't. I had already started to get worried, to get used to that noxious taste of doubt in the back of my throat, weeks before the night they slept over at my house.

In some ways though, I was happy. A simple, straightforward happiness, something I couldn't remember feeling before. Something I haven't experienced since.

That first lunchtime, the day after the career expo, I took my place with them on the damp grass of the oval. I was so used to watching their little triangle from a distance that it was surreal to be a part of it. To make it a square. I sat with my arms around my knees, grinning, while terrified they were going to tell me to go away.

"These are cool." Mel tapped a black varnished fingertip onto my Doc Marten boots. She pulled her bag open and fished in the bottom for her Wite-Out pen. Shaking it, she leaned down over my feet. I looked at the top of her shiny head. Down her part, I could see rows and rows of hair follicles like shark teeth.

"Better." She clicked the lid back on and returned the pen to her bag. She'd drawn a white love heart onto the cracked leather, with an arrow puncturing the middle. I'd already noticed the heart on all of their Docs. It was like a gang tattoo, a cattle stamp. It meant I was part of them. I was in.

Over the next month they taught me how to drink and how to do my hair. They introduced me to the band MGMT, and we screamed along to the words in bedrooms and cars and made plans to try ecstasy together. I learned that everything from the seventies was cool, the eighties were lame, it was okay to like Katy Perry ironically, but never Taylor Swift.

The first time we cut class we went to Saanvi's house. I didn't really want to cut, but I was elated just to be going along. Saanvi was the least sure on me. She'd never actually said anything, but I could tell that she didn't really think I belonged. Still, they both followed whatever Mel said, so she couldn't have the two of them over without inviting me as well.

Saanvi's house was on a slim tree-lined grove off the grungy bars and cafés of Brunswick Street. From the outside, it didn't look like a house, just a high dark brick wall with a door set into it. It went as long as three of the terrace houses before it though. When she pulled out her keys, I was glad, relieved to get off the street. I was trying to seem as relaxed as the rest of them, but I kept flinching every time I heard the crunch of a car turning onto the road, worried it would be a teacher.

Inside, her house was incredible. I'd never been to a place like this before. Usually we went to Mel's and sometimes Cass's, though not often because her mum was always crying. Mel and Cass both lived in houses about a million times nicer than mine, but not like this. Saanvi's house was so modern, so full of big open spaces. The middle section was hollowed out through the whole three stories. There was a skylight, as well as huge windows around the top and a mezzanine entirely made up of bookshelves.

Mel and Cass flopped down on one of the pristine white sofas.

"Wish it was warm enough to go in the pool." Saanvi threw off her bag and lay down on the cream carpet.

I knew I should sit down too, but I couldn't stop looking around, wondering how it all worked. "Why do you have so many books?"

"Duh, so my parents can pretend to be smart."

I shrugged and sat down on the very edge of the sofa, worried my dark jeans might leave a mark. Mel didn't seem to care, she had her boots up on the cushion next to her, and was plaiting a lock of her hair in front of her face. I noticed that this was something she did when she was bored; the others seemed to always take it as a sign that they had to do something to entertain her. A light drizzle of rain began falling against the skylight above us, making that big airy house feel somehow dark and sinister.

"What do you guys want to do?" Cass asked, looking between Saanvi and me for ideas.

★ ★ ★

Just a few hours later I was standing over the toilet bowl, my jeans crumpled across the shiny white tiles.

"Are you doing it?" Mel called through the door.

"I don't think it's going to work. It's too big."

"We all did it! Of course it will work."

I held the tampon in front of me by the string. It was puffed up like a cloud, almost an inch in width. Every few seconds a drip of vodka would fall from it, splashing into the toilet water.

It had been Mel's idea. She said she'd seen it on some British current affairs program. It had been called a "youth epidemic," but she'd never heard of anyone actually doing it. At first, Cass and Saanvi said no. I was relieved. I definitely didn't want to try it either, but knew I would have to if the rest of them did. But somehow, while I was out of the room, she seemed to convince them.

We had slipped into Saanvi's dad's study.

"I know he keeps a bottle in here somewhere. I can smell it on his breath."

"I can't believe we are really doing this!" Mel put her arm around my waist and squeezed. I noticed Cass was quiet, and I tried to catch her eye. If I could get her to say she didn't want to, then maybe I could get out of it too. She didn't look at me.

Saanvi began looking through the drawers of the huge wooden desk. I wanted to ask what her dad did to warrant such an amazing home office. It must have been important.

"If it's anywhere it's got to be in here. Dad wouldn't leave it somewhere my mum could find it. Bingo!" She pulled out a bottle of whiskey. The dark amber liquid rippled as she set it on top of a neat pile of papers.

"I don't know." My thighs clenched together protectively. "Does he have anything less...intense?"

"What? You want me to see if he's got wine? Or beer? That would just be gross as well as pointless."

"Yeah." Mel let go of me. "Plus do you really want to put fermented grapes up your whoo-ha. I reckon that would give you thrush."

"Whoo-ha?" Saanvi laughed, and begun rummaging through the next drawer, her face lit up. "Here. Perfect."

She pulled out a slim frosted glass bottle. Belvedere vodka. Mel said she'd go first.

Cass, Saanvi and I sat waiting in Saanvi's room while Mel had disappeared into the bathroom with the bottle and a tampon.

"Why do people even do this?" Cass asked. She still wasn't looking at me. She was sitting on the chair at Saanvi's desk, picking at her cuticles.

"I think it's so you can't smell the booze on their breath," Saanvi told her.

"Nah." Mel opened the bathroom door. "It means it absorbs faster. Plus, less calories."

Mel's eyes were glowing. She grinned at me, then threw a tampon to Cass.

"You're up. The bottle's in there."

Cass and Saanvi each took their turn, barely staying in the bathroom a few minutes each. They both said it was easy, it didn't feel weird or anything. I was desperately hoping one of them would chicken out, but they didn't.

"Bring the bottle in here," Mel called to Saanvi when she came out. Mel looked up at me, that cold flicker in her eye, a look I wasn't used to yet but came to know well. Saanvi passed the bottle over to her and Mel unscrewed the lid and took a sip.

"Not too much!"

"We can fill it up with water."

"Yeah, I know, but if it's more than a couple of inches he'll notice."

Mel just rolled her eyes. She put the bottle between her knees and unwrapped a tampon. Holding on to the string she let it fall in with a plop, like she was fishing.

"I can do it myself." I reached for the bottle, but she jerked it out of the way.

"No. I know you'll just leave it in for two seconds and not do it properly."

That hurt, even if it was partly true. "I wasn't going to do that."

She ignored me, watching as the tampon began to bloat.

"Hurry up!" she was saying now, jiggling the handle. "Do you need me to come in and help you?"

"No!" I yelled, still staring at the dripping pendulum. "I just don't know how you guys managed to get it in."

"If a dick can fit in there, that thing definitely can," Saanvi called.

"Ew," I heard Cass say.

There was no point in hesitating. I knew I had to do it. I put one foot up on the toilet seat and tried to stuff the wet cotton inside me. A trickle of cold vodka ran through my fingers onto the plastic seat.

"It's working," I called. Sort of, at least. I heard them laughing and whispering, but couldn't make out what they were saying. It was already starting to burn, but I pushed it up farther. Tears sprang to my eyes and I tried to blink them away. In that moment I wished more than anything I was still at school, bored at the back of English class.

I grabbed some toilet paper and rubbed at the liquid that was dribbling down my thighs, then pulled my jeans back on. It felt horrible. Like something big and sharp prickling at my insides.

When I opened the door Mel looked at me closely. "You did it?"

I nodded and she laughed again. I tried to laugh along with her. This was fun after all, an adventure. This was what I wanted. To be daring, to reach my full potential. To not be a scared little nerd just watching anymore. To really live.

"Is yours hurting at all?" I asked them.

"Mine is tingling a little bit," Saanvi said.

"Yeah, I bet you love it too. It's tingling in all the right places," Mel said.

"Shut up!"

Mel grabbed my hand. "Let's go out."

I had to hold the banister as I walked down the spiral staircase. My legs were heavy, and my head woozy already. I reached for my backpack.

Mel pushed it out of the way with her foot. "Leave it. It makes it so obvious that we're still at school."

Walking back out through the door, my eyes hurt from the light. It wasn't even five o'clock yet, and though it was overcast and still spitting with rain, the day felt too bright. I pulled my hood over my head and tugged at the cords so it tightened around my face.

"I think she's smashed already," I heard Cass whisper. I turned to them, wondering which one of us she meant.

"Come on." Mel pushed me along. "Apparently they never bother to check for IDs at Bar Open before dark."

I could hear them giggling and whispering again, but I didn't listen. I raised my face up to the sky and felt the coldness of the misty rain on my cheeks. My insides were still burning a little, but otherwise I felt good. Light and free, the nervousness abated. I knew it had been a test; Mel didn't think I would do it for some reason. But I had done it. I'd proven myself.

Cars whizzed down Brunswick Street, flicking dirty water up from the gutters. The four of us raced across the road, darting quickly in front of the cars. I almost slipped over on the wet tram tracks, then began laughing, almost hysterically.

"Stop it." Mel's face was humorless. "We won't get in if you act so obviously drunk."

"But don't you guys feel it too?"

Cass put her hand on my shoulder and a finger to her lips. That made me want to giggle again, but I kept it in, nodding instead. A dampness was beginning to collect in my underwear, thank God I was wearing black jeans.

Bar Open had a small hand-painted sign in its grimy front window. Mel led the way, and we walked in without anyone seeming to notice. A noisy-sounding punk band squealed from the speakers as soon as we pulled the door open. It was dingy inside, with a long bar across one side and small tables on the other. Past that, there were the toilets with painted murals on the doors and an outdoor area with a few heaters that was about a quarter full of people smoking. We took a table near two guys. They were much older than us, probably early thirties. One of them had a thick brown beard and the other was clean-shaven, but they were both wearing black denim jackets. They spoke slowly, sipping their beers and smoking, obviously good enough friends that they weren't trying to entertain one another.

Mel looked over at them and smiled. "Hey."

They nodded at her, then went back to their conversation. The dampness was worse now. It was beginning to inch down my leg, and the soggy denim felt horrible against my skin. Plus, the burning was getting worse. What before had been a sting, now felt scalding. I reshuffled myself on the bench, trying to somehow stifle it.

"Is yours burning? Mine is really burning."

"Shut up," Mel hissed, then turned back to the guys. She shot them a half smile and brushed her fingers through her hair. "Can I bum a cigarette?"

"Sure." The guy with the beard leaned toward her with the packet outstretched. She slid the cigarette out slowly. He raised an eyebrow at her and turned back to his mate.

I twisted on my seat a bit more. It was really hurting. I

gripped onto the table, the pain shooting through my abdomen. I looked over at the bathroom doors, the murals swimming slightly. I could duck in there and get rid of it; maybe the others would want to as well.

"I think I might take it out."

"Don't be such a fucking pussy," Mel said, lighting the cigarette. "It's fine. We're fine and we did the same thing."

It was true. Saanvi's eyes looked alert, Cass was staring at the table but she looked like she was handling it okay.

"Maybe mine soaked up more or something?"

Mel didn't answer. She was getting sick of me. I could tell. I was complaining too much. I was being annoying. She was right; the others had done the same thing and they weren't whining like I was. My head was starting to pound, but I forced myself just to breathe. I clenched my thigh muscles but that only seemed to make it worse.

The tattooed bartender came out and began stacking glasses at the table next to us. He watched us intensely as he did it. No one spoke. The two men next to us had stopped talking to one another. Now they were looking between him and us, smiling in a sort of pitying way. The barman stopped stacking, straightened up and stared at us, eyes challenging. Mel slowly finished her cigarette. It felt like everyone was watching her do it, waiting. Finally, she stubbed it out in the ashtray.

"Let's get out of here, guys. This place smells like piss."

We rose up and slowly walked back toward the door. Once we were back out onto the street they all starting laughing again.

"I can't believe you said that!" Cass beamed at Mel.

Mel put her arm around me. "Come on, let's go fish these things out."

My insides felt like they were blistering the whole way back to Saanvi's, but I didn't rush. I stayed in step with the others, trying my hardest to smile.

When we got back inside, I didn't race to the toilet. I followed them quietly up the stairs. No more complaining. Once we were in Saanvi's room, I went straight into her en suite and locked the door. Trying to pull my jeans down I staggered on the spot. Finally, I sat heavily onto the toilet. The smell of the vodka stung my nose. It made me want to gag. I pulled the string and for one sickening moment, I thought it was stuck. But finally, the thing began to slide slowly out. I didn't want to even look at it as I opened the bin next to the toilet to throw it away, but I did notice the contents of the bin.

On top of a pile of screwed-up tissues and cotton swabs were three brand-new, unused tampons.

16

"Do you have any booze?" Saanvi asked. She was sitting in my window, staring out at the sheet of black. It was two weeks later, the night they stayed over at my house.

"Nope," I said.

She sighed dramatically and pulled out her iPhone. Saanvi was the only one in our year to have one, and she didn't waste an opportunity to show it off.

There was no way I was going to let her have any of the bottle of gin my mum kept in the back of the kitchen cabinet for special occasions and really bad days. Weeks had passed since the day we'd done the tampon experiment, and I was still feeling a bit confused about the whole thing. The way they'd told and retold the story since, we'd all done it, we'd all felt it burning, we'd all gotten really drunk. The way they talked about it made it seem true. Every time I remembered those three white little tampons, I told myself that they could have been there for ages, that they didn't mean anything. After all, they wouldn't lie to me; they were my best friends.

Mel and I were lying shoulder to shoulder on my bed working on her invite list. Her party was the next weekend. We were rewriting the list in order of who we wanted to come the most to the least.

"Not Veronica, she's a skank," Mel said.

"I thought you liked Veronica," I said. "Anyway, Laura is boring—that's way worse."

"Cass?" asked Mel.

Cass was sitting on one of the mattresses on the floor, on her laptop. Chucky was asleep against her leg.

"Skank beats boring," she said, not looking up.

It was overwhelming having them in my room. It was both intensely wonderful and excruciatingly nerve-racking. There had been always been an ache in my chest. I hadn't known it was there until now, when it was gone. I knew all I had to do was relax, not say or do the wrong thing, and every moment would be entirely perfect. Ever since the tampons, they'd been even nicer to me than before. As long as I didn't muck it up, things would stay golden. Mel's hair tickled my cheek; her warm arm rested against mine. I wanted to pause this moment, because I knew, inevitably, I'd somehow do something to ruin it.

"What about your mum, does she have any booze?" Saanvi seemed suspicious, like somehow she knew about the gin. But that was impossible.

"Nah, I doubt it. She's always on call at the hospital, so she can't really drink."

"I didn't know your mum was a doctor." Mel turned to me.

"She's not. She's a nurse."

"What about your sister? She must have something."

"I dunno—we can ask her."

"Oh my God!" Cass shrieked, waking up Chucky.

"What?" asked Saanvi. "Please, entertain me! I'm dying of boredom."

That taste rose up again in the back of my throat. I had been sure we were having fun.

"Shut up, Saanvi," said Mel.

"Look." Cass flipped her laptop around and we all dropped down onto her mattress to see.

Cass pressed Play and the all too familiar scene appeared. The shadows of the underneath of the stage. The square of yellow, lighting up Mr. Bitto's face. The back of my school sports shirt. Hip-hop played over the top and it'd been edited so Mr. Bitto lunged in and out for the kiss in time to the beat, that horrible hungry expression on his face.

"It's a mash-up!" said Cass. "It already has thirty thousand views."

"That's awesome," said Mel.

"You're famous." Saanvi looked at me. I smiled back at her, and tried not to watch it. I hadn't seen Mr. Bitto again after he got off the bus that day. Counselors descended on the school almost instantly. All the girls got pulled out of our classes in small groups to "share their feelings." The counselors wanted us to talk about whether we'd ever felt uncomfortable with any of the teachers. They always referred to what had happened as "recent events," or "the current situation." They never said his name. Outside of those groups, his name was everywhere. It was like he was famous. The only one eclipsing him was me. The Girl in the Video. She was a celebrity, a mystery. She was all anyone could talk about. They all had a theory on who the girl was. I could tell the counselors were dying to know as well.

When the clip was finally over, Saanvi leaned her head onto my mattress.

"Let's go out," said Mel, a flash in her eyes.

It was different being out in the dark with them. My morning scamper to the bus stop was nothing like this. Now the estate hummed with an energy, a feeling of possibility and adventure. Cass and Saanvi walked ahead, looking into windows of the empty houses and laughing, making ghost noises, "OOOOoooooo OOOOOoooo."

The three of them were just shadows out here. Black shapes.

The gloss of their hair reflected the moonlight. The cold air made my skin prickle under my jacket.

Mel kept in step with me. She linked her arm with mine.

"You know I love Cass and Saanvi more than anything—" even a whisper was loud out there "—but it always felt like something was missing."

"What was missing?" I asked.

"You, stupid!" she said.

I never thought it would be this good. Never, in my most ludicrous fantasies had I put those words in her mouth.

I couldn't speak.

"There was something uneven about us—we would fight sometimes. Three is a bad number. You've evened us out. Plus, I know you understand me in a way they can't."

"How?" was all I could manage.

"What went down with Mr. Bitto—that was the worst thing that ever happened to me. And now it's the worst thing that ever happened to you too."

Mel pulled my linked arm closer to her body. I could feel her warmth through our jackets.

"Guys!" Saanvi's hushed call.

She and Cass were squatting in the bushes outside a house. It was the one where the man lived by himself. He'd driven past me a few times on my walk up the hill in the evening. There was a very faint silver glow coming through the curtains. Mel's arm unlinked from mine. She sprinted forward and ducked down behind them. I followed, crouched down next to her, the wet leaves prickly around me.

"Look," said Saanvi.

Mel and I raised our head slowly to the window. It was like looking into my own living room; it was identical. Same cream carpet, same white walls—I could see the corner of the kitchen through the doorway, tiled in the same drab gray. The television was on, casting silvery-blue shapes across the room.

A man sat on the sofa in front of it. The way he was looking at the screen was strange. His eyes were so empty, like he was dead. I ducked back down.

"Did you see the pictures?" asked Cass.

I sneaked another quick look. On the wall were framed pictures of a family. A man, his wife and two young children. They were formal photographs, the family's smiles slightly strained. They looked Middle Eastern, but I didn't know from where exactly. The clothing they had on was traditional. Then I noticed that the man in the picture was the man sitting in front of the television.

"Have you ever seen his family?" Mel asked, as she ducked back down.

"No, just him."

"He probably killed them," said Cass.

"Their bodies are probably buried under the house." Saanvi's eyes were sparkling.

"Don't say that!" That wasn't something I wanted to have to think about on my walk to the bus stop in the mornings.

"Come on, let's keep going," said Mel.

"Okay," I said, getting up to walk next to her.

We made a beeline for the next occupied house. Where the two women lived. Nancy and her great-aunt, but I didn't know that then. Our hushed giggles echoed in the silence. Saanvi was having fun now, I could tell. They were all having fun.

We looked in through the window. But all their lights were off. They must be asleep. Mel stood up.

"Get down!" squawked Saanvi.

"Shh!"

"I want to see inside." Mel strode around to the back, looking through the windows as she went. I watched the way she walked so confidently in the dark. I would never look like that.

"She's crazy." Saanvi shook her head.

I snorted. "I thought you wanted to have fun?"

"Yeah, getting done for breaking and entering wasn't what I was picturing," she hissed.

Cass gasped. The sound of it bounced around the silence. I jumped, trying to see what she had. A face was looming on the other side of the window. Two inches from my nose. I jolted backward, then I heard the cackle of Saanvi's laughter.

It was Mel behind the glass. She grinned at us and pointed to the left. Cass and Saanvi got up and went the way she did. I froze for a moment. Going into the house seemed too far. But Mel was still watching me through the window, her face hovering in the black. I had no choice.

The back door was open. I guessed they must have forgotten to lock it.

The women had picked a slightly different model out of the catalog. Their house still had the same walls, the same carpet, but even in the dark I could see the living room was bigger. The countertops in the kitchen were stainless steel, and there was muck and splatter all over them.

"Let's go."

"Don't be a pussy," Saanvi hissed at me.

I bit back my reply as I followed them. It wasn't that I was scared; I had to live with these people. I didn't want to see accusing faces every day. I didn't want to ruin this place for myself already. We came to the stairs. Saanvi placed her foot onto the bottom one, and then hesitated.

"Go on," I said, knowing she wouldn't.

She turned back to me, but as she opened her mouth to say something, a light upstairs flicked on.

"Nancy?" a woman's voice called.

We stared at each other, frozen.

"What are you doing down there in the dark, you twat?"

Cass slapped a hand to her mouth like she might laugh. That did it. We ran out of the house. By the time we rounded the corner to my street, we were giggling breathlessly.

"Look what I got." Mel pulled a large brass statue of a cat out from under her jacket.

"You stole it?"

She passed it to me. It was heavier than I expected.

"A gift," she whispered.

I tucked it under my jacket, trying not to let my emotions show on my face. I could feel the cold brass pressing through my T-shirt onto the skin across my ribs. No matter what happened after this, even if we drifted apart after high school or she moved away, I had something now. Something that proved that this was real. Every time I looked at it I would remember how amazing our friendship was, how lucky I was.

"Thanks," I whispered back.

A boy was standing under the front light of one of the houses, looking over at us. Evan. I'd heard Aiden call his name so I knew it, but I'd never spoken to him before. Every time I'd seen him, I'd quickly looked away.

Mel slowed down as we approached him, and so I did too.

"Hey," she called over to him.

"Hi." His voice was deeper than I had expected.

"Hi." I hoped like hell he hadn't seen anything. "I'm Ava. Do you live here?"

"Nah, I just heard this was a really fun place to hang out."

I blinked at him. "Yeah, you do. I see you all the time."

"Then why did you ask?" he said.

"Why did you lie?"

He shrugged.

I pulled at Mel's arm. I didn't want this weird guy getting involved in our night. I didn't trust Mel not to do something unexpected, like invite him to my house or dare me to kiss him.

"He's hot," Cass murmured.

The guy looked at her, then back at me, and smirked.

"See ya," I said, and kept on walking. Eventually the rest of them followed.

17

I could hear the sounds of their breathing. All deep and long and out of time with one another, filling my room with a peace I hadn't ever felt before. Cass was on the mattress on the floor. Mel, Saanvi and I were squashed into my bed all together, with Mel in the middle. I didn't think I would have been able to sleep this way, but I had. The tiredness I carried with me now was greedy. If I closed my eyes for even a few minutes, its tide would pull me into unconsciousness.

The sun was starting to creep through the blinds, just touching the edges of things. The light made the sheets around me look like sand dunes, the crinkles becoming peaks and crevices across the mountains of my body and Mel's next to me, and the ravine of the gap between us. It made the black glass eyes of the cat statue glint.

Mel's breathing must have changed, but I hadn't noticed. It was something about her stillness, a sudden rigidity of her muscles next to mine that made me look up at her face. She was lying on her side, hair across her face, but her eyes were open. She was looking at me in that same way she had that day with the tampons, with that strange cold flicker in her eyes. I smiled at her and pushed her hair back onto the pillow. I was thinking she'd laugh but she didn't. She closed her eyes, as though my touch was doing something to her. She grabbed my hand before I could pull it away and held it to her face.

I watched her eyes blink back open, looking at the little speckle of gold that was in one iris but not the other. She leaned forward, and grazed her lips against mine. It wasn't at all like Mr. Bitto. Her mouth felt soft. Her lips pressed onto mine, holding there for one long second, and then she pulled back to look at me again. Her expression was still cold. It was a dare, another trial, like she wanted to see what I would do. She leaned over again. This time her lips parted and I felt the hot wetness of the inside of her mouth. She gripped my bottom lip for half a second between her teeth.

She wanted me to kiss her back, so I did. I reached my hand under the sheet to touch her waist. She gasped against my mouth as my skin touched hers. I let my hand slide up until it touched the bottom of her breast and the tiniest of whimpers escaped her. I liked that, hearing the sound that she made.

Movement. Saanvi was stirring in the bed next to Mel. We didn't move. Then, very softly, I stroked my thumb over her nipple, just to see what she would do. Her mouth opened next to mine, but no sound came out. My whole body felt like it was throbbing with a new energy, like I was hyperawake. Her hair was in both our faces now, and we weren't kissing. We just stared at one another, my thumb still resting on her nipple. Her leg moved, her knee prying itself between mine. I didn't resist. Her thigh rose up until it was between my legs and I pushed myself against it.

I closed my eyes, rocking myself into her, letting my hand brush down toward her belly button. I found the elastic of her pajamas, and slid my hand beneath them. I wanted to put my hand inside her underpants, but I was too scared. I'd never done anything like this before. I could feel the pressure of my heart thudding against my ribs. The outside of her underpants felt clammy. I pressed my fingers down between her legs for just a second and I felt her whole body tense. A groan escaped her, too loud.

"God, what time is it?" Cass's voice.

Mel's knee disappeared, I pulled my hand away.

"I don't know," Mel said, and she sat up. "I think Ava's having a sex dream. She's making the weirdest noises."

"Really, who about?"

"I'm not!"

"You were. I could hear it."

I could still feel the sweaty heat of Mel on my hand, but she was looking around the room as though nothing had happened.

"Shut up, guys!" Saanvi said.

"Ava was having a sexy dream," Cass said.

"Gross!"

Mel pulled herself out of the bed, wriggling out between the two of us. She climbed over to the end of the mattress and went to the window, leaning against the frame and looking out at the cold morning light.

"The wife killer's gone out," she said.

"Really?" Cass jumped up to look. "It's like 7:00 a.m. Where would he have gone?"

"Maybe there is a secret mistress."

"Oh yeah, and they can't see each other at regular times because then the police will get suspicious."

Saanvi covered her head with her pillow next to me.

"I'm going to have a shower," I said, my heart still not beating right. "We should leave before eight if we're going to get to school on time."

"Eight? That's insane!" Saanvi's muffled voice moaned from under the pillow.

Things were different with Mel that day, and again the next. All week she was dismissive of me. Cold. There was no holding my hand or gripping my waist. She'd talk to the other two like I wasn't even there. I couldn't understand why she was angry with me. I knew she'd only done it to make things right, to make up for Mr. Bitto being my first kiss, to teach me how good things could be. I wanted to tell her I understood, but she didn't seem to want to talk about it.

I tried not to worry. I tried to just be excited about the party like the rest of them were. She'd been planning it for months. Saanvi had managed to convince her brother to buy us a bottle of spirits. We'd asked for vodka, but he'd gotten us whiskey. I was secretly glad, I never wanted to touch vodka again.

"Probably didn't want to buy a girl drink in front of the bottle shop guy. Idiot," Saanvi said, when she showed us.

After school we all went back to Mel's. I'd been there a few times now, but still never really felt very comfortable. It looked just like my old house from the street: a two-story terrace sandwiched tightly by its neighbors. However, inside, it had been gutted and replaced with the interior of a mansion. It didn't have the same cracked kitchen tiles and dusty old ceiling roses like my old house. Instead, everything was brand-new and almost regal. The whole house looked like it had been coated in a thick layer of varnish; the floorboards were so shiny it was like the floor was wet. It all smelled of pine cleaning spray.

Her bedroom was surprisingly tidy, not what I used to imagine before we were friends. On the wall was a framed painting of her family. I'd stood and looked at it when I first saw it, about to make a crack about how stiff it was, but the others hadn't even looked up at it. I'd thought that maybe they all had portraits like this in their houses.

The only part of the room that looked like it was really owned by Mel was the bedside table. Above it was a photo of her, Saanvi and Cass pulling dumb faces, stuck to the wall with blue tack. Next to the lamp were a few used tissues, a *Cleo* magazine, a lighter and a pink box.

I sat on her bed, while Saanvi went straight to the mirror and perched in front of it.

"You better have some makeup that doesn't look stupid on my skin tone," she said. Cass pushed her with her hip and tried to balance next to her on the chair.

"Oh God, I'm having such a bad face day today," she said.

"Oh fuck off, you never even wear makeup and you look awesome. I have to wear it every single day."

"You don't *have* to do anything."

"Easy for you to say." Saanvi elbowed her and Cass fell off the side of the chair onto the carpet.

"Whoopsy, my elbow slipped."

"So who are you going to kiss tonight?" Mel asked, flicking through her closet.

"I dunno." Cass arranged herself into cross legs. "Maybe Alessandro?"

"He's a really good kisser," Mel said, pulling out a hanger. "What do you think of this?"

It was a grungy-looking dress. Mismatched florals in dingy browns. I thought it was ugly.

"Awesome," Cass said.

"What about you, Ava?" Saanvi said, looking at her own face as she said it. "Who are you going to hook up with?"

There wasn't one guy at school that I liked. They all seemed a bit grimy, like they didn't shower enough. But it seemed like I had to pick someone, and I tried to think of a guy that wouldn't be too bad if I ended up having to go through with it.

"Oh come on," Mel said, hanging the dress onto the doorknob. "Who's going to want to kiss that?"

Saanvi snorted a laugh, but Cass looked around to me, confused. I stared down to my hands in my lap.

"Shall we make some drinkies?" Mel asked, walking down the stairs without looking at me. The others followed.

I listened to them for a minute, their chatter echoing up the staircase. Carefully I opened the lid of the pink box on the bedside table. All I noticed was a strip of condoms before a ballerina flicked to a standing position. It started to twirl and a single note sounded before I slammed the lid back down.

18

I've been waiting for you for hours now. The sky outside that tiny window is pitch-black. I'm getting tired. This isn't how I thought this would go. Pictures of Mel have been everywhere. The black-and-white photo she used as a headshot pinned up inside shop windows, on lampposts. *Missing*, they say. *Melissa Moore.* The photograph, the perfect alliteration—it's like she was made for this.

It's been a week now, and everyone is fearing the worst. It's started to fade out of the news. The posters are starting to get soggy, her self-photoshopped image blurring and running. It's been the longest week of my life.

I spent a long time standing outside the station, deliberating, you know. I thought for sure that the minute I came in, the minute I said the words I'd been practicing in my head— *I'm here about Mel. Mel Moore*—handcuffs would be slapped on my wrists. I wouldn't have hesitated for so long if I'd known that I'd be waiting all this time. If I'd known that there would be hours to plan, to decide exactly what I'd say to you. To remember all the things I'd much rather forget.

I was already drunk by the time people began to arrive at the party. It might have been part exhaustion after another darkened start to the day, but after only two drinks the world was sliding and shifting around me. I'd forgotten that I didn't know what to do at parties. I sat beside Cass and Veronica Britson on the couch, smiling and nodding along to what Veronica was saying even though I was barely listening. I'd always hated Veronica Britson, even though I didn't know her, really. The bass of the music thumped through the room. People I saw every day at school were transformed. The girls wore thick makeup and tiny skirts; the boys' voices sounded deeper as they ogled the girls from afar. Even over the music, I could hear Mel squealing from the kitchen. Ever since he arrived, she'd been so close to Theodore she was almost on his lap. I sneaked glances over to them, watched as she laughed too loudly at some story he was telling.

Everyone seemed to always have so much to say at parties. It seemed to be what everyone did at these things: just drink and talk and laugh. I wish I knew what they were all talking about that was so interesting. The only thing I could think to mention was school. I took another sip of my drink. Mel said something to Theodore, and he turned around. They were both staring at me, staring at them, and I began to feel dizzy. I tried smiling at her, but she just looked at me with that cold flicker in her eye again. It made my stomach twist with unease.

"I feel shit," I said to Cass, interrupting whatever it was she was talking to the other girl about.

"Oh no! You going to puke?"

"It's only ten o'clock," Veronica said, and I shot her a dirty look.

"You should go lie down in Mel's bed for a bit."

"Do you think that'll piss her off?"

"As if."

"I don't know. She seems angry with me for some reason."

"Yeah, I noticed that. I think she's on her rag—she gets like that. Don't even worry about it."

"Yeah, Mel's a moody bitch," Veronica said.

I gave her a death stare and stood up, the room tipping around me.

Holding tightly on to the banister, I climbed up the stairs, trying to figure out if I was very drunk or just really tired. Pushing Mel's door shut behind me I sat down on her bed. The room was a haven away from it all. The music was subdued, the only light came from her bedside lamp. Making sure my shoes stayed off the bed, I lay down. The pillow smelled like her. Clammy and sweet. I closed my eyes and it all felt so good, so right, and I knew I shouldn't sleep but I couldn't help it.

I woke to the feeling of something warm on my face. A hand. Mel's hand, probably. Maybe she'd come and found me there, curled in beside me, and now it was morning.

"Shh…shh…she'll wake up."

"That's so gross."

"Shh."

The bass of the music was still bouncing around the room. It hadn't stopped. The party was still going. Something smelled disgusting.

"Just a little bit more."

The warmth on my face again. The smell intensified. I opened my eyes. Theodore was standing over me. He took a quick step back.

"Quick, quick, take a picture."

I looked around, trying to understand what was happening. Theodore had on one pink washing-up glove. Something was going on. I sat up, feeling a lurch in my stomach. The smell was horrible.

Then I heard the click.

That unmistakable fake click of a camera phone. Mel was holding Saanvi's iPhone in her hands. She looked down at the screen, the blue light on her face. On her grin. It was the same smile she'd had when they threw meat at Miranda.

I jumped up, adrenaline racing through me. Something really bad was happening. I didn't know what it was, but I knew I needed that phone. I lurched toward her and wrestled the phone out of her hands before she had a chance to react.

"Careful!" Saanvi yelled. I hadn't even noticed her there by the door.

"Hey!" Mel said, glaring at me like I was disgusting. "Don't even touch that!"

I looked down on the screen. She was writing a Facebook post. It just had two words in it and a picture. *Shit Head.* The picture underneath was my face, brown smudges across my cheeks.

I looked up at her.

"Can you give the phone back, please?" she said, stretching out her hand. Theodore laughed stupidly next to her, but I ignored him. Her eyes were too bright, too focused on my face.

"Give me back the phone, shit head."

Saanvi started laughing too.

I grabbed the phone tightly in my palm, and smashed it with all my strength against the side of Mel's bedside table. The screen exploded into a spiderweb, but the picture was still there behind it.

"What the fuck! Stop it!" Saanvi screamed.

"Give it back, psycho!" Mel tried to grab it out of my hands but I pushed her away and smashed it again and again against the wood.

"You're a bitch!" I said, my voice sounding strangled as I smashed the phone again. "A bitch!"

The three of them weren't smiling at me now. They were backing away from me, as though I was some crazed animal. I threw the remnants of phone onto the floor. I ran past them to the bathroom and begun rubbing water and hand soap onto my face. The smell of it hit my nostrils again and I vomited into the sink, the water running it quickly down the drain. As soon as my stomach was empty I washed my face again, the hand soap burning my eyes, getting into my mouth, but I didn't care. When my face felt raw I stopped, tears already threatening. But I had to get out of there first.

Grabbing a towel, I rubbed my face as I half tripped my way down the stairs to the front door.

"Hey, we're having champagne!" Cass yelled, and I heard a loud bang. I ducked and put a hand over my head defensively, as cold liquid sprinkled up my arm and shoulder. Looking around I saw Cass staring at me, confused, the bottle in her hand. Other people were looking at me too.

"Fuck off!" I screamed, and threw the towel on the floor as I left.

When I reached the end of Mel's street, I started to run. My breath quickly became ragged and my face dried, but that smell was still in my nose. The main road was up ahead, but before that was the turnoff to my old street. I turned my run into a jog and took the turnoff. The familiarity was waiting for me. Nothing had changed. I got to my house and began to walk down the path to the front door. I don't know what I was thinking. I guess I wasn't thinking at all, just wishing my life was back the way it had been before everything got so complicated.

There was a light on inside. I could see into my living room. There was a couple in there, on a couch I'd never seen before. Her head resting on his shoulder. This wasn't my house anymore. I turned around before they noticed me out there. I needed to get home.

The main road was deserted. All the shops were closed. I already knew before I checked the tram timetable. The small numbers only confirmed it. The last tram was gone, long gone, as well as the last bus connecting from the city.

Pulling out my phone, I called Bea.

It was freezing cold already.

No answer.

I called my mum.

People got murdered in Melbourne all the time.

No answer.

They'd both be asleep, their phones on silent. I couldn't wait until morning, I couldn't be out here by myself for all that time. I would be murdered. They'd never caught the guy who had broken into our house. He was still out there, somewhere.

Then I saw it. Golden headlights and a dim Taxi sign crawling toward me. I threw out my arm and its indicator blinked.

When the meter flicked over from ninety-nine dollars to one hundred, I realized I had to think of a plan. I had spent the last hour staring blankly out the window, watching as the houses began to disappear and then the streetlights. Now there was nothing outside the window but black. My neck and arm were sticky from the champagne, my head was throbbing, and every time I thought about what happened in Mel's bedroom I was sure I was going to be sick all over the driver's faded floor mats.

I looked up at the driver. He hadn't said a word to me since I first got in, but I had felt his eyes flick over to me many times.

"We're almost there," I said to him. He just nodded.

His high beams lit up a farmhouse. I'd seen it from the bus window; it wasn't far, maybe the closest I could get without him knowing where I really lived.

"It's just this one here."

He nodded and slipped on the indicator with his pinkie finger. The *ticktock* of it filled the car. He turned onto the long driveway, stopping just outside the house. I went to open my door, but he pushed a button and all the locks snapped shut.

"Don't even think about doing a runner."

We locked eyes.

"I just have to go and get my dad," I said, trying to sound as childlike as possible. "He's got the money."

He sighed and unlocked the doors. I forced myself not to fling it open. Instead, I smiled at him and slowly unclipped my seat belt. I pushed the door and got out. Not hurrying, I walked all the way up to the porch. The thick bush was right there, beckoning me. Instead of taking the step up to the front door I darted away. Throwing myself into the sticks and branches.

"Fuck! Not again."

I stumbled through the bush, trying to push myself to move as fast as I could and not vomit or cry or scream. Just move. My breathing was coming in pants. It was too dark. So dark I could barely see. I pushed blindly ahead through the trees, praying I wouldn't trip. I could hear his footsteps now too. They were heavier than mine. And faster. He was catching up with me; I wasn't going to be able to outrun him. Veering to the left I jumped down behind some dense scrub, flattening myself against the ground. I tried not to breathe.

The bush turned silent. He had stopped to listen. He could do anything to me out there. No one would ever know. I should have stayed closer to the farmhouse. I was far away enough from it now that I could scream my lungs out and, if anyone was awake, they would think it was the faint sound of an exotic bird. The slow crunching sound of his footsteps was getting louder. He was standing almost on top of me. If he took two more steps forward his boot would land on my skull. Another crunch of his boot against the undergrowth. I could hear him panting, puffed out from running.

"Fuck!"

Another step, but in the other direction.

I didn't breathe again until I heard the ignition start.

It was a long walk up the road of Lakeside Estate. I was covered in dirt and muck. My teeth were chattering from the cold, my breath rising above me in white puffs. There were small scratches all down my legs and arms. My T-shirt was ripped.

The champagne smelled sickly sweet. My house was up ahead; I was almost there. The thought of being in bed, the soft blanket over my head and being safe and warm and alone, made me run. Strength I didn't know I had bubbled up to the surface and I pushed forward. Down my street and in through the front door, up the stairs and into my room. I pulled off my clothes and got into bed, curling up under the blanket, my head on my knees.

Finally, I could allow myself to cry. I could look back at the night, at what I'd ruined, at how horrible school was going to be now, at the look on Cass's face. At how scared I was. At what Mel did. I could let out the sobs I'd had trapped in my throat all night.

But it was too late by then. I was all dried up on the inside.

This is where I'll end the story of what happened that year. I won't tell you what happened next in the weeks and months that followed. You don't need to know about all that. Really, it's none of your business. It's what I've done since then that I've come here to tell you. I'm not here to make you feel sorry for me—you shouldn't. I'm here to take responsibility.

Part 4

PARASITIC LIFESTYLE

2013

19

Saanvi wore black exclusively. It seemed she had decided that she wouldn't be taken seriously as an architect if she didn't. She wore black tailored pants and black leather ankle boots and black silk tops.

The black didn't seem to be working. She'd always be the one that rode the elevator three times a day to the coffee shop next door to juggle three espressos, two soy lattes and a ristretto back up to the office.

Even now that the sun was high and bright in the sky each day, she'd never leave the office before dark. When she finally emerged, she'd walk at a brisk pace with her head down to her one-bedroom apartment, which was only fifteen minutes out of the city center. It was tiny and soulless and on the ground floor, its windows glowing out into the alleyway behind.

She'd pick up takeaway from the greasy Thai restaurant around the corner. They'd greet her warmly, try to ask about her day, but she'd be stiff and formal every time. She didn't want to be a regular. At home, she'd eat the takeout sitting at the small desk she had crammed into the already-tiny space of her apartment. When she was finished she'd often open Facebook, and go to the profile of someone called Matt Solloway. She'd always go to the same image. It was a picture of a young man, Matt presumably, standing and smiling into the camera. He was holding an architectural model in front of him, simple with sweeping curves against sharp edges that matched his haircut. She'd stare at the boy in this photo for a long time, as though she was looking for something in his face. Then she'd swap over to YouTube and watch video after video of pimples being popped and blackheads being extracted in close-up.

It was usually around then that the lights would go off. The first time this happened, she had gotten up from her chair, gone from light switch to light switch, flicking them up and down. Now she just waited. Sometimes tensing her body and closing her eyes. The lights would go on and off, on and off, on and off, for minutes at a time.

If she had looked up, looked out the window when it was darker inside than out, she might have even seen me there, watching, hand inside the fuse box.

20

"It's show-and-tell time, Ava-babe!" Celia yelled down the stairs.

I was meant to be cooking for her but I knew there was no point asking if we could do it later. I turned the stove to simmer, put a lid over the ginger and pumpkin soup I was making, took my laptop off the table and climbed the stairs.

Initially, I was surprised by how nuts Nancy's great-aunt turned out to be. I was even more surprised that, almost immediately, I liked her. She would do things I would never dream of doing, like sunbathe in her underwear in the front yard or spend the whole day making herself look fabulous only to do the dishes.

I'm not demented, she'd told me my first day in her strong English accent. *I don't know what that square has told you, but it's not true.*

That square. That's what she always called Nancy, or sometimes *that twat* if she was really annoyed.

When I got to Celia's room she was wearing her crimson silk dressing gown, and it fanned elegantly around her. The effect was slightly ruined by the dark stains down the front from where she'd missed her mouth with her breakfast this morning, but I didn't point them out.

"There you are, duck. I've been waiting hours," she said, and patted the mattress next to her.

I got up on the bed to sit next to her. Her room was actually the same as mine, but flipped. The windows on the left of my room were on the right of hers, the mirrored doors of the built-in wardrobes reflected the west instead of the east. Celia took the leather-bound album from her bedside table.

"Did you take your pills?" I asked her.

"Oh yes, yes," she said, waving a hand dismissively, "don't you worry about that, nursey."

I'd been Celia's nurse for two years by then. I'm fairly sure she knew I was bullshitting about being a nursing student, but I also think she liked that. Celia had an appreciation for the unexpected.

"I'll go first," she said, and opened the album.

I knew Celia's story well, since she'd told me more times that I could count. She had come to Australia from England in the middle of the 1950s to follow the love of her life, a bushranger named Bullseye Bob. When she'd arrived, she'd discovered that he was actually a married accountant named Robert. Celia liked it here in Australia, so she'd stayed on anyway.

"Guess how old I am in this picture?" she asked me, pointing to a photograph of her smiling toothily in a jacket with broad shoulder pads next to a man in a well-cut suit.

"Maybe thirty?" I asked.

"Fifty!" she said. "I was beautiful, wasn't I?"

"You're still beautiful."

"Pfft, don't you even try," she said, turning the page. On the next one was another picture of her and a man. This one with salt-and-pepper hair. He looked vaguely familiar, but I couldn't pick from where. She turned the page again, to the image of her with an arm around a little girl with a big scowl. Nancy.

"This was just after she'd arrived and look at the face on her! Shipped off to Australia to live with crazy Great-aunt Celia. You'd think she would have rebelled, but no."

She turned the next page. Nancy's long navy formal dress and butterfly clips were outshone by Celia's hot pink blazer.

"Look at that." Celia's voice was laden with disgust. "Who wears navy to their first big dance? Hideous."

"I think she looks okay," I said.

"Oh, don't even start with that, Ava-babe. You're not fooling anyone." She snapped the album shut. "It's your turn."

I crossed my legs on the mattress and pulled the laptop closer, opening Facebook. I went to Mel's page first, like I always did. There she was, sitting on her balcony, sunny Paris in the background, a smile on her face.

"Is this the girl that kidnapped poor kitty?" she asked.

"Yeah."

I'd left the brass ornament on their doorstep after high school had finished. I didn't like having it in my room anymore, staring at me with its shiny black eyes. Now it stood on Celia's dressing table, next to all her makeup.

"What does it say?" Celia peered at the photograph on the screen. She wasn't wearing her glasses. Celia never wore her glasses.

"It says, *How did I ever deserve all this?*"

"Little brat is asking for a slap," she said. "And your architect friend?"

"She's not much fun," I told her. "Goes to bed early every night."

"What's wrong with young women these days? Where's the sex? When I was a girl we were bonking left, right and center."

I opened Cass's Facebook, but there was nothing new there since the image of her sitting at a café with her boyfriend from a few months back.

"That one's a bit of a bore," Celia said. "I like the French one the best. I'd love to see you knock that smirk off her pretty little face right under the Eiffel Tower. Serve her right for steal-ing from me."

"One day," I said, shutting the laptop down and hopping off the bed to go and finish cooking our soup.

21

When I got home, Bea was waiting for me.

"Guess what?" she said.

"Oh God, you're not pregnant, are you?"

The way she and Aiden had been going at it, it wouldn't have surprised me.

"No!" she said. "No, listen. You know how I submitted my illustrations to that agent?"

"Yeah?"

"She agreed to take me on!"

"Really?" I asked. "That's so great!"

"Come on," she said, "I've been dying to tell the boys but I wanted to wait for you."

She took my hand and pulled me out the door and across the road.

When she told Aiden, he pulled her into his arms and started kissing her. I stood by the screen door, waiting for their lips to part. It didn't happen, so I squeezed past them and went up the stairs.

Evan was sitting at his computer, and I rapped one knuckle on the door.

"Auntie Ava," he said, leaning back in his chair, "how are you?"

"Not good," I said, and went to lie down on his bed. "I

think I just saw the back of your dad's tongue. That's how far it was in Bea's mouth."

"Well, thanks for that image."

"You're welcome."

He spun his chair around. "How's the old bat? Still think Nancy's poisoning her food?"

"I think she was just joking about that."

He turned back to his computer. He was on one of his gambling sites. He was so good at it he didn't even need to work. He told me he would show me how to do it; it was actually a lot more complicated than I thought. He had explained the basics to me once and I couldn't keep up, but hadn't wanted to admit it.

"You know there was this old lady in Sydney in the 1950s." I was speaking to the back of his head. "She was the sweetest, nicest-looking woman. Perm and cardigans and all of that. All her neighbors started going blind and losing their hair, and then her nephew did as well, and he was only in his thirties. She kept bringing over tea to them and being lovely, but her nephew realized that he always got sicker after she visited. Turns out she was actually putting rat poison in their tea."

"Isn't it true that women poison more than men? They like it because it's more passive or something," Evan said, as the numbers in the corner of the screen suddenly went up by hundreds. He turned around, smiling, and stretched out his fingers. "I swear, this is getting too easy."

"No, idiot. It's because women aren't as strong. It's not like they can overpower a guy. If we want to kill someone, we have to be sneaky."

"Do you reckon the old bat is doing that to you? Except instead of rat poison it's LSD in your tea and that's why you are so crazy?"

I looked around at him sharply. He'd never said he thought

I was crazy before. He caught my change of expression and got up to sit next to me on the bed.

"I'm just kidding," he said, and messed up my hair. "I'm just as nuts as you."

I shifted away from him. He'd been doing this a lot lately. Touching me when he didn't have to.

"What are you doing tonight?" he asked. "I don't really want to spend another evening listening to the soundtrack of rigorous copulation."

"Fuck, Evan!"

He shrugged, grinned. "Should we do it?"

I looked to the carpet. "Not tonight."

"You keep saying that. I'm a good teacher, promise. We have to do it sometime."

"We don't have to."

"Come on, we'll just go out for an hour. I bet it won't take you long to pick up."

I'd stupidly admitted to him that I couldn't ride a bike. Now he was insisting on teaching me.

"I just don't feel like it."

"Fine, fine. We could watch a movie?"

Originally we'd watched movies based on the stories we swapped, but eventually it had just become part of our week that we'd hole up together on his couch or in his room, and watch whatever film he'd downloaded. Lately, we'd been going down the Ingrid Bergman rabbit hole. First it was *Casablanca*, then *Anastasia*. A few months back we'd watched *Gaslight*, a film about a woman whose husband makes her think she is going mad.

"I'm busy tonight. Later in the week maybe."

"What are you up to?"

He was looking at me intensely now. We were too close to each other on the bed. I stood.

"Just seeing friends."

"You know, you are being really evasive lately. What's the big secret?"

He was smiling still, but there was an edge to his voice. I hovered in his door frame, one hand resting on the white painted wood.

"No secret, and why do you care?"

I was expecting him to bite back, but he didn't. He put his head down, so I couldn't see his face, and said quietly, "Are you seeing someone?"

"Huh?" I asked, the question taking me by surprise.

He looked up at me, pain flashing across his face. "I don't care. I just don't know why you don't tell me."

I felt a stab of my own.

"I'm not," I said, not able to look at him. "Not that it would be any of your business."

I walked back down the stairs, trying my hardest to remain composed.

"Hang on," Bea said as I passed. "I thought we were going to celebrate?"

Her hand was still resting lightly against Aiden's neck, like it was the easiest thing in the world.

"I've got to go. Maybe tomorrow?"

"Yeah." Aiden pulled Bea into him, his arms wrapping softly around her stomach. "Let's do it properly. Maybe we could all go out for dinner or something?"

They looked at each other, and the moment felt meaningful.

"Sounds good," I said, and went out to the car.

I'd learned to drive by then. It made everything a lot easier. No more early-morning bus rides. No more lifts with Nancy. As I drove to Saanvi's that night, I pushed my foot on the accelerator hard. I took the turns too quickly. People like me can't feel emotional pain. They can't get their feelings hurt. I knew that. I also knew that me and Evan could never be together.

I could never be like Bea and just open myself up. Inside, she was as soft and loving as she seemed from the outside. There was no shadow following her. Not like me. If Evan knew who I was, what I really was, he'd run. I knew he'd be able to feel it eventually, the coldness, the evil I carried around inside me, just by touching my skin.

When I got to Saanvi's she hadn't even turned the light on. She was just sitting there, in the dark, staring at that picture of the boy. I stared at him too, through the window. I wondered if they used to date, if that's what it was. If she had thought she was in love with him, but it had ended, and now all that was left was that picture.

I felt my stomach unclench as I stood there, nose inches from the glass. The tension left my neck, my shoulder blades dropped loose, my muscles melted. I could breathe.

Saanvi snapped her laptop closed and picked up her hand-bag from where she'd dumped it near the door. She pulled a string shopping bag from the coatrack and left the apartment.

I walked on the other side of the road to her. I'd learned that. People only think they are being followed if you are walking behind them. The echo of footsteps in the dark. The sound stopping when you stop, quickening when you quicken. No. That wasn't how it worked. Or at least, it wasn't how it worked for me. It was easiest in crowds, on transport, in the light. People don't look around them anymore. They don't no-tice the same face pop up again and again; they don't feel the prickle on the backs of their necks. They only see the screens in their hands, hear the music in their ears, feel the stress in their shoulders.

I reached the small supermarket before she arrived, and took my own basket from next to the security gates. It was quiet in there, despite around twenty people being inside. Most were alone—this wasn't really a family area. There were a few young couples who spoke quietly as they traipsed from aisle to aisle, their skin looking pallid and tired in the fluorescents. The same Lorde song that seemed to be everywhere that year sounded tinny through the speakers.

I began filling my basket. My mother had gotten irritated with me only a few days before for not making enough of an effort. Now that I was working, if I still wanted to live at home, she expected me to contribute. The fridge wouldn't fill itself, she said. I knew that, of course I did, but since I'd started following Saanvi I'd let things slip.

It wasn't something I'd wanted to happen—you will need to know that. It wasn't like I sat down and planned it. I just had to know, I needed to know, what she was doing. It's a hard thing to describe; it was like a pull, a magnetic force. It was something I couldn't control. Like having that second drink. Once you've had a taste, you want more.

It felt like I'd righted a wrong with Theodore. It had been the first time in years that I'd felt empowered, that the world had seemed to make sense. After Theodore, I knew what I was going to do. I knew it was only a matter of time.

I filled my basket. Milk, cheese, bread, pasta, tomatoes, basil, coffee, cereal and a ten-pack of batteries.

Saanvi. Always so sure of herself. Always convinced she was right, and everyone else was crazy. She was twenty-three now, but she was just the same. That's something else I have learned: people don't change. Her life had been on track. Like Theodore, there had been no cosmic karma, no punishment from the universe. Like Theodore, the only karma would be of my making.

Saanvi was staring down into a freezer full of microwave dinners, her eyes unfocused. I slid past her, close enough that my body made contact with hers just slightly, so she'd mistake the twitch of her handbag as my hand entered it for the brush of my shoulder against her.

"Sorry," I said.

"No worries," she muttered, not turning.

I paid for my groceries and went to the liquor section that adjoined the supermarket. Saanvi took a long time to get to the checkout with her two microwave meals.

Rubbing her eyes, she placed them on the counter and put her string bag down next to them.

"Card or cash?" the checkout girl said, on autopilot.

"Card."

"Do you want a bag?"

Saanvi looked from her to the counter, and pointed to the string bag. "Clearly not," she said.

"Oh yeah. Sorry," the girl said, putting the frozen meals inside and coloring.

Saanvi dug into her handbag for her wallet. I stood behind the wine, and held my breath. She took her wallet out, face not changing, and offered the girl her credit card. I began to smile.

She swung the string bag onto her shoulder and headed toward the door. When she went through the security gates, the effect was instant. The alarm was piercing, shrieking through the quiet. The lights flashed; every head turned. Saanvi glared around, shaken but angry.

"I'll have to check your bag, sorry," the checkout girl said, looking embarrassed as she approached.

"Check it," Saanvi said, throwing her handbag onto the counter. She glanced around then, and I ducked back behind the wine shelves just in time.

I looked back to see the girl withdraw the packet of batteries from Saanvi's bag.

"What?" Saanvi's face was stricken. "I didn't. I mean, they must have fallen in there or something, honestly."

"I have to call my manager," the girl said.

"Seriously, I didn't mean to," Saanvi was whispering now, clearly mortified.

"I have to call my manager," the girl said again, raising her eyebrows.

22

@EllieDore: Looking forward to drinks tonight with @SaanviChabra. It's been too long! Meyers Place?

@SaanviChabra: Yeah, sounds good. I need a drink. Or ten.

Meyers. It'd taken me a while to find the right place. There was no bar called Meyers Place, only an alleyway with that name at the north end of the city. Eventually I found it, on a blog of course. It was a tiny hole-in-the-wall that was too cool to even have a name, so everyone just called it by the name of the alleyway.

After leaving Celia's house, I went straight home to get ready. I slicked my hair back tight, and was in the midst of piling on some eye makeup when Bea came into my room.

"Oh. That looks…different," she said.

I sniggered. I looked like an absolute poser, which was the point. The bar was tiny, so it was going to be hard to prevent Saanvi from seeing me at all. With my hair like this, plus the makeup, I looked nothing like I had back in high school. If I wanted to remain invisible, I had to fit in.

"You don't have to go to so much effort though," Bea said. "It's just dinner."

I turned to look at her, the question on my lips, when I remembered. Fuck. The stupid celebration dinner.

"I mean," she continued, "it's nice though. Aiden says he wants to go somewhere really good and even Evan is coming. Poor Mum isn't going to know what to do. She never gets the house all to herself."

"Where are we going?" I asked, trying desperately to think of a way out of it.

"I dunno. Somewhere not too far away I guess. Although, everywhere remotely close is pretty crap. Greensborough, maybe?"

I stared at her for a moment and saw her face changing, as though she could sense my head rattling around for excuses. I could already see disappointment there.

"Fuck Greensborough," I said instead. "Let's go to the city! There's this Mexican place that's meant to be really good."

"But it's ages away!"

"Not really, once you get on the freeway it's basically the same. Plus if it's going to be a celebration, we've got to do it properly."

Her face lit up and she ran over to hug me. I felt myself stiffen, but she didn't seem to notice.

"How lucky am I?" she asked, her cheek pressed to mine.

We all piled into Aiden's car. Him and Bea in the front, me and Evan in the back, like children being ferried to school by their parents.

"New look?" Evan asked me.

I shrugged.

"I like it," he said, and smiled. "Makes you look sort of like a raccoon."

He was acting as if yesterday hadn't happened, which I was grateful for.

"Fuck off," I said.

"It was a compliment! I love raccoons. They're probably the best-looking pests in the world. Think about it. Rats, horrible. Locusts, worse. No one wants to look like a locust."

"What about rabbits?" Bea turned to ask, as Aiden started up the car.

"Bea, why did you go there? I was trying to be nice to your sister. We all know there's nothing cuter than a rabbit."

"Just shut up," I said.

"I like it when they clean their little ears with their paws," Bea said.

They spoke about rabbits for a while, but I stopped reacting, so they got tired of it. I was trying to think of a way to get away. To find an excuse to leave them so I could go to the bar. I could fake an important phone call from a friend maybe. Or say I wasn't feeling well and wanted a walk by myself to get some air.

"These tacos better be worth it," Evan said, after we'd been driving for twenty minutes. They were starting to get restless.

"They'll be great!" I said.

"Maybe we should play a car game?" Bea asked.

"No bloody way," I said.

We sat in silence for a while, listening to the low voices on the talk radio Aiden had tuned into. Evan turned to me.

"Have you ever heard of Mr. Cruel?" he asked.

"Nah. Stupid name."

"Yeah."

"Who's he?"

"He's a Melbourne one, you know? He abducted three kids from their houses in the eighties. He'd just go right into their homes while their family was asleep and take them, then would drop them off somewhere different the next day."

"Dead?"

"Nah, alive. Until the third one, who they couldn't find for a year, but then a bush walker tripped on a little skull. Scariest bit is, they never caught him."

"So he could still be alive?" I asked.

"Evan, what the hell is wrong with you?" Aiden snapped from the front.

Evan shrugged. "Are you actually asking me? The list is pretty long. Hey, maybe that could be the car game? Guess all the things that are fucked-up about Evan."

"Um, bad dental hygiene?" I asked.

He bared his teeth at me. "Nope. Brush twice a day."

"I know—weird taste in music."

"That's actually true," Bea said from the front, looking over her shoulder with a twitch of a smile.

"No way. You guys don't know what you're talking about."

"You have the musical taste of a twelve-year-old girl," I told him.

He nudged me with his shoulder. "Not true."

"Very true. I think I actually heard you listening to Shakira once? Shakira? I don't think twelve-year-olds even listen to her anymore."

"One, Shakira is awesome," he said. "Two, you think you're so funny, don't you?"

He leaned over me, his seat belt making a ripping sound, and started trying to tickle me. He smelled so good.

"Stop it!" I said, batting him away. His hands were hot against my skin.

His tickles changed, and his finger traced the skin next to the strap of my singlet softly. I wanted to close my eyes, to really feel the jolt in my stomach, the prickles in my skin.

"Stop!" I said. "I haven't shaved my underarms in months."

That worked. He pulled away, looked at me surprised, then sat back on his side. I caught a look between Bea and Aiden.

When we got to the restaurant, there was a line up the stairs.

"Don't need to line up in Greensborough," Aiden said.

"It'll be worth it, trust me," I said. "Apparently the food here is amazing."

Really, I had no idea. I only knew of it because it had been mentioned in the same blog post as Meyers Place. I also still had no idea how I was going to get from here to the bar. I couldn't leave by myself—it would never work. They could come with me, but then what would be the point? I wouldn't be able to hear a word Saanvi and her friend were saying. Plus, Bea had met Saanvi once. It was only briefly, that night they slept over at my house, but it was still possible they might recognize one another.

The line didn't last long, and soon we were seated near one of the two huge square windows. Luckily for me, it was really nice. The lights were low orbs, filling the place with a soft, warm glow. The furniture was a mix of light wood and soft leather, and behind the bar was a huge black-and-white photograph of a Mexican woman in the 1940s. The air was filled with a spicy scent, and the music was only just rising above the rumble of different conversations around us.

"This is actually pretty cool," Evan said.

"Yeah, good one, Ava." Bea was grinning as she looked around. "I'm glad we picked somewhere special."

The waitress approached, large paper menus tucked under her arm. She put them on the table and asked if we wanted any drinks.

"I'll have a margarita!" Bea said. She'd been doing well lately; she hadn't had a seizure since the one in the shower almost two years ago.

"Me too," I said.

"Make that three," Evan said.

"I'm fine with water," Aiden told her, and then off Bea's look, "I'm driving!"

"Oh come on," she said, "you'll be okay with just one."

"Alright," he said, "four."

"And some guacamole!" I added.

★ ★ ★

The drinks were amazing, and the food was going to be great if the guacamole was anything to go by. Bea was talking happily about her agent, and about how they were putting her forward to illustrate a picture book this week.

"Honestly," she said, "it's like all my dreams are coming true."

"What about you?" Aiden asked me. "Do you think you'll go back to uni, finish your degree?"

"Dunno," I said. "Maybe."

"You'll probably have to," Bea was saying. "Nancy's giving you a great deal, but it can't last forever."

"Yeah, I guess."

It felt like everyone had suddenly gotten obsessed with jobs and careers and success in the last few years. I took a sip of my drink and checked the time under the table. Saanvi would probably be at the bar by now. She'd be sitting with her friend, telling her all about her life. No matter how much you watched someone, you could never see inside their head. I needed to know how Saanvi was feeling, what she thought about everything that I had been doing to her. I needed to get out of here.

"I guess this is as good a time as any," Bea was saying. I realized I'd tuned out.

"Hang on, what?" I said.

"Aiden and I have some news."

"Fuck," said Evan, "you're not pregnant, are you?"

"No!" said Bea, picking up her margarita glass and shaking the ice at him.

"We've decided to move in together," Aiden said, watching Evan carefully.

"Oh," I said.

"Yeah," Evan said.

"Wait, in our house or theirs?" I asked.

"In mine," Aiden said.

I didn't want Bea to move. I didn't want anything to change, but I forced a grin. "That's really great! At least we'll still be neighbors."

At the same time, Evan's chair pulled back, squeaking on the floor. He didn't say anything, just rose up turned his back and walked down the stairs. We all stared after him.

"Oh no." Bea's forehead furrowed. "I hope he doesn't think we wanted him to move out. I would never want that!"

It was my chance.

"I'm really, really happy for you," I said, "but I think I should go after him."

"No," said Aiden, "I will."

I stood up before he could. "Honestly, he'll be more likely to talk to me. He just needs some time to process it."

"She's probably right," Bea said, looking like she might burst into tears.

I took her hand and squeezed it. "Order dinner, have fun. We'll go for a walk or something and come back. Okay?"

I didn't wait for an answer. I went straight down the stairs, shimmying and nudging past the people waiting for a table, and out into the hot summer night.

I found Evan sitting at the tram stop across the road. I crossed over and sat down next to him, the silver metal of the seat feeling cold against my thighs.

"That was really juvenile," he said, staring at his knees.

"Sort of, but who cares," I told him. "Where are you going?"

"Home, I guess."

"You could do that," I said. "It'll take you ages though."

"Are you going to try to convince me to go back up? It's not about Bea—really I like her—it's just…"

"No," I said, "I was thinking maybe we should go get a drink somewhere?"

He looked up at me, surprised. "That'd be great."

"I know a place that's close."

"Awesome," he said, eyes smiling. I led the way.

I'd found the bar on my map before we came, but still I wasn't sure if we were in the right place. There was a high brick wall on one side of the lane, and small alleyways coming off on the other that stank of piss.

"I knew it," Evan said.

"Knew what?"

"You never wanted a drink. You brought me here to kill me."

"I think it's just across there," I said, as we went past a parking lot. I was expecting another dirty alley, but sure enough, there were lights and some people sitting on upturned milk crates smoking cigarettes.

As we got closer my heart started thumping. I was afraid the bar was going to be too small, that Saanvi would see me straightaway. That she'd recognize me. We rounded into it, and to my relief I saw the back of her glossy-haired head. She was sitting up at the bar, talking to a girl on the stool next to hers, her back to the entrance.

"This place looks great," Evan said, smiling widely at me.

The bar was small, with just a few booths, shrouded from each other with low bookcases. It was a bit grimy, but with its warm orange lights and wood-paneled walls, it felt cozy.

"Beer?" I asked.

"Sure. I'm going to go wee."

"Don't call it that."

I leaned against the bar. Saanvi was so close I could have reached out and touched her, but her back was to me and she didn't turn around. Luckily, the bartenders seemed more interested in talking to each other than looking at me, so I could listen.

"Are you sure?" Saanvi was saying.

"Absolutely. If you want to."

"I do. Really, that would be fantastic."

"I'll text the others but I'm sure it'll be fine. But I thought you liked your own space?"

"I thought I did too. But I dunno—"

"Hey." The bartender was looking at me.

"Hi," I said. "Two pints?"

"Coming right up." He winked at me as he flicked the beer tap, which was weird. I turned away.

"It's just so odd," Saanvi's friend was saying.

"I know."

"No, I don't mean going crazy. Anyone would go crazy working for that jerk-off. I can't believe he still has you doing renders—that's so shit. And still only being paid as a student is probably illegal you know."

"I know, but he said he'd look over my designs, which is good. And really, I'm lucky to even have the job."

"I don't know. I was miserable for ages graduating and not finding work, but to be honest I think I prefer what I'm doing now."

"Really?"

"Yeah. But anyway, that's not what's odd. I just think it's bizarre that you chose batteries. Who steals batteries? Avocados, sure, they're like five dollars each these days. But batteries? Plus they are like the only thing that has a security—"

"Sixteen bucks," the bartender said.

I looked at him, not comprehending for a minute. He looked from me down to the beers.

"Oh yeah," I said, pulling out my wallet.

"Long day?" he asked.

"Not really," I said, passing him a twenty. He sniggered as he put my money into the till.

"Anytime really would be—" I heard.

"Here's your change," he said, smiling at me again.

"Great."

I slid the beers off the bar. Evan was sitting at the closest booth, within hearing distance of Saanvi and her friend. I slid in across from him and set down the drinks on the table between us.

"I think that bartender was flirting with you," he said.

"Don't think so," I said, feeling so happy I could burst. It was working. She thought she was crazy.

"Why wouldn't he be? You look hot."

My face went cold, but I laughed as if I thought he was teasing me. "Fuck off."

He held up his hands. "Just saying."

I took a gulp of my beer and winced at the bitterness of it. "Not really as good as the margarita."

"I guess," he said. "God, you know, now I feel terrible."

"They don't want to kick you out or anything," I said, only half listening. I was trying to think of something. Another way of making Saanvi think she was crazy. Make her friend think it too.

"That's good," he said, then he rubbed his hands down his face. "I'm being stupid. I guess it's just because my mum didn't want me around and it never felt like my dad did, and now I feel like I should probably move out."

"Don't move out," I said, focusing now. "Seriously, it'd be shit there without you."

"Really?"

"Yeah. Plus, I'm too old to be living at home too. You're younger than me."

"Barely."

"Yeah, but still. If Bea moves out, then you move out, I'll have to move out, and I don't want to."

"Why?" he said. "I mean, Lakeside sucks. There's not even a lake, for one! I would have thought you'd be dying to move back closer to the city. Live with friends and stuff."

"Nah," I said, "I hated it to begin with, but not anymore. But why don't you want to?"

He looked at me as if he was going to say something serious, but he didn't.

"Dunno," was all he said, and took a sip of his beer. "There are some things about it I like."

I had a feeling I knew where this was going, and it couldn't go there. We couldn't have that kind of conversation.

"Do you want to do a dare?" I asked.

"What?"

"You know. To get your mind off things."

"How old are you?" he asked.

"Are you chicken?"

"Chicken? Are you five?"

I shrugged, leaned back, sipped my beer.

"She just texted me back and she said it's fine," the girl was saying from behind me.

"That's so great!" Saanvi's voice.

"Fine!" he said. "Tell me, what is it?"

"Hmm," I said, pretending to look around carefully. Really my mind was racing.

I turned my attention back to him. "See that girl over there."

"At the bar?" he said.

"Yeah." I leaned in close, spoke mock conspiratorially. "The one wearing black, facing toward us."

He craned his neck to see past the bookcase. "Yep."

"Her name is Saanvi. I used to know her."

"Really?"

"Yeah," I said, "at uni. I met her a whole bunch of times and she always forgot who I was."

"How could she forget who you are?" he said in pretend shock-horror.

"So the dare is. Go up to her and pretend to know her."

He cocked his head. "Huh?"

"You know how when someone says hi to you and you have no idea who they are and you just have to play along. It'll be so funny."

"Surely that won't work."

"It will. Say you did architecture with her at school—that's what she studied."

He looked from me, to her.

"Say…" I continued, "say you were friends with Matt Solloway. That was her boyfriend. He was one year ahead of her."

"I don't know."

"C'mon," I said, leaning even closer, "it'll be so funny."

"Saanvi?" he asked.

"Saanvi."

He took a gulp of beer and got up, crossing through the screen once again.

"Saanvi!" he said.

I peered through the bookcase, and saw her look up at him in surprise.

"Hi," she said.

"How are you?" he asked.

Saanvi looked between him and her friend, and laughed. "I'm okay."

"Still doing architecture?"

"Yeah," she said, looking really confused now. "I'm working for King & Dinisen."

"That's awesome. Good on you."

"Thanks," she said. "Um, and you?"

"Same old," he said. His eyes slid from her to me and I smiled at him. "God, it's so good to see you."

"Yeah," she said slowly, "you too."

"I miss architecture school so much. Good old days, right?"

"Dunno about that," her friend said. "I don't remember you. Were you in our year?"

He was stricken then, but only for half a second.

"Nah, year above. I was Matt's mate, remember? Matt Solloway."

It was perfect. So perfect. Her face fell.

"Anyway," he continued, "I've gotta go. Hot date."

They turned to me and I shrank into the shadows.

"But we should totally catch up sometime," he continued.

"Yeah," she said, struggling to recover, "yeah, that would be nice."

"Cool. Well, you've got my number."

And then he actually did it. He actually leaned in and kissed her on the cheek.

He came back down and sat across from me. I put a finger to my lips, and we listened.

"Do you know him?" her friend whispered.

"Yeah," Saanvi whispered back, "sort of. I guess I must."

I put a hand over my mouth to stop from laughing.

"I don't remember him hanging out with Matt."

Saanvi didn't reply.

"Where is Matt anyway? He was so, so good. Totally the last person I'd thought would have dropped out."

"I think he's in Canada," Saanvi said, her voice sounding strained. "I should probably head home. Early start."

I looked at Evan and shook my head.

"I can't believe you," I whispered. "That was so good. You're so fucking good, it's unbelievable."

"I've got a dare for you," he said.

"What?"

"Kiss me."

23

I shouldn't have done it. I knew it straightaway. Not in the moment of course. In the moment it was simple. I wanted him. I leaned over our beers, put one hand to the side of his neck and pulled his mouth to mine. His lips were warm and soft, but not gentle. We kissed each other urgently, we couldn't get enough. There was no hesitation, no second thoughts, only butterflies and fireworks and weak knees. All the things that you are meant to feel. All the things I could never have.

We went back to the restaurant and Evan said congratulations like he meant it and Bea was smiling and Aiden was pleased. Evan grinned every time he caught my eye and I knew it was wrong but it had felt so good.

"I've got a present for you," Celia told me the next morning. We were sitting on her couch, where she was telling me about one of the many marriage proposals she had gotten. I was only half listening. I couldn't stop thinking about last night. About the kiss. About Evan.

"Great," I said.

Celia had given me presents before. One was a record, even though she knew I didn't have a record player. And after she'd seen me talking to Evan out the window, she gave me a black lace G-string, which may have originally been Nancy's. Or hers.

Now she was passing me a parcel wrapped in squashy red wrapping paper. The paper was crumpled, with bits of sticky tape stuck to it. She'd obviously saved it from a gift someone had given to her.

"Thanks," I said, and put it into my bag. "Time for your meds."

"I already took them."

"Why is it you always take them before I get here?"

"Do you want to count the pills in the bottle? You can if you like. While you're at it why don't you smell my breath to make sure I've brushed my teeth and inspect my bottom to make sure I've wiped."

"That's just gross."

"Is it time for our walk?" she asked.

"Okay," I said. I got out my laptop and opened up Facebook. I went to Mel Moore's profile page. I visited it so often, it was almost automatic. I scrolled down through the changes to her profile picture, the dumb comments in French that I'd already Google translated. I went to the picture of Mel standing outside a house, the caption reading *My new home. Mon Amour!* I studied the house again, although I knew it so well I could probably draw it from memory. It was two stories, painted a crisp white, with a blue door and two circular windows on the second level. I opened Google Maps. Keying in the train station Mel had mentioned in her tweets, I switched over to Street View. We panned up at the building, then began moving down the street.

This was another one of Celia and my routines that we'd somehow fallen into. Every few days, we'd take a "walk" on Google Maps. I knew Mel's house must not be too far from the station. We just had to find it.

"Let's turn off at Rue Saint-Hubert today, Ava-babe."

"Alright."

The apartments were so different to anything in Melbourne. Set close to the road and four stories high. All the tiny balconies had ornate railings, some with plants trailing down from them. A man leaned out from his balcony, his face blurred. A woman crossed the street, frozen in midstride. As we ventured farther down we saw cafés with seats outside the front, all facing out to the street rather than toward each other. I wondered if Mel ever sat in those chairs. I wondered if she ever looked at the passing crowd and thought of how she got to live in such a beautiful place. Thought of how it wasn't luck, it wasn't skill. It was because of me. Because of what I'd done all that time ago. What I'd done after the party, in the weeks before we graduated high school.

"I went to France once," Celia told me. "It wasn't really my cup of tea, but I think you'll enjoy yourself."

"Yeah, one day."

My phone buzzed and I looked down to it. A text from Evan: Movie tonight?

"Who was that?" she asked, trying to look over my shoulder at the screen.

I slid the phone back in my pocket.

"Do you want to play cards?" I didn't want to answer her question. I just needed some distraction, for a moment; everything was spinning too quickly. Before she could answer I got the packet of cards and moved to sit down on the carpet on the other side of the coffee table. I began stacking the cards into piles. It was a game called Spite and Malice, or Cat and Mouse. Celia had been the one to teach me, and we played it together often now. It was a bit complicated, but definitely beat Snap.

"Ready?"

"Yes." She picked up her cards and held them close to her nose so she could see them.

"You can go first."

She nodded and put an ace down in the center.

I put mine next to hers, trying to focus on the game and not the thoughts pinwheeling in my head. I wanted Evan. I wanted to run over to his house and into his room and push him into bed and climb onto him and kiss him and never stop. I wanted to walk down the street hand in hand. I wanted to be the good, nice, normal person he thought I was. But I wasn't. If I let him in, he'd see that. He'd see what I really was. The thought of it made me feel sick.

I looked up at Celia. "Can I ask you something?"

"You just did. But you can ask me something else too, duck, as long as it's something interesting."

I swallowed. "Do you think it's obvious to people what I'm really like?"

"And what are you really like?"

"I mean, do you think people can tell that I do things like—" I waved my hand toward the image of the Parisian street on the screen. "Like that. Do you think I'll ever be able to be like everyone else? Be normal?"

She put down three of her cards, when she was only meant to be playing one at a time. She was cheating, right in front of me, but I didn't care. Once she'd inspected her new hand, Celia surveyed me, pursing her lips, which she'd painted a dark maroon to match her bra straps that were peeking out of her low-cut top.

"I'll tell you something, Ava-babe. It's important, so make sure you're listening. When I was a kid they called me different. When I was a teenager they said I was wild. When I was a young woman they called me eccentric. When I turned sixty I was batty. Now they say I'm demented."

She leaned forward, her perfume so strong up close it stung my nostrils, and whispered, "I don't think I'm the right person to ask about being normal, but I've always thought the best way to live is to embrace your crazy. I'll tell you now it's always a hell of a lot more fun."

I went by the grocery store on my way to Saanvi's to buy bleach. It was Saturday, which was usually when she did her washing in the machines in the basement of her complex. Just one load of all black.

My phone buzzed in my pocket. Evan again: I downloaded Spellbound. I imagined it, sitting with Evan in his warm house. Eating crappy food and making jokes. Maybe leaning into him on the sofa, feeling his warm stomach against my back, his breath on my neck. I closed my eyes, focused.

That wasn't who I was.

I went around to the back of Saanvi's apartment block. Found my spot in the laneway, expecting to find her as I usually did: sitting in front of her computer, eating bad takeout. I'd do something to her, and I'd feel better. I'd get a release from the pressure that had been building up in my skull all day.

But Saanvi wasn't alone. The girl from the bar was with her. They were playing that godawful Selena Gomez song up loud, drinking red wine out of tumblers and packing Saanvi's things into large cardboard boxes.

Saanvi was moving. She was leaving. And she looked happy. I'd failed.

If Mel was there she'd be laughing and calling me an idiot. I could hear the contempt in her voice, *You loser, how are you still so pathetic?*

My phone rang. Evan.

I ducked out of the laneway, answered, worried they might see the light.

"Hey! Did you get my messages? I've got *Spellbound*, corn chips and some terrifying-looking liquid cheese. Are you in or what?"

Couldn't he see? Couldn't he see what I was? Not only a monster, but a failure. A bitch. A creep. A psycho.

"Just leave me alone!" I yelled at the phone.

I didn't go over to Evan's house after that, and he didn't come to mine. I kept telling myself it was for the best. I was protecting him from myself. Still, it felt nice to know he was close, to be able to look out my window down the street at night and see that his light was on. But that changed.

I'd just finished for the day with Celia. It had been a tough one. She'd told me the lunch I made tasted like dog shit and refused to eat it. I'd tried to give her the pain medication she was meant to have with meals, but she wouldn't take it, insisting she'd have it once I left. It was blisteringly hot, but I was glad to get out of the stale air-conditioned air of her house. I didn't have my sunglasses, so I was squinting into the sunlight, walking slowly up the hill back to my house. I was staring up at the bluest of skies that seemed to go on forever and ever. As I turned onto my street, I thought about how I'd pass Evan's house. He might be in his kitchen and maybe if I looked inside, he'd smile at me. That's all I wanted. Just a smile.

As I approached, I heard his and Aiden's voices.

"Just one more."

"Are you serious, Evan? There's no way it will fit."

"There's stacks of room."

"Yeah, but I need to see out the back."

"No, you don't. Live dangerously."

"That's so reckless."

I turned the corner and stopped. My feet glued to the hot cement, my breath stuck inside my throat. I felt a coldness oozing down my arms, getting into my veins, freezing my stomach, making my skin turn to gooseflesh. Their car was packed with boxes. Aiden was by the boot, trying to rearrange the items squashed inside.

Evan came out of the house, another cardboard box in his arms.

"I'm serious," Aiden said when he saw him. "I'm not driving if I can't see. It's completely irresponsible."

"I'll put it in my lap. Don't stress so much, old man. God, you're really going to miss me, aren't you?"

Aiden was about to retort, when he stopped. He'd seen me

standing there by the road, staring at them. He raised a hand in greeting. Evan turned to me. I tried to think of something to say. Anything. Something that would fix all of it. But he turned back before I could even open my mouth.

"Come on," he said to Aiden, then got into the passenger seat, and snapped the door closed behind him.

I found out from Bea that he was moving into a share house near the city and that he'd enrolled in an accredited course. He was starting over. It was like the cards were reshuffling in the worst way. Bea left. Evan left.

Bea was only over the road, but it wasn't the same. Mum worked nights so most evenings it was just me, alone in the house, gorging myself on photographs of Mel in Paris. Making stupid fake plans of what I'd say to her if I ever saw her again. What I'd do to her. I knew how pathetic I was, but I couldn't stop.

Evan didn't text or call. He didn't want to be my friend, and I didn't blame him. I tried not to even think of him—it was too hard. He had allowed me some glimmer of hope, and now that had been snuffed out. Things were never going to get better for me, I'd always be broken inside, no one could fix that. The only change in my life would be for the worse.

Things changed for Saanvi too. Every few days would be another post on her Facebook. Her and two other girls sitting around a fire: *Best housemates ever!* Out on the town, with drunk eyes, and cheeks pressed together: *It's official! King & Dinisen promoted me! They are using my design! Who wants to come help me celebrate?*

I knew I was in the past for her, long forgotten. But still, these posts felt like they were directed at me. Like she was mocking me. It was done. I couldn't make things right, but I couldn't move on either. Sometimes I'd wake up in the middle of the night sweating, terrified that I'd be stuck in this lonely limbo forever.

24

Three Little Lizards. That's what Bea's book was called. I didn't
believe it was real until I saw the books piled high at the entrance of the store; her drawing was right there on the cover.
I could recognize her style anywhere. Three lizards standing
on their hind legs, wearing little hats and bow ties. *Illustrations
by Beatrice Berne.*

The bookstore where they were doing the launch was small
but inviting. It was squeezed between two Italian restaurants
on Lygon Street, fifteen minutes out of the city center. Every
corner was filled to the brim with books, which made fitting
a crowd in difficult.

"Sorry," someone said, as they elbowed me in the ribs.

"'Scuse me," came another voice, right after they'd stepped
on my toes.

I managed to get my mum and myself a glass each of cheap
pink wine. I'd wanted to reach the whole way to the front so I
could congratulate Bea and wish her luck before the speeches
started, but there was no way I could make it up there. I was
trying my hardest not to push as I attempted to get back to
where my mother was standing.

"Hi," a voice said. A voice I knew well. Looking to my left,
there he was. Evan.

"Hey!" I said, my excitement seeming out of place compared
to his neutral expression. "How are you?"

"Good," he said. "I thought it would be nice to show my support to my stepmum-to-be."

"Of course! I wasn't sure if you'd come, but it's so good you're here."

I knew he was coming, I'd asked Bea more than once. I'd been thinking that I'd see if he wanted to go for a drink after. Enough time had passed now; he couldn't be angry with me anymore.

"Not hard anymore. I only live ten minutes from here," he said.

"God, don't rub it in." I tried to sound nonchalant. "So what are you doing after this?"

"Don't know. Did you have something in mind?" At first I thought he was talking to me, and I opened my mouth to answer, but he'd turned to the person standing next to him. A girl, about our age.

"Maybe grab some dinner?" she said. She smiled at me, then looked at Evan, as though waiting for an introduction, but he didn't make one. I looked at her hand, clasped around a copy of Bea's book. Her fingernails were perfectly rounded, with a shiny polish that made them glimmer in the light. My fingers had never looked like that.

"Better get this to my mum before it starts," I said, then scurried past them, not caring how many feet I stepped on.

I sipped at my wine as the speeches began. It was warm, and sickeningly sweet. The author spoke first and I tried to focus. It was obvious she was nervous; her voice was thick, like she had a lump in her throat. I couldn't bear to look at her, just seeing her so anxious was making my heart race. The people were pressing in all around me. It was so hot in here. Everyone applauded and the author sat down and Bea stood up. There was sweat on her forehead. I could see the shiny gleam of it all the way back from where I was standing. She started talking, but I could barely hear her. I could hear only the rush of my own blood in my ears. I don't know if it was the wine or the closeness of the people next to me in the hot room, but I was sure I was going to throw up. Bea kept speaking, laughing nervously after each sentence. The people around laughed politely along with her. I stared down at the ankles of the person standing in front of me until, finally, it was over.

"Back in a sec," I said to my mum.

I ran toward the entrance, nearly tripping over a kid sitting on the floor. Putting my wineglass on the front counter I rushed out of the store. The night air was cold against my hot skin. I kept walking, as quickly as I could, away from the store. Away from Evan and that girl. I'd go back; I'd have to. But I couldn't be there in that crowd. I couldn't be there for a polite conversation with Evan. A conversation with no humor, no trying to scare each other with dumb stories, no smiles or glittering eyes. I felt like it would kill me.

I kept walking, away from the shops and restaurants, down toward the main road. Where there were no people, just cars and exhaust fumes and building sites. I tried to breathe, but I couldn't. I hadn't been able to breathe properly since that last night outside Saanvi's window. Even sitting at home, watching television alone, my breath felt too shallow, my neck and back aching with tension. The tension of nothing. Of doing nothing, being nothing.

I got to one of the building sites and reached a hand out to support myself. Pressing my hand onto the white plastic sign attached to the fence, I clenched my eyes shut and tried to force my breath to slow down. I had to get back. It was Bea's night. I didn't want her to even notice my absence. I let the exhaust-

fumed air fill my lungs as slowly as I could manage, then released it. I could do this. I had to.

I took my hand away from the sign and turned back to the road,
squinting as a car came past with bright headlights. The lights lit
up the sign next to me. I only saw it out of my peripheral vision,
but that was enough to make me stop. Turn back. I could have
so easily missed it. I could have walked back to the bookstore
and not even noticed. But I did. I took a step backward toward
the road, balanced my feet on the edge of the curb. There it was,
right in front of me. The sign I had been resting on had a large
architectural rendering of the building that was going to exist in
the brown cavern behind it. When I stared at it, my breath came
out in a whoosh. My lungs opened up. I could breathe again.

I knew that building. I knew its smooth curves against sharp
edges. It was almost an exact replica of the model that Matt Solloway was holding in the Facebook picture. Saanvi had never
been looking at him in the picture; she'd been looking at his
assignment. On the top of the sign in front of me, in big bold
letters was *King & Dinisen*.

You may have heard about what happened next. I wonder
if I'll have to remind you? It was in the newspaper at the time:
Vigilante Vandal was the heading, or something like that. Perhaps I shouldn't admit to it. Vandalism is illegal after all. But
compared to what I've done since, it doesn't seem too serious.
I wonder if you'll remember the photograph that went underneath the heading in the paper. It was taken from across the
street, I think. The construction site, the large King & Dinisen
sign and, next to it, a black-and-white photograph of poor old
Matt Solloway, proudly holding the replica. I'd had it printed to
be a meter square, and pasted it right next to the sign with the
word *STOLEN* at the top in the same font as King & Dinisen.

Poor Saanvi. I could have almost felt sorry for her.

I'd stayed awake until 4:00 a.m. in order to do it. That road was never entirely empty, but I pulled up my hood and took the risk. A few cars passed me while I pasted up the sign of Matt; one even slowed down. But no one stopped.

I slept in my car for what was left of darkness. There was no point going home. When the sun was rising and people began emerging in suits and heels I joined them. I went to the city and waited outside her office building, wishing I could see through the steel and concrete to what was going on inside. She went up the elevator at eight thirty. By nine o'clock she came back down. Her arms were crossed over her body and her shoulders were rounded. She walked slowly toward the tram that took her back to her share house. I was expecting tears and anger, but she just looked dazed. Someone was calling her again and again, but she just kept muting the ringer and putting it back in her pocket. Eventually she answered, sitting down on one of the benches of the tram stop. I sat on the bench behind it.

"So I'm guessing you heard?" she said into her phone. I wondered who was on the other line.

"Yep, I'm definitely fired. Definitely."

She listened to what the other person was saying for a while, then she seemed like she was sick of it.

"No. It's done. I'll never get another job in architecture, no way. They aren't going to wear this—don't you get it? They are going to put it all on me. Everyone will know. My future is fucked."

She paused for a moment, then cut in again. "I don't want to talk about it anymore, Mum. There's nothing to say. Anyway, my tram is here."

She hung up and flung the phone back into her bag.

I didn't follow her onto the tram. I didn't need to. We were even.

25

"Why are you back here, Ava-babe? I thought you'd be butter-ing your croissants by now," Celia said to me as I walked back in from the pharmacy. I forced the annoyance from my face. She'd starting asking me why I wasn't in France at least three times a day, even after just going to the bathroom.

"I've barely been gone an hour," I told her. "The pharma-cist reckons we are getting through these pills too quickly by the way."

"What does she know? I've never even met her."

I unpacked the painkillers into the cupboard, aware of Celia eyeing me from the couch. The thrill of ruining Saanvi had started to wear off by then. I was beginning to feel stuck again. Stuck in my house, stuck in this job. Now that I didn't have Saanvi to follow, I had no reason to go anywhere. I hadn't left Lakeside for a whole two weeks, and the future was beginning to look terrifyingly long.

"Hand me that bottle," Celia said, pointing to a bottle of amber-colored sherry that was on the top shelf of the pantry.

"I think that Nancy has put it up there so you can't have it. You aren't meant to mix it with your meds," I told her. It was start-ing to get annoying to always have to be responsible. I'd never wanted Mum's job, and somehow I'd ended up with it anyway.

"Fuck it," I said, and grabbed the sherry down and pulled two clean glasses out of the dishwasher.

"Much better," Celia said, and poured us two fingers each.

I took a sip. It was syrupy and burnt my throat, but somehow made the dull ache that had been pulsing in my temples ease.

"Ah!" said Celia, smacking her lips together. "That's much better. Now, I'm not going to ask you why you are in one of your muddy moods again, because you are meant to be looking after me, not the other way around. I don't have enough time left to be helping you out of a sulk."

I laughed and lay back. "You're not planning on dying soon, are you?"

"Not in the next month, if that helps. Long-term, I'm afraid I can't make any promises."

"I think I'm going to have a major career crisis when it happens, so try to hold out as long as you can, alright?"

Celia scoffed, sipped at her sherry, then spoke low. "When I was young you were only given three choices—nurse, teacher or secretary. There was a fourth choice too, of course. Still is."

"What was it?"

"Deviant."

She let out one of her signature cackling laughs, and chugged the rest of her sherry.

"What in hell are you still doing here anyway, Ava-babe?"

"God, don't ask me about Paris again. Please, I want to go. I do."

"I know you want me to tell you that life is short, but I won't. It's tediously long-winded. Only thing I bothered to stay around for are presents. Did you like my last one?"

She reached for the sherry bottle again but I snatched it away from her in time.

When I got home the first thing I did was dig into the back of my closet. Underneath my winter coat and odd socks was Celia's present; I'd never bothered to unwrap it. I ripped open the scrunched wrapping paper. Inside, it was filled with money. Twenty-dollar, fifty-dollar and hundred-dollar notes crammed tight.

Part 5

SEXUAL PROMISCUITY

2014

26

It was just like in the movies. The streets were cobblestoned. The buildings were from another time. People's breath rose above them in white clouds as they strode briskly past the huge brass statues of men on horseback and grand soldiers without even looking up. Cars honked, and pedestrians yelled, *"Merde!"* and *"Qu'est-ce que tu fous?"* as they walked straight into the oncoming traffic.

The bluestone building had been quiet for the last hour. Now people poured from its doors. Some of the passersby did double takes. All of the people leaving the building were women. All of them were approximately five feet seven inches and sixty kilos. They had straight brown hair and were wearing blue jeans and plain white T-shirts under their assorted jackets.

Among the different-shaped eyes, the different-sized noses, the varying skin colors, the moles, the blue eyes and the brown, was her. The one. Mel. Real and wholly from a dream all at once.

She turned left and made for the Metro station. Her flat-soled boots clapping against each stair as she descended. The first step light and the second heavy, a lopsided rhythm, *clip-clop, clip-clop, clip-clop*. She slipped a thin white card into the machine and the gates opened for her.

Her phone rang as the train arrived. She withdrew it from

her bag and her face lit up. She stepped onto the train as she answered.

"Hello?" Her voice reverberated around the half-full carriage. People spoke in low French, a couple kissed and giggled in the back.

"Yeah, fine," she said, her voice rising. "I was just at an audition...Good, I think. What about you?"

An older man turned to her, but she didn't notice. She remained standing, despite the surplus of empty seats, holding one of the handles from the upper rails, her body undulating with the train's movement.

"Tonight?...I'd love to! Coltrane?...Yeah, I think I know it. It's on Rue Notre-Dame, right?...Alright, see you at eight."

She took her phone from her ear and grinned, looking around to see who had been listening.

Mel got off at Republique station. The crowd ebbed and flowed around her, turning her head into a bobbing buoy, disappearing and resurfacing. Across the public square where kids in puffy jackets chased pigeons. Past the *boucherie* on the corner, its window full of headless, gutted pigs, its smell of flesh. Down a narrow pathway, up a hill. And then, we were there. In the photograph I'd seen before. The one I'd spent so long staring at that I'd memorized every detail. The white facade, the windows like two gaping eye sockets. She took her keys from her bag and the air caught their jingle. She entered the house and was gone.

I'd been so close on my walks with Celia. Even closer this past week, when I'd wandered the streets myself. Scarf around my head, ears stinging pink from the cold. Winter was different here. Back home it was drizzle and flapping wind; here it was ice and heavy white mist. My feet felt rigid from cold through the thin soles of my shoes; my nose was often numb.

But I didn't care. I was here. I was going to destroy Mel. She was the one who really mattered. If I could repay her, finally get even, I knew that I could move on. Then I would finally be free.

27

For twenty-seven hours I had waited in the dark. I had watched bad American comedies on the screen that was inches from my nose. I had contorted myself into every position I could think of on my seat, trying to find one that didn't deepen the ache in my lower back. Eventually, I turned the screen off and sat in still silence, staring numbly out the window to the tiny dots of lights as we got closer and closer to our destination. Paris. I had imagined it so many times it had become like a dream place. In the black limbo of the plane, hovering above the world, it didn't feel like we'd ever arrive anywhere. Like we were in a timeless, spaceless purgatory. Like this could just go on indefinitely.

But at last, the lights flickered on. A ding sounded, and the seat belt sign turned orange. We began our descent. Within minutes, we were shuffling out into the arrivals terminal, all of us tousled and stinking. I stood in line at immigration, the straps of my backpack digging into my shoulders. Despite people speaking French all around me, it still didn't seem real.

When I grabbed my suitcase from the luggage conveyor, I noticed a group of policemen standing near one of the doors. Their guns were huge, almost as long as my forearm. I tried not to look at them as I passed. I walked through to the huge cavern of the airport. It looked like some kind of spacecraft, the roof a net of fluorescent lighting that made my eyes sting even more. It was all too bright.

At the bottom of the escalator at the Metro, the woman in the small glass service booth glared at me.

"Je peux vous aider?"

"Oh, um." I cleared my throat, I hadn't used my voice since I'd left Melbourne and it sounded thick and rasping. "Sorry. English?"

"Yes." She raised an eyebrow at me.

"Great. Thanks. Um, one to Republique station? Can I get one train there or do I need to swap?"

"Gare du Nord, ten euro thirty," she snapped.

I dug through my backpack for my wallet and pulled out some notes for her. For some reason, her abruptness made me want to cry. I tried to tell myself it was just fatigue, just the weight of the bag on my back and the awkwardness of carrying the suitcase.

As I sat on the train into Paris, I stared out into the dark streets. It looked terrifying out there, dangerous. My stomach was cringing from the bad airplane food, my mouth was clammy and my skin was gummy with dried sweat. I wished violently I was still at home, in the safety of Lakeside. Wrapped up in the January warmth. I was sure that I'd made a terrible mistake coming here, that it was all going to be a disaster, that something awful might happen.

After finally figuring out the trains and getting lost dragging my suitcase in the cold, I found my hostel. Outside, everything had been closed down and dark. Only a few bars were still open, drunks yelling words I didn't understand. I'd kept my head down, the sound of my suitcase's wheels against the pavement marking me as a tourist, a target.

I entered the dim lights of the hostel, ears bitten from the chill, eyes watering, feeling conspicuous and stupid. The tattooed woman behind the reception desk had shaken her head at me when I'd begun talking in English. When I fumbled through my bag to find the computer printout of the reservation she'd looked at it for only a moment before handing me a silver key attached to a heavy piece of wood with the number seventeen on it. I had climbed the steep stairs, wincing as my suitcase banged loudly against each, and made it to the room. It was quiet and warm. There were three sets of bunks, only one bed empty. I didn't care that this room was alien, that I didn't even know the faces of the people I was sharing it with—I just wanted sleep. I tugged off my sticky jeans, pulled on the pyjama pants from my backpack and took my bra off from under my top. I burrowed into the clean sheets of the bed and could have groaned with bliss. Sleep pulled me under almost instantly.

I'd woken early the next day, the room still almost dark. A square of pale gray framed the blackout blinds. Pulling myself from the bed, I'd padded down the stairs. Passing the front desk, I'd smiled at the new girl who sat behind it; she smiled back. Then I pushed open the front doors, just to have a look.

I can't describe the feeling of that moment. Of standing out there, the cold going straight through my cotton pants, the air smelling different to anything else. The menacing foreignness of last night was like a bad dream. It wasn't anything like that anymore.

I'd spent so much time looking at these streets with Celia, but this was something else entirely. Before, the people had been frozen midstride, the watering can hovering forever above a window box, a woman's hands held high in paralyzed gesticulation outside a coffee shop. Now everything was moving. It was like someone had pressed Play. People spoke loudly in French, the scent of baking hovered in the air, making my mouth water. The banister was wet against my palm. The world had become real and I was real within it.

28

"Aber es kostet so viel Geld!"

"Was soll's, wir müßen das erleben. Es ist doch schließlich der Louvre!"

"Nun ja, aber man sagt, daß die Mona Lisa *nur so groß wie eine Briefmarke ist!"*

"Trotzdem können wir nicht nach Hause fahren, ohne sie gesehen zu haben: man wird uns bestimmt danach fragen."

I sat on my bunk, trying to ignore the whispered argument going on in the corner of the room. The two German girls had only arrived yesterday, taking over the bunks vacated by the Chilean woman and the British teenager who were here when I'd first arrived.

I was still exhausted, but trying hard not to fall asleep as it was only midday. I'd found if I didn't come back to the room for a few hours each day my head would start spinning. Still, I was often falling asleep before dark and waking at dawn.

I'd been in Paris for five days by then. While I was waiting for Mel to post a clue online, I'd played tourist. I'd even climbed the Eiffel Tower, the view from the top too magical to comprehend.

But I'm starting to get off topic, aren't I? I need to stick to the facts. You won't want to hear about the wonder I felt of being somewhere so different from home. You won't want to know about getting lost on the Metro, or eating fresh bread and thick cheese in the mornings, or learning the simplest of French but being too embarrassed to use it. We aren't going to be trading holiday happy snaps. I'll only be wasting your time. You want to hear about what matters here, about what happened with Mel.

Coltrane was a small bar only twenty minutes' walk from the hostel. It looked a lot like other places in the area. Seats out front, large red awnings with the bar's name in block white letters. Inside, it was crammed with young people. There was a bar near the entrance, backlit so that the glass bottles glowed. On the other side was a long mirror that took up most of the wall. I was sitting right near the back, with a small table all to myself. You couldn't see me from the entrance, and to the people around me I looked as though I was just sipping my drink, staring at nothing in particular. What do they say about capturing beauty? It's all about angles.

I was at the perfect angle to see the front half of the bar in the mirror. Mel and the guy she'd met came in and out of view as the people around them moved and parted. He was grinning at her to begin with, one hand stroking her arm while she spoke. The next time I got a look at them, she was still talking and he was sitting back in his chair. I didn't need to be able to hear them to see that he'd stopped paying her much attention. He was good-looking, in an affected sort of way. He had long hair tied into a bun and an oversize black T-shirt that made his arms look thin and spindly.

I had ordered a red wine and was sipping it slowly. Since they were sitting right near the bar, I wouldn't be able to go up and get another one without risking Mel seeing me. Part of me wanted that. To push past her with just an *excusez-moi*. Let her recognize me, fake a coincidence.

Or I could go straight up to her, throw my arms around her. After all, I was only keeping my promise. The promise she'd begged me to make back in school, that I'd come with her here to Paris.

The guy was now twirling the stem of his wineglass between his thumb and forefinger, staring absently into the shallow crimson pool. Then, his gaze lifted and set straight onto me. He smiled and I looked away quickly. I took a sip of my wine, tried to swallow it, though my throat had tightened. Surely, it wasn't me he was looking at, but his own reflection. Taking a breath, I let my gaze rise, for a moment convinced I'd see them both staring at me through the reflection. But they weren't. They were kissing on each cheek and he was putting a hand on her lower back. They were leaving. I was going to follow them; that wasn't even a question. Now that I'd seen Mel I was hungry for her. Hungry to see every piece of her new existence, to understand who she had become. To know if she'd changed.

I forced myself to pause, to give it at least thirty seconds. He'd noticed me; if I tailed them straightaway he might recognize me again and point it out to her. I took a drink from my wine. Someone came to stand in front of my table, blocking the mirror from view.

"*Je devais me débarrasser d'elle.*"

I'm not sure what I was expecting, a waiter perhaps. But I would never have thought it would be him. Mel's date. Standing in front of my small table and looking straight at me. No mirror between us. No nothing. He was so much taller than I'd thought.

"*Tu es très belle.*" He leaned forward so I could hear him over the conversations all around us, and rested his hands on the tabletop. His hands were big, with wide fingernails cut short and a tiny sprinkle of hair above each knuckle.

"*Désolé, mais est-ce que tu parles français?*" he asked.

My mind wasn't working quickly enough to begin to understand, so I just shook my head.

"Anglais?"

I knew that word, so I nodded. "English, yes."

He took that as an invitation, and squeezed in next to me. I shifted away from him. My mind still whirring. He had been there with Mel, a flat image. Now I could feel the hard bone of his knee touching mine; I could smell the slight spiciness of his cologne.

"I thought you were French." His accent was thick. "You looked like a French girl sitting here alone so confidently."

"No," I said.

Up close I could see he had fine stubble on his face, a thin silver ring in his nose.

"You are very beautiful."

"Um, thanks," I said, certain suddenly that Mel must have put him up to it somehow. That this was a trick.

"Where are you from?"

"I'm Australian."

"Australie?" His brow furrowed, then he laughed. "The girl I was just with. She was also Australian."

"Really?" I asked. "Where did she go?"

"Quelle?"

He was barely listening to me, I noticed. Instead, he was looking at me in *that* way. His eyes flicking down my body and back to my face. It wasn't a trick. This guy was trying to pick me up. He wanted to sleep with me.

"The girl you were with." I spoke slowly and smiled coyly. "Where did she go?"

He shrugged. "Home, I suppose."

"But not with you?"

"No." He shot me a boyish grin. "I saw you looking at me again and again. You Australian girls are not very subtle."

"Is she your girlfriend?"

"Pas du tout, I met her only once before. She is very pretty, but very boring."

"Really?"

"*Oui*, she goes on and on about acting, but she is not working. She tries to speak French, but she cannot. I told her to stop,
but she continues anyway. It's very annoying."

"She's an actress?"

"No, she is just trying. Anyway, who cares about that girl.
I want to know about you. Everything, tell me."

He reached up to touch my arm, his fingers tracing down-
ward just as he had done to Mel less than twenty minutes ago.
It had been so long since I'd been touched, by anyone. I'd
begun to think of my skin as hard and stiff. I resisted my urge
to flinch, to pull back. To make an excuse. To run. Instead, I
held still and let myself feel the fizz of nerves.

His name was Clem, I soon found out, and within the hour
we were making our way to his house, my thick jacket on, the
air cold on my cheeks. He wanted me to meet his housemates,
he said, since he'd told me so much about them. Plus he had a
bottle of wine at home.

I didn't give a shit about his housemates, or the fact that he
was in the middle of putting his demo together, or his opinions
on French politics. I wanted to know more about Mel, what
she'd told him, how they'd met. But I won't lie. I was also cu-
rious. I'd never gone home with a guy before. I wanted to see
what would happen, to know what I would do.

Clem was right. His house was only a few minutes' walk
away. He led me past the propped-up bicycles into a tiny wire
elevator. We had to squeeze in to fit together with our big coats
on. He looked at me under his lids, like he might want to kiss
me in that confined space. I turned my face away.

He opened the door to his apartment to the smell of cooked
food. It was small inside, the corridor tight enough so that my
shoulders could almost touch both sides. He put his coat on
the hook.

"Clem?"

"*Salut!*" he called, and pulled off his shoes. I did the same, leaving my coat on top of his and my shoes among the many other pairs in various colors and sizes. I felt a little trapped then, without any coat or shoes. I couldn't just run away if I needed to.

I followed him into the small kitchen.

"*C'est Ava,*" he said casually.

"*Salut,*" both the housemates said. They were sitting at the table eating together. They grinned at me over their meals. I tried to smile back, but I was sure I was wearing my fear and awkwardness all over my face. Clem took a bottle of red wine down from the shelf.

"*En voulez-vous?*" he asked them, but they shook their heads.

He plucked two glass tumblers from the overflowing drying rack. "*Ça sent bon. Est-ce que tu m'as laissé?*"

One of the housemates scoffed, "*En aucune façon.*"

I leaned against the sink, wishing I could understand even a word or two of what they were saying, wondering if they were making fun of me.

"We will drink this in my room if that's okay?" he said. "They don't want any."

I shrugged, trying to look relaxed. "Okay."

I followed him into his bedroom and he closed the door behind us. I was surprised at how big his room was, three times larger than the kitchen. He had a desk with a laptop and some stray papers littering it and a corner of the room set up with what looked like musical equipment. The only place to sit was the bed. He put on music, then poured the wine, overfilling each glass. He put the glass into my hand and sat down heavily next to me.

"Cheers," he said to me. I smiled at him and took a gulp.

"You like it?"

"Yes, it's nice."

"It's Côte Du Rhône. Do you have French wine at home?"

"A bit."

"Do you have a boyfriend at home?"

I shook my head, took another gulp.

He put a hand to my face. Again, I fought the urge to run, remembering my shoes on the floor near the door.

"How is someone so beautiful all alone?"

I tightened my hand around the glass to try to stop it from shaking. Clem took my silence as an invitation; his hand slid from my cheek to the back of my skull and he pulled me toward him. My stomach lifted in the same way as when an airplane suddenly drops in altitude. His mouth tasted of the wine. I pulled away to take another sip, emptying the glass. I couldn't help but think of Evan.

"Here," Clem said, and took my glass and put it on the bedside table.

He leaned in to kiss me again. I moved my head away and he began kissing my neck instead.

"So where did you meet her?"

"Who?"

He lifted my woollen sweater and T-shirt off over my head at once. He went to kiss me again, but again I moved my cheek away. He continued kissing my neck, squeezing my breast with his hand as he did.

"The girl you were with tonight."

"Mel? At a party."

"You liked her at first?"

He stopped what he was doing and looked at me. "It turns you on to talk of her?"

"Yeah," I said. He liked that.

Pulling me down with him onto the bed, he continued kissing me, his hand stroking up and down my body. And I started feeling something then. Something in my skin when he touched me. I didn't want to run anymore.

He began reaching behind me, trying to unhook my bra.

"Did you kiss her?" I breathed into his neck.

"Yes, we made love," he said, pulling off my bra. "Do you want to?"

He brushed a hand over my bare breast, looking from it back up into my eyes, his breathing fast. I'd never done this before. But I wanted to. I wanted to see if I could. I wanted to see if it would reveal the nastiness that was inside me somehow. If I didn't do it right then, right in that moment, I knew I never would. So I nodded.

29

You won't really want to hear about my sex life though, will you? You won't want to hear about the grunts, the sweat, the fumbling fingers as Clem tried to squeeze himself in, not knowing why it was so difficult. It hurt, more than I expected, and as soon as the first shock of pain started to die away enough for me to begin to enjoy it, his body was rippling and he was pulling himself off me.

"T'es si serrée," he'd groaned.

"What?"

"That was amazing."

He'd wanted me to stay, but I didn't. Even though it had been far from amazing, I felt dazzled. Free from my own fear. He hadn't looked at me any differently afterward. I hadn't revealed the monster inside me. Nothing bad had happened.

I was happy for the aching pulse between my legs as I walked down the quiet street alone. I was happy for the cold, for my stinging cheeks and ears, happy to hear the sounds of cars far-off, the sounds of French conversations I couldn't understand. There were fairy lights in the trees around me and they twinkled at me, like a million tiny eyes winking.

I knew I could never be in a relationship. People like me weren't capable of real love. Plus, no one would be able to love me if they knew who I really was or the things I did. I'd always thought that love and sex went hand in hand, but I realized then that they didn't have to. There was part of the human experience that I was allowed to be included in after all.

I walked until I reached Mel's place. The windows were dark. I stood in the middle of the narrow street, looking up at it. This street had a dark hush about it. There were no lights in the trees here, only the blue-orbed streetlights. She was only meters away from me, if only I could see her. Peering over the roof of her house were the tops of a building clad in mesh panels and scaffolding. It wasn't something I would have usually risked doing. But that night, anything felt possible.

I circled around to the street behind Mel's. The scaffolding caged a crumbling gray stone building, a few levels higher than the two-story house Mel lived in. It wasn't hard to climb. Pulling my weight up with my arms, my muscles shook with the effort. Sidling across the metal bars in my boots, elated by my own daring. Sweat building under my thick jacket, I squeezed around to the back. The white roof of Mel's house opened out in front of me like an ice-skating rink. There were some pigeons nesting in a corner, a chimney sticking up the middle and, to the left, a black square. I hopped onto the roof, treading softly so that my footsteps wouldn't be heard in the rooms below. The black square was actually not black at all, but a panel of glass. It wasn't big, less than a meter each way. Crouching next to it, I saw down onto her bed. Mel was lying there, the laptop on her chest illuminating her face a pale blue.

I watched her for a long time, imagining many things. Stomping through the glass and falling onto her bed, smacking her across the face with her laptop. Or perhaps the glass would do enough, its jagged pieces falling over her, cutting her up into small pieces.

Eventually she closed her laptop, slid it under her pillow and turned onto her side, eyes closed. Without the light from the screen, I could barely see her in the dark. She was only a dark shape against the white sheets. I stood, bones crackling from immobility, and made my way gingerly back down to the ground.

30

When I got back to the hostel that night, no one was awake. I showered in the empty communal bathroom, then slept deeply for a few hours. I got up with the sun, and returned to Mel's house. I was cleaned out, refreshed inside and out.

For days, I trailed Mel's every move. She didn't go out much, but when she did, she was always alone. She'd sit by herself in cafés, scooping the foam of her coffee into her mouth and then tonguing the spoon. Then she would eat a buttery croissant with her hands and lick her fingers, one at a time. She never went back to the bluestone building where I'd first seen her, and I noticed she'd deleted the post about her audition from Instagram, which I guess meant she didn't get the part. A couple of times she went to the Pathé-Wepler Cinema, a huge complex that played blockbusters and stank of stale popcorn. She avoided the French films, watching movies in English with French subtitles. I'd sneak into the back row after the trailers were finished and the lights had gone down, and watch the back of her head as she ate popcorn and leaned back in her seat. It made me think of that night we'd watched *Cloverfield* together on her laptop, weeks after that awful party. I sat in the dark, seething at the memory of it.

Sometimes she'd spend hours just walking. She'd walk and walk and I'd follow, but she never seemed to go anywhere. Just endless loops through the city. Still, after all this time, I didn't understand her. I didn't know why she did the things she did, and if I didn't get her, how was I ever going to pay her back.

Just as I was beginning to despair, just as I was sure Celia's money would dry up before I found an opportunity, that I would fail at this and have to go home, Mel left the house with makeup on. She walked with purpose. She was finally going somewhere.

I followed her to the neighborhood of Pigalle. We passed brothels and sex shops and I began to get excited. Maybe Mel's Paris life was going to prove to be salacious after all. But no, she turned off into a bistro, La Cantine de la Cigale. It was a red-walled little place with low-hanging lights and large black-boards with specials. Outside, there were rows of heavy steel chairs, all facing outward as they did in Paris, where people watching seemed to be part of the culture.

I hoped she'd take one of those chairs, where it would be easier to eavesdrop. But of course she headed inside instead, choosing a table by the window. I pulled my jacket tighter and took a seat outside. Mel was facing away from the glass, but I hoped that catching glimpses of the face of whoever she was meeting might give me a hint to what was going on. I had to twist my body to see inside so instead I watched the door. Within minutes, a young woman approached. I knew her face well, but she looked different in three dimensions. I had seen her smile, flattened and filtered, many times on Mel's Face-book. She was one of her best friends, Léa. As she passed me, she caught my eye. I looked away quickly.

I'd had a look at Léa's Facebook page a few times as well in those long hours at home alone. I always checked out anyone Mel posted about. Léa was French, but her English seemed to be flawless. From what I'd gathered, it seemed like she'd studied acting along with Mel, but given up on it soon after. Now she was a production manager on a French soap opera, spending her days running around with a headset on and dealing with actors' tantrums and costuming catastrophes.

At the bistro, she shared a cold cuts platter with Mel. I just had a black coffee, wrapping my hands around it to keep them warm. I wished there was some way I could sit inside. Mel was probably spilling all her secrets to her friend right now.

I twisted around to look at them. Mel was dipping a pickle in the pâté, and gesturing with it as she talked. She got her phone out and was showing something on the screen to Léa. I could almost see it. I wrenched around even farther. The chair's legs on the opposite side lifted off the ground. I was suspended for a moment, scrambling to readjust. It was too late. I fell, arm scraping against the ground, chair falling next to me with a loud crack. Fuck. I lay still on the pavement for a moment. She'd seen. Surely, she'd seen.

"*Ça va?*" The waiter had emerged.

"Fine." I waved him away. "Sorry. Yeah. Totally fine."

My cheeks burned. Slowly, I looked up at the window, expecting to see her face, mouth open in shock and disgust and fear. But she was facing away from me. She was still looking at the screen of her phone. Léa on the other hand was looking straight at me, an expression somewhere between concern and amusement playing on her face. I threw some money on the table and rushed away from my upturned chair, heart pounding. I rounded the corner, then leaned against a wall, my breath coming in bursts, skin prickling with panic, hot against the chilled air. That had been so close. Too close.

I inspected the damage. My coat wasn't ripped, thank God. There was blood dripping down my arm though. My wrist and the side of my forearm had gotten the worst of it, a dirt-encrusted graze throbbing painfully. I looked through my bag and recovered a scrunched-up tissue from the bottom. I held it to the wound, wincing.

Fifteen minutes later, Mel and Léa emerged. They kissed on each cheek, then walked in opposite directions. I followed Léa. She walked north, in the direction of Montmartre. I still felt too shaken to follow Mel, too worried that I might do something stupid again, that she might see me.

Léa seemed to be window-shopping. She went inside a bookstore for fifteen minutes, idly flipping through paperbacks. She went to a dress store, and spent a while inspecting an edgy-looking leather bag while talking to the salesgirl in clipped French, but she didn't end up buying it. I waited outside, too afraid that she'd recognize me again, or that my bloodied wrist would attract the chagrin of the salesgirl. Léa hesitated outside a small shop, then went inside. Looking up, I noticed the neon cross that connoted a pharmacy. I paused, an idea forming in my head. Then I took a deep breath, tried to conjure back some kind of confidence and followed her.

She was standing in front of the skin-care section, sniffing hand creams. The bell sounded as I entered, and I let her catch me notice her. She looked away quickly. I went over to where the Band-Aids were and took some off the shelf. Then I turned to her again. She looked up at me, and I smiled.

"Anglais?" I asked.

She nodded.

"You saw that, at the bistro, didn't you?" I pretended to be embarrassed.

"Yes." She smiled. "I don't know how you managed it. It was a spectacular fall."

I put my hand to my head, angled it so she could see my

injured wrist. "So embarrassing! I think I should just go back to Australia now."

I saw her eyes flick to the graze. "You hurt yourself?"

"Oh—" I looked at it "—it's nothing. Actually...could you help me?"

A weariness flashed across her face. "With what?"

"It's okay, actually, don't worry. Sorry, I shouldn't be bothering you. I just can't figure out which one is antiseptic, but it's fine."

I turned away from her, went back toward the Band-Aids. I stood there for a moment, pretending to be focused on the vials and bottles. I heard movement behind me. Léa came to stand next to me. She was taller than me and, turning toward her, I noticed a small mole just below her bottom lip. I felt a warmth go through me, a wanting. That pull toward someone I hadn't felt since Evan.

"This one," she said, pulling a red-and-white bottle from the shelf and handing it to me. I took it from her, let my hand touch hers just slightly.

"Thanks," I said.

"She said he just suddenly jumped out of his chair and said he had to go, but as soon as they were outside he said he needed to use the bathroom and he went back in."

"Strange."

"Yeah, she thinks that maybe he spotted someone else in there he liked the look of better."

"Did she go and check?"

"Don't think so but I think she's been texting him." She pulled the blanket until it reached our chins. "I don't usually do this in the middle of the day, you know."

I rolled onto my stomach and grinned at her. "Me neither."

"So, how long have you guys been friends?"

She looked at me out of the corner of her eye, and I knew I

was starting to push it. I kissed her bare shoulder. "Don't know why I'm so interested. I guess it's nice to hear about another Australian in this city."

"Which city are you from?"

"Perth," I lied. "What about her? How strange would it be if we knew each other."

"No, she's from Melbourne."

"Did you guys ever...?" I let the question hang.

"Oh God no," she laughed. "That girl is as straight as they come. The only reason she'd show me any of that kind of interest is if she thought I could get her a role."

I resisted any remark.

"How long are you staying for?" she was asking me. "I'd like to see you again. You're sweet."

We were in her studio apartment. It had large windows and sheer white curtains, one wall was stacked high with magazines, a mixture of the white spines of art journals and the yellow of *National Geographic*.

"A week or so," I said. "Not long."

"Can I convince you to extend?"

I'd been considering it. I was only just starting to get a sense of how Mel lived now. I still had no idea what I was going to do to her, but Celia's money was starting to run dry.

"Maybe."

I had a long hot shower at Léa's place, whose bathroom was much nicer than the mildewy tiles at the hostel. My flesh was feeling reawakened. Cleansed. I wasn't afraid of being touched anymore. It had been different with Léa than it had been with Clem—better. I had actually enjoyed it, actually let myself forget everything for a few moments and just be in my body. Her skin was so warm and soft, her touches so tender. As I washed myself with her expensive, creamy soap it struck me that I hadn't felt this good in a long, long time. Maybe it was because I was so close. Once I got back at Mel, made her feel how I had felt, even for an instant, then I knew I could move on. And for the first time it felt like there was something for me after all this, that despite everything I knew about myself, I might be able to have some sort of life of my own after all.

Re-dressed I sat down on the bed, where Léa was sitting up with a blanket around her waist, not seeming at all self-conscious of her exposed breasts. I gave her my email address—I had no French phone—and kissed her goodbye before making my way back down to the street.

There was a café nearby. I found a seat under the heater outside and ordered a coffee and crepe, even though it was late afternoon. I was ravenous.

Something was changing in me. Being here, seeing how big the world was, how different things could be, it was making me see things differently. An idea was fluttering around inside me, the idea that maybe it was possible for me to be something else, to do something else. Maybe it was possible for there to be a different life out there for me. Once I got even with Mel, made amends for what had happened between us, then maybe I could start over.

The waiter slid the crepe and coffee down in front of me.

"Merci," I said.

When I cut the crepe into bits, melted cheese oozed out of my incisions. It was hot and creamy against the crispy dough. The tomatoes squirted their juices between my teeth as I chewed. In front of me, two women talked in quick French. One of them was standing with her back to me, balancing a baby on her hip. On the back of her arm, just above the elbow, was a tattoo done in fine black ink. Thin circular lines that looked like a solar system maybe, or perhaps just a design, I wasn't sure. Whatever it was, it meant something to the woman, whose face I couldn't even see. It was significant enough to her to want to stamp it onto her flesh forever. And the baby. He was permanent. This woman had that confidence. She could make a mark on her own life, shape it, make decisions that lasted forever. For a moment I envied her fiercely. I wanted that tattoo. I wanted that baby on my hip. I wanted to be hemmed in by my choices, have a set path in front of me. But then the baby turned to look at me. Its cheeks were wobbling over a small chin. It surveyed me with its beady little eyes. Then, its eyes squished closed, its skin turned red and blotchy, its mouth opened huge and wet and pink. It let out a piercing cry. The woman began bouncing it in front of her. She began making low soothing noises as she tried to pacify the red, screaming thing.

I downed the remainder of the coffee and left some money on the shiny tabletop. Making my way back to my hostel, my ears were still ringing from the baby's cries.

31

I was starting to find it hard to fill my days. The construction site behind Mel's house had workers on it until nightfall, and Mel was going out less and less. At night, I'd watch her. She did strange things in that room, alone. To begin with, she was always just watching television and eating takeout. But now, it was different. It was like she'd sensed the change in me, that somehow she'd felt my shift after I'd made love with Léa that day.

Since then, she'd started turning her heater on high, I'd seen her fiddle with the knob. Then, she'd strip all her clothes off. In her underwear, she'd read French novels or drink glasses of whiskey and suck on the ice. It was as if she was posing, expecting some fashion photographer to be in the corner of her bedroom snapping pictures of her.

Saanvi and Theodore had so much more in their lives, things that they'd worked for, things I could take away. But not Mel. Like me, she didn't seem to have put down roots. On those long, cold nights staring into that square of light. Mel lying across her bed in the false heat in her matching lace underwear, my limbs stiffening and my nose running, I'd started thinking more and more about the future. Watching people had used to make me feel so good, so powerful and fulfilled. But for some reason, watching Mel wasn't working. But I couldn't stop now, I was here, I was so close.

I'd been saving up my coins to call Bea. My bag was heavy with them. The straps bit into my shoulder and the contents jangled as I walked. It took me a while to find a phone booth. Now that everyone had mobile phones, they were starting to become redundant. Eventually, I found one with cracked glass and graffiti, on the corner of a busy intersection.

Feeding coin after coin into to it, I dialed the country code, then Bea's home number, crossing my fingers that she'd be in.

The phone beeped, went silent for a few seconds, then began to ring.

"Hello?"

"Bea!"

"Ava?"

Just the sound of her voice made me want to cry; I hadn't realized how much I'd been missing her.

"Yep, it's me! How are you? I'm just at a phone booth, not sure how long I've got."

On cue, the phone beeped. I fed some more coins in and pressed the plastic black receiver tightly to my ear as a motorcycle bellowed past.

"It's so good to hear from you! How is it going there?"

"It's great. The food here is amazing, I…" But then I hesitated; her voice had sounded strange. Something wasn't right.

"Are you okay?"

"Yep, course," she said. "What were you saying?"

I fed some more coins in.

"Are you sure?"

I could hear the crackle of a heavy breath. "I didn't know whether I should tell you. I think you should just have fun while you're there. Evan was here for dinner last night and—"

The phone beeped again, and her voice cut off. I quickly shoved in the coins. My hands were shaking.

"Bea?"

Why did she mention Evan? My throat felt tight, I was

sweating, and I felt a deep longing and pain stronger than I thought I could feel.

I pushed in more coins.

"Ava?"

"Hi! You're there! What were you saying?"

"Oh. Well, it's not good news. I didn't want to tell you but Evan said he thought you'd want to know."

"What is it? Just tell me!"

"It's Celia."

"What about her?"

"She's really not doing well, Ava. I'm sorry."

That was just like Bea, being so overly vague and nice. "What do you mean not doing well? Can you be specific? Is she just sick or do you mean she's dying or what?"

"The cancer has come back. Aggressively. They're saying if she doesn't do chemotherapy now she'll only have a few months. Even if she does do the chemo, it's not looking very good."

I couldn't say anything.

"Ava?"

"I'm here." I tried to clear my throat. "So is she going to do it?"

"Nancy is trying to make her, but you know what she's like."

"She doesn't want to lose her hair?"

"Bingo. But listen, A—"

The phone beeped again, and I put the remainder of the coins in.

"Bea? What did you say?" I asked.

"I said try not to think about it. Don't let it ruin your—"

The phone beeped once more, and then returned to a dial tone. I stayed where I was, phone to ear, watching the traffic careen by around me.

In Paris, people leave their garbage on the street. They don't fill plastic bins like we do. They don't wheel them out only once a week and leave them standing in neat rows like soldiers out front of their houses. No. Every night, there are bags of garbage piled on the footpath. The crows get into them. Slicing the plastic with their sharp beaks, pulling it apart with their razor claws. Then it's the rats' turn. They sniff and prod with their little noses, worming their way into the crows' holes and scampering off in front of you, a furry blur, as you walk past.

I watched my feet as I walked to Mel's. I'd almost screamed when I'd accidentally kicked a bag I hadn't seen last week and a crow, impenetrably black and huge, flapped and thrashed from it. At least it wasn't a rat.

For some reason, the crow made me think of the ones that were always foraging in the mud of the empty lake back home. I never thought I'd miss that place. But for a moment, I did.

The scaffolding was waiting for me, like the nest of a funnel-web spider. The moonlight glinted off its edges. I didn't even look around anymore to see if anyone was watching. I didn't even care. This city had started to feel different to me in the days since my conversation with Bea. Before I'd felt independent and free; now I just felt alone.

I pulled myself up, using the route I knew. The beams I was confident could hold my weight, that wouldn't wobble. I was used to the coldness of the beams against my palms, to the stretch of my muscles as I pulled up my own weight. I was starting to get good at climbing. Jumping onto the roof I fell silently, then trod as softly as I could over to the square. It was lit up, bright and white. Mel's light must be on.

Bending down I looked in through the glass. She was in there alright, and she wasn't alone. She was lying on her back, totally naked, a man crouching between her thighs. She bit her lip, arched her back, gripped onto the sheets with her fingers. I couldn't hear her, but I could imagine what she'd sound like—*Oh yes, baby, just like that.* She'd be making those girlish little mews that sounded just right, breathing heavy. He got up from between her legs and clambered on top of her, began kissing her neck.

I looked a little closer. I couldn't see his face, but I recognized the body. I recognized the messy bun of his hair. It was Clem. I leaned even closer, just to be sure, putting my nose right up to the glass. It was definitely him.

Mel looked right up. She looked right into my face, which was being framed by the skylight. I knew I should duck away, but I couldn't. I was frozen in shock. Clem was thrusting into her now, and her whole body was jiggling with each plunge. But she barely seemed to notice him. She was looking at me, and smiling that smile that brought back so many memories.

It was the smile that said she'd won.

32

Celia's funeral could have been for anyone. People wore black; they spoke sedately and quietly. The priest spoke of God and Jesus, and I imagined how much she would have cackled if she'd been there next to me.

Evan came. I appreciated that. He didn't have to. It lessened the sting a little. Nancy wouldn't speak to me at all. In fact, she looked at me as if I shouldn't have been there, which was something I could understand.

After the service finished, people made their way in dribs and drabs back to Celia's house, where Nancy was holding the wake. I managed to stay awhile, nodding along to some old codger who talked about Celia like she was the one that got away. But then the lump in my throat got too painful. I ran over to what I still thought of as Evan's house. The half-built one he used to sleep in after fights with Aiden. I jumped in through the glassless window and sat down on the floor. It was even dirtier than before.

I'd gone there to cry, to try to get it all out so I didn't have to do it in front of everyone. But now that I was there I couldn't.

"Thought you might be here."

Evan was standing there in his suit, leaning in through the empty window.

"Do you want company?"

I wanted to shake my head no. I didn't want anyone to see me like this, least of all him. But his face set me off. The simplicity of his worry, the kind way he was looking at me. That was when the tears started to come. He jumped in through the window and got down next to me on the dirty floorboards, not even hesitating as he pulled me into his shoulder. If Celia was there, she would have told me to cry demurely. She would have wanted me to let one tragic tear drop down my cheek and ask him to ravish me right there on the floor. I could just imagine her saying something like that. But I couldn't. I cried loudly and messily. It felt like purging, like vomiting, in the way it took over my body. The heat of his skin through his shirt, the tight hold of his arm, only made it worse.

"It's okay," he said, stroking my hair. "It's going to be okay."

The way he did it reminded me of the woman at the French café and her ugly, screaming baby. My cries started turning to laughter then. Weird, hysterical laughter. I hiccuped, pulled away from him and rubbed my palms over my face.

"Sorry," I said, "really. That was full-on."

"Don't say sorry. I know you really loved her."

I shook my head. He still didn't understand. People like me couldn't love.

"It isn't that," I said. "I'm not sad. I'm angry. That whole service was so impersonal, so not her. No one had more personality than Celia, and then that's all she gets?"

I was half yelling, but Evan was nodding at me, his eyes still painfully empathetic.

"I'm sorry about everything," I said, more quietly, "for being such an asshole to you."

He looked away, uncomfortable. Then, "It's fine."

"It's not."

He still wasn't looking at me.

"You know I heard this story the other day. About a couple that were murdered at a ski resort."

He didn't even say anything. I tried another tactic. I needed him back in my life. It wasn't an option to continue only seeing him awkwardly when we really had to with Bea and Aiden.

"I miss what we used to be. Do you remember the crazy shit we used to do?"

"What, like taking roofies together right here?" he asked.

"Yeah, or…I dunno, remember when you pretended you knew that old friend of mine at the bar? Just dumb stuff like that."

I cursed myself. I was still doing it. Seeing everything through the lens of my stupid revenge plot.

"Just, everything," I said, then forced myself to say it. "I miss you."

He grinned. "God, you spend a few weeks in France and you come back all touchy-feely? What happened to you, Auntie Ava?"

There was so much I could have said, so I just looked down, saying nothing.

"I guess we should go back."

"Yeah."

"Nancy probably wants your help with things, right?"

"Um. No. She doesn't even want to look at me."

"Why?"

I guess he didn't know how Celia really died. Nancy had been keeping a tight lid on that one. It seemed that Celia hadn't been taking her meds at all; she'd been hoarding them, just in case something like this were to happen.

It was my job to make sure she took them. To watch her take them, but I didn't.

"Don't know," I said.

"Maybe she's worried that the old bat is going to give you all her millions?"

I tried to laugh as Evan pulled me up.

Part 6

JUVENILE DELINQUENCY

2008

33

Did you know that chickens are cannibals? If a chicken has a scratch on it, even a small one, you have to separate it from the others. They can smell blood. At first it will just be one bird pecking at the injured chicken, but poultry tend to imitate each other. Soon, the whole flock will be on it, pecking, scratching and tearing at its feathers, its tissue, its organs, until all that is left is just a big bloody mess. It's in their nature.

I thought I wouldn't tell you what happened next. That explaining the night of Mel's party was enough for you to understand. But really, I have to, don't I? If you're going to understand any of it, I'm going to have to tell you what happened after that night. I'm going to have to tell you all of it.

The night of the party changed my life irrevocably, you see. There was no going back from something like that. If you've woken up with shit on your face, then you'll understand, but I'm guessing that you haven't. The months that followed it were blurry and indistinct. The pain became numbness, a necessary shield from the cruelty.

But the first Monday, I remember. The first Monday I still had hope, stupid misguided hope, that maybe everything might be okay.

The weekend before it had been drained of color. I had put the shower on as hot as I could stand on Saturday morning and watched as the dirt and sticky champagne disappeared down the drain. After that, I barely left my bedroom. Bea knocked, asked if I was okay. I ignored her. When my alarm clock went off that Monday, the first Monday, I didn't wake with a jolt, I didn't lie in bed stiff with worry. I remember getting up straightaway with empty acceptance. The cold didn't creep into my bones as I walked down to the bus. I wasn't scared of the black morning like I had been.

The first pain of the day hit me as the farmhouse flicked past the bus window. I looked away like I'd been slapped.

It was second period when I knew for sure. PE. They'd all covered their bodies when I walked into the change room. Not just Saanvi and Mel. Not just Cass. Almost all the girls covered themselves and glared at me. The story of what happened in that room must have spread. Morphed and mutated like Chinese Whispers. I put my bag on the bench and tried to ignore them.

"Don't look at me, weirdo!" whispered Saanvi. "You owe me a fucking phone."

The toxic taste was in my mouth again, gripping my throat. Threatening to strangle me. I changed my clothes quickly, staring at my feet, just trying to breathe. As I walked out of the room, I caught Mel's eye.

"Psycho."

That word caught on. *Psycho.* It was yelled, jeered and hissed at me every day by people I had never even spoken to, and every night when I got home, I could hear it echoing back in my head. Numbness didn't make the time go faster. This was the time that should have been a blur. Should have disappeared in a montage of my sad face and their maniacal cackles. It wasn't like that. Each minute was painfully, achingly slow. Each class was a combat, something to be dreaded. I would stare down at my book, while inside I was crouched, ready and waiting for the inevitable.

Through the fog, I even attempted to reconcile with Ashleigh and Ling. Ashleigh had given me a half smile, but Ling just looked annoyed.

"You can't do that, Ava. You can't ditch us without a word, and then come back like it never happened. That's not fair."

She was right. I could have kept trying, made the effort to make amends, told them what had happened and how sorry I was. But it was too hard; I was too tired. Just existing was exhausting.

Sometimes the only thing worse than the names was the silence. In science we had a class exercise in which we had to play "genetics bingo." We had a list of different genetic traits, things like tongue-rolling, earlobe attachment, dimples, left-handedness, and we had to find a student that fit each one.

"Ready?" our science teacher said. "Go!"

People leaped from the seats, paper in hand. Quickly, the room got very loud, everyone talking to each other at once, filling in names and moving on. I tried. First, I approached Evelyn, a shy girl with auburn ringlets who had always seemed friendly.

"Can I write you down for curly hair?" I asked.

She just looked at me, then turned to someone else. I tried once more, with a guy called Rob. He was known as the nice guy at school; he was kind to everyone.

"You've got dimples, right, Rob?" My voice was already cracking.

He didn't even look at me. I retreated back to my seat, staring at my empty worksheet.

"Bingo!" someone called eventually.

When everyone had returned to their spots, the teacher had each person stand up and say how many traits they'd ticked off.

"How about you, Ava?" he asked.

I stayed sitting, shook my head. "None," I whispered.

"You didn't participate?" he asked. I shrugged, not wanting to meet his eye, hoping no one would call out, *None of us wants to talk to the psycho!* No one said anything. The teacher looked around awkwardly, and then moved on to the next person. Somehow, that was even more humiliating.

For the rest of the day, my throat was clogged with sharp stones. As I walked up the hill to Lakeside the tears finally came. I was so wretched, so conspicuous in isolation at school. I looked so stupid all the time. There was no respite from it. When I got home, I'd turn on my computer. There'd be messages there, comments on Facebook, that had banked up throughout the day. *Can't you afford new clothes?* And *You're such a fucking joke.* And *If I was you I'd kill myself.* And always *Psycho, Psycho, Psycho.* I knew that I'd read them all, each and every one of them. Then tomorrow, it would start all over again.

"You okay?"

I looked up. The guy from across the road, Evan, was standing in his kitchen by the open window. He peered at me with real concern. I rubbed at my wet cheeks.

"Yeah."

He offered me a sad smile, and I retuned it and kept walking before he could say anything else.

I couldn't tell anyone what had happened, not even Bea. I knew I should. I wanted to. But how could I? Where could I start the story that ended with my face smeared with shit? I always wondered whether it was Theodore's or someone else's. I hoped it was an animal's. That felt like the best option.

Bea stopped asking me eventually. One day after school she heard me crying in my room. The crying never helped, but my body kept on doing it anyway. Over my own pathetic blubbering, I heard her knock lightly.

"Go away! I'm fine."

I tried to hold the crying in, but it made my throat burn so much that another sob escaped anyway.

The door pushed open. I hid my face in my hands. I knew I was snotty and disgusting; I didn't want her to see. The bed squeaked as she sat down next to me. She pulled me into her. Wrapped her arms gently around me.

"It's going to be okay," she said.

I tried to tell her that it wasn't, but I couldn't speak. She rubbed my back. Eventually the crying eased.

"It's those girls, isn't it? I knew they were bitches."

I pulled back to see her expression. "How?"

"I could just tell. The way they swanned in here that night like we were so far beneath them. Honestly, Ava, you are so better off without them."

"You don't get it," I said, nestling back into her shoulder. "Everyone at school hates me."

"Who cares?" she said. "You've only got four months left."

"I should have swapped schools."

"Yeah, but it's too late now. Just focus on getting good grades. As soon as high school finishes it stops mattering. Seriously."

I nodded and she stayed for a while longer and patted my hair. It was nice, so I didn't ruin it by saying anything more. When she went back to her room, the numbness was still there.

I got out my science textbook and tried to study, but I couldn't make sense of any of it. I used to be so good at science.

I remember clearly the moment that the numbness dissolved. It was like I had been wearing a thick, heavy veil and all of a sudden, after all those months, it was snatched off. When I finished my media class, I began my funeral march toward PE, which was always the worst class. The corridor was empty, except for Mel. She was standing against the wall outside the drama room and she looked up as I approached. Hurriedly I averted my eyes and quickened my pace.

I half expected her to stick out a leg to try to trip me, but she didn't.

"Hey," she said, instead.

I looked up at her, but didn't slow or reply. She began walking next to me.

"How's it going?"

She was talking to me like she used to, like nothing had ever happened. I sneaked a look at her and she was staring right at me, smiling.

"Okay," I answered.

"Listen, I'm sorry for being kinda mean lately. And God, Saanvi and Theodore were such assholes at the party, right?"

I didn't respond. Instead, I bowed my head and tried to walk faster. She kept pace with me.

"Anyway," she said, "you should come over after school."

"Really?"

"Yeah!" She shrugged. "Why not?"

I didn't answer; there wasn't time. She'd already jogged ahead of me to reach the change room. My head was clattering, trying to understand what had just happened. I started wondering if it was possible that I had misunderstood all of it. That it had been all Saanvi and Theodore, that Mel hadn't been involved at all. More than anything I wanted that to be true. But it couldn't be. She was the one holding the phone, she'd been the one to first call me psycho. I didn't understand.

When I entered the change room, she was in the corner with Saanvi and Cass. I stared at her.

"What are you looking at, psycho?" Saanvi snapped.

I looked away and started changing, but then I caught Mel's eye. She made a face at the back of Saanvi's head. We both smiled.

When I went out to the oval, I felt everything. The air on my face, the smell of the grass, the blaring whistle of the PE teacher. Somehow, while I had been consumed by survival, the weather had changed. It was almost summer, and I was still wearing the gray hooded jacket I'd had on all through winter. Sweat was prickling underneath it and I hadn't even noticed it. I pulled the jacket off and tied it around my waist. The sun caressed my bare arms. I wasn't stupid. I knew it might be a trick. I knew that none of it made any sense. But I didn't care. At least there was a chance the torment would stop. Now I had the possibility of redemption, where before I'd had none.

The rest of the day disappeared and soon I was making my way to her house.

I knocked on the door. I had the whole thing worked out in my head. She'd lead me into the living room, where Cass and Saanvi would be waiting. Cass wouldn't mind, but Saanvi would be angry that I was there. She'd come around. She always did what Mel wanted eventually.

Then there was the other option. That I'd come into the living room and they'd all be hiding, waiting. That they'd jump out and throw something disgusting all over me and it would be my fault for being so stupid to come here.

The door swung open. It wasn't Mel; it was her mother.

"Hi, Ava," she said, stepping back so I could get inside. "How are you, honey? I haven't seen you in a while."

"I've been really busy," I said.

"Mel's up in her room."

"Thanks," I said, and walked quietly up the stairs.

If this were a trick, surely Mel wouldn't do it when her parents were in the house. Mel's door was open and she was sitting on the bed painting her nails in a dark red color.

"There you are," she said. "I thought maybe you'd forgotten."

"Nah," I said, barely able to look at her. This room was where it all happened. It didn't seem like the same place with the afternoon sunlight flooding through the curtains, her Beach House album playing softly on the stereo.

"Can you do my toes?" she said, holding out the polish.

Dumping my bag on the carpet and pulling off my shoes, I clambered onto the end of her bed. I took the polish from her hand and she put her foot in my lap, pointing it like a ballet dancer. Unscrewing the tiny brush out of the bottle, I carefully applied the polish to her smallest toenail, which curved like the letter *c* under the toe next to it.

"Your pinkie toes are all wonky," I said.

"Shut up," she said, kicking my knee and leaving a red line on my skin.

"Don't, it'll smear!"

"Sorry," she said, and lay back into the pillow.

Staring up at the roof, she said quietly, "I missed you."

I didn't reply.

When I finished the second coat I blew on it, then put her foot down on the bed next to me.

"Do you want to watch a movie?"

"Yeah," I said.

Using only her palms, she pulled her computer onto her belly. "I've got *The Dark Knight* but I've already seen it. And *The Sex and the City* movie, but apparently that's shit."

I watched her scroll down, stared at the careful way she touched the keys with her finger pads so as not to smudge her nails.

"How about *Cloverfield*?"

"Alright."

"Close the curtains," she said.

I got up and pulled the curtains shut, then lay down next to her on the bed. At first I felt uncomfortable, not being able to stop thinking about the last time I'd lain in this bed in the dark. After a while, I started to get drawn into the movie. I sank down into the pillows to watch the small screen as it rose and fell with Mel's breath.

It was a good film. We got up to the bit where they were in the tunnel and the camera switches to night vision, and you see all the spidery aliens around them. Mel and I both screamed, then we looked at each other and started to laugh.

"That girl is a good actress," she said about the screaming one.

"She looks a bit like you," I told her.

"Really?"

"Yeah."

Pushing the laptop onto the bed, she turned to look at me.

"Do you think I'm going to be able to make it?"

"As an actress?"

"Yeah," she said. "I can't imagine what I'll do if it doesn't happen."

"Why wouldn't it happen?"

"I dunno, you hear about it all the time. All these girls that want to be actors and they move to America and end up just being waitresses and stuff and then they get old and ugly but still think they're going to make it and it ends up being really pathetic."

I stared into her beautiful face. "That won't happen to you."

"Really?"

"Yeah."

She smiled at me, then rolled onto her back again. "I'm going to start with theater anyway. That's what you are meant to do. You start with theater in Europe and then some talent scout finds you and casts you in some shitty franchise movie, and then you get really famous but everyone remembers you started in theater so they know you are actually a serious actor."

I didn't really know what to say, so I just shrugged. "Cool."

"So are you going to come and visit me in Europe?"

I stared at her.

"Dinner's ready!" her mum called up the stairs.

"I should probably go," I said.

"Why?" Mel whined. "I already told Mum you were staying for dinner."

"I don't want to miss my bus."

"You're not sleeping over?" she asked.

I stood up, starting to get frustrated. I wanted to fix things, but this was starting to feel weird. It was too much like nothing had happened, but it had.

"I have to go."

"Ava, don't."

I turned to look at her.

"I'm sorry," she said. "Really. I've been so sad without you as a friend. I really just want us to go back to the way things were. Do you think we can do that?"

I had two choices. I could go back to being friendless. To hiding in the toilets at lunchtime, to going into every day like it was a battle, to wanting to die rather than go to school the next day. Or, I could believe her. I could believe her version of how things were and pretend it had all been some bad dream.

"Come on," she said, grinning. "It'll be so much easier for you to get to school from here. Plus, we still have to watch the second half of the movie."

I barely slept that night. I was too afraid I would wake up to another trick. I kept far away from Mel, lying on my side on the very edge of the bed, ready to jump out and run. The air conditioner whirred quietly. She said she always kept it on, because she liked sleeping with thick quilts, even in summer.

Mel seemed to sleep soundly, tugging at the blanket as she rolled, and was breathing deeply. In the middle of the night, she turned toward me. Her hand fell onto my waist and stayed there. Her breathing didn't seem as even in that moment, and I wondered if she was really asleep or if she was testing me, seeing how I would react. I tensed my muscles, staying perfectly and completely still, until eventually I must have fallen asleep too because the next thing I remembered was her alarm going off.

"Errgh," she said, "it's too early."

I rolled over and stretched. "Not for me!"

The morning sun was squeezing through the edges of her curtains. I hadn't been tricked; I'd passed the test.

"I wish I had different clothes," I said, thinking about spending another day in the same thing I had on yesterday. I didn't want to smell.

"Are you asking to borrow some undies?"

"No!"

"You can," she said, smiling at me and getting up. "It's gross to wear the same pair two days in a row."

We walked to school side by side. At first we chatted about the movie, but as we got closer Mel got quieter. I kept talking, trying to draw her out. When we turned the corner onto the street the school was on she started to walk really fast.

"I'm going to be late for homeroom," she said.

"What do you mean?" I asked, trying to keep up. "The bell hasn't rung yet and we're almost there."

She kept rushing ahead, almost running. Once we got in front of the school, she turned on me.

"Fuck off!" she spat.

A few guys that were hanging out near the fence laughed loudly.

"Psycho!" one yelled.

By the time school ended, it had circulated. I had cornered Mel outside school that morning and begged her to be my friend again. But I didn't withdraw back into myself again. No, that was over.

I wasn't numb anymore.

34

I remembered what I used to do when I lay in bed on a Saturday morning back at my old house. I would scratch at these small little mounds on my wall, where tiny star-shaped stickers had been painted over. I was slowly working through them, the ones that I had already scratched the paint off would glow at nighttime, but there was a whole galaxy left to uncover. I would imagine how the room would have looked when they'd put on the stars. No magazine cutouts on the walls, no clothes on the floor. A baby's cot in the corner and the walls alight with stars. I liked that the house had history. That it had the ghosts of previous residents frozen inside it. I'd left part of myself there.

The walls of the Lakeside Estate house were blank.

I opened the lid of my old black laptop. First I opened Facebook, just from reflex. Six new messages, four new notifications. I knew what they'd say: *fucking psycho, psycho freak, why are you such a psycho?* I'd read them later. Instead, I went into Google. With one finger I typed the word into the search engine, one letter at a time: *p, s, y, c, h, o.* My computer whirred and the results appeared. *Characteristics of a psychopath.* I clicked on it.

I scanned down until I reached the list.

Lack of empathy.

Pathological lying.

Impulsivity.

Parasitic lifestyle.

Sexual promiscuity.

Juvenile delinquency.

Poor behavioral controls.

Cunning.

Scanning the list, my response wasn't what I'd thought it would be. I had worried so much about being a "psycho," but maybe I shouldn't have. I'd be happier if I was one, that was for sure. If I was a psycho, I'd do something to Mel. I'd get even. I'd been worrying so much that there was something terribly wrong with me. But maybe the thing that was wrong with me was the only thing that was right.

I remembered the power I'd felt when we'd destroyed Mr. Bitto. If I could do it to him, a fully grown man, surely I could do it to Mel, who was only a simpering, shallow teenager. I just had to come up with a plan.

Bea rushed into my room and I snapped my laptop shut.

"Come with me!" she said, leaning in the door. She had the glowing look about her that I hadn't seen in ages.

"Where?"

"Just outside, dummy—calm down. I know you're a recluse these days."

"Shut up."

"Come on!" She grabbed my hand and pulled me up. We walked down the stairs together and outside.

"Dah dah!" she said, opening her arms up to a crappy-looking car on the curb.

"Yours?" I asked.

"Yep!"

"But how?"

"Well, you might be spending all your time mooching around, but I've been job hunting. I got a job as a secretary, but it's impossible by public transport so I got a loan."

I looked between the beat-up-looking car and her smiling face. "You could get a way better job than being a secretary."

"Yeah, I know—" she rolled her eyes "—but right now, this means freedom!"

She walked over to the car and unlocked it.

"Get in."

"Where are we going?"

"Anywhere, who cares?"

I shrugged. She had a point. I got in the car next to her and we took off. She went through the gates and we were free. We rolled down the windows and the hot air felt cool as it made our hair dance. The main road was empty and she sped along it, probably going over the speed limit but I loved it.

"Do you want to see somewhere weird?" she said.

"Yeah!"

Taking the next turn, she swung into a parking lot.

"Whoa," I said.

I'd thought Lakeside Estate was an eyesore. I hadn't expected this.

We sat in silence for a second, looking at the large, gray shopping square. Or at least what was once a shopping square. All the shops were closed down; some with papered windows and all with doors locked with thick silver chains. The car park out front was completely empty except for our car.

"Do you want to go exploring?"

I shrugged. "Sure."

Opening the door, I felt a wave of heat. It was way hotter here than it had been outside our house. Maybe the bitumen soaked up the week's sun, and was now spitting it back out at us, its trespassers. We walked up toward the buildings, dwarfed by the huge empty space.

"What happened here?" I asked Bea, and she shrugged.

"Apparently businesses are closing down all over the place. I think this used to be the central hub when this was all farmland, but now there's that mega mall half an hour away."

The shop windows were frosted with grime, but I could still

see inside the ones that weren't papered up. I tried to imagine what it would have looked like here before it closed. There was a hairdresser's shop, where farmer's wives would have come to get their hair done, a bakery next door. Their kids might have waited in there for their mums, blowing bubbles in their milkshakes.

We walked past the fish-and-chips shop. If the kids were good, their mums would probably pick up fish-and-chips for dinner. Bea leaned forward, trying to see inside.

"Do you remember when we used to have fish-and-chips for dinner?" Bea asked, and it was like she was reading my mind. *Sister moments*, we would call them. We hadn't had one in a while.

"Every Sunday night," I said. "I miss that."

"Me too."

I remembered sitting in the car, the box wrapped in white paper on my knees. After a while it would burn my thighs, but I didn't mind. That was a part of it. We'd park the car outside our house and I'd hand the box over to my mum, carefully, like there was a small animal asleep inside. There would be a pink rectangle left on my legs, still warm to touch, and it would take a full ten minutes to fade away. When we opened the box it was like pulling the wrapping off a present. We'd sit in front of the TV and eat and no one would even be thinking of the week to come.

Bea and I kept walking.

"It's kind of sad here," I said after a while.

"Yeah." Bea stared straight ahead. "I always wonder how long the shop owners waited here until they decided to shut it down. Like, if there were a few months where they all sat in their empty shops just waiting for their regulars, still fooling themselves with the notion of loyalty, the realization slowly sinking in."

I watched her profile as she spoke.

"You've been here before?" I asked.

She shrugged.

"How'd you even find it?"

"I've been going for walks with Chucky," she said. "I've had a lot of time to kill. Sitting in that house alone all day job hunting is too depressing."

"Sorry," I said, feeling like I might cry all of a sudden. She'd probably look forward to me coming home, and then I'd just lock myself in my room and ignore her.

"Doesn't matter now! A job and a car all in one day is pretty good!"

"Yeah, no more wandering around this creepy place like a weirdo."

"Maybe just on weekends," she said, then laughed.

We kept walking, the silence between us comfortable now. I was surprised that there wasn't more graffiti here. It was almost like someone pressed Pause and just let the elements take over. Like when they abandoned it they just left it to its own devices, like if they didn't look at it then it wouldn't exist anymore. But even if everyone wants you to be invisible, even if you want it too, that doesn't make it happen. Somehow it just made you more conspicuous, because it felt so wrong that you existed at all. I ran my hand over the red bricks, feeling the warmth coming from inside them. It was like this place still had a pulse. It hadn't given up yet.

"Should we get out of here?" she asked.

"Yeah."

"Hey, what's that?" She was looking at my leg. "Did you scratch yourself?"

I looked down and noticed the red line on my knee. It was Mel's nail polish. I hadn't had a shower this morning. In fact, I was still wearing her underwear.

"Yeah," I said, putting my hand over it. For some reason I didn't want Bea to know what it was. I looked around, and noticed a public toilet block.

"I'll be one sec!" I said, rushing toward it.

"Yuck, Ava, that place will be rank!"

I ignored her and went inside, scratching the nail polish off with my fingernail. She was right; the place was filthy. I didn't care. I turned on the tap, but no water came out. Looking up at my reflection I saw my own shock. Written across the mirror in front of me was *UGLY*. The toilets were absolutely covered in graffiti. Scrawled in different handwriting and markers were phrases like *ur a fuckn ugly sluzza, Ellie Stewert is a whore!* Almost laughing, the image of the farmer's wife and her cute kids disappeared from my mind. The writing was everywhere, one overlapping the other and sometimes almost frightening in some of its intensity. Words that felt like violence just in themselves.

"Oh wow," Bea said as she followed me in.

"Let's go," I said. "This place is freaking me out."

We went to the supermarket and got some food, then made Mum dinner. It was the first night in the new house that felt normal, like nothing had changed, like we were us again. But I wasn't me. I was different. While we were walking down the aisles of the supermarket, an idea was forming in my head. When we were listening to music and chopping up vegetables, I was planning. While we sat around the table with our mum, laughing as she told us a funny story about a patient she'd had that day, half my mind was on tomorrow, imagining how Mel would react.

35

The note was folded into a neat square. It fit easily in my palm. I could put it into my backpack but I liked the feeling of it between my fingers. The softness of the paper. Knowing the secret folded inside gave me strange little tingles where its corners touched my skin.

"'Dear Mel, I've always liked you—'" Mel began. I couldn't see her face but I knew it was glowing.

"What a Romeo!"

"Shut up, Cass!"

Their voices echoed around the change room. I sat on the closed toilet seat, still and silent, my knees up by my ears, my arms wrapped around my legs.

"'—I've always liked you but never known what to say,'" Mel continued. "'I guess I'm your secret admirer. You are the most beautiful girl I've ever seen. Just thought I should let you know.'"

Silence. Then their laughter exploded like a pyramid of champagne flutes crashing to the ground.

"That's so tacky!"

"It's sweet!"

"Holy fuck, I bet it's some loser!"

"I had science before this. Maybe they put it in then?" Mel said. "I sit next to Theodore."

She was half right.

"He looooves you!"

"Shut up!"

The next day I heard a shriek from across the oval. It was coming from Cass. They had found my latest letter in Mel's bag. They were all huddled together over it. A few minutes later Cass pretended to swoon and they all laughed. I looked carefully at Mel. She had a private little smile on her face. I imagined her in her bedroom, air-conditioning on full blast, holding the letter to her heart. Idiot.

"Another one!" Mel exclaimed. I was back in my spot on the toilet seat, waiting.

"What, where?"

"In my bag again, right down at the bottom."

"Does that mean he sneaked in here?"

"Whatever, read it!" Cass's squeak.

"Gee, calm down."

"Shut up!"

"Shut up, listen. 'Dear Mel, I watch you smile and it's like an electric surge straight to my heart—'"

"Wow!"

"Shut up!"

"'I want to talk to you.'" Mel's voice was serious now. "'Somewhere we can be private. Meet me behind the school tonight at 8pm.'"

"Fuck. I don't know Mel—that sounds creepy." I knew Saanvi would be against it.

"But it's Theodore—it has to be!" And I knew Cass would be on my side.

"Don't go!"

"Shut up—it's romantic!"

I had to hold back my laughter.

Part of me had thought about sticking around school. Waiting until night fell and Mel came out to wait for her secret admirer. It would be hilarious. But it was almost better not to wait. Just to be at home hanging out with Bea and watching television, knowing she was out there in the dark.

When I fell asleep that night my dreams were violent. I was hitting Mel with a bat and she was screaming for help and I was laughing. Enjoying the sound of her bones crackling with each blow.

I woke up in a cold sweat. I tried to calm myself. Breathed in and out deeply. If I really was a psychopath, I wouldn't feel guilty about what I was doing. Mel probably didn't even show up. If she did, Cass and Saanvi would have accompanied her; it would have all been a big fun joke. I remembered when we had run around the estate in the dark, making ghost noises and trying to scare each other. I wanted to cry. Instead I got up.

For the first time since we'd moved in, there was a glimmer of dawn as I walked down the hill through Lakeside Estate. The sky was graphite rather than the impenetrable black that I was used to. I could see the edges of window frames, the detail of grass and cement and brick. The air didn't have the same bite to it.

They hadn't made any progress on the half-built houses. Some were so close, just missing glass in the windows and doors in the door frames. I wondered if it made my mother sad, to see all this wasted potential.

Through a glassless window I saw a movement. I froze, primed to run. But I was a psychopath now, and psychopaths didn't feel fear. So I took a step closer. I pulled my phone out of my pocket and shone the light into the square. It lit up a book, some scrunched-up food wrappers, then, the corner of something bigger. The light traced up the folds of fabric until it reached the top. It was a sleeping bag. A full one. The person inside it stared up at me. Then I was running. Running out the gates to the bus stop.

It wasn't until I boarded the bus that I realized I knew that face. It wasn't some drifter or homeless man or crazed murderer watching and waiting. It was the boy from across the road. Evan.

In science class Mel looked sad. She must have gone last night after all. Other people might not have noticed the change in her. But I'd studied the back of her shoulders all year. The set of them today, as the teacher mumbled about atoms or whatever, told me she'd spent last night waiting alone in the dark.

After class, when she bent to put her books in her bag, she caught my eye.

"Wait," she mouthed.

"See ya," Theodore said.

"Bye," she called after him.

After everyone else was gone, she turned to me. "What are you doing tonight?" she asked.

"So, what do you think?" she asked me later, as we sat on her bed. The notes were spread out all around us, my left-handed scrawlings of sweet nothings.

I shrugged, and pretended to have a closer look at the most recent letter, the one that asked her to meet at the school yard at night. Since I'd gotten there she'd kept telling me she had a secret. We'd had dinner with her parents and then she'd pulled me upstairs, saying she was ready to tell me and made me swear I would never tell another living soul, saying I was the only one she trusted. I knew there was no point in calling her out, asking her about why she would be so awful to me at school and so overly nice to me here. I was playing my own game now, and she was the one who didn't know the rules.

I pretended to read them as she'd changed into the gray marle men's T-shirt she always wore to bed, its cotton overstretched and saggy.

"It's definitely a guy," I said after I'd finished the final letter.

"Obviously. The handwriting is too terrible to be a girl's."

"Do you think it's Theodore?"

"Dunno. Want one?" she asked, holding out a bowl of miniature green pears. "They're organic."

I picked one out and took a bite; the sweet juicy flavor exploded in my mouth. I wiped my chin and smiled at her.

"They're awesome, aren't they? So much better than the usual supermarket shit. You know the pesticides can give you a hairy chest? And give men man-boobs."

"Isn't that chicken?" I said, only half listening as I pretended to be fascinated by the contents of the most recent note. She looked at it over my shoulder.

"The weirdest thing," she said, leaning close, mouth full. "I swear he was there watching me."

"Really?"

"Yeah. There was someone in the shadows. I saw them."

"What about Cass and Saanvi—didn't they come with you?"

Mel rolled her eyes and took another bite. I could hear her chewing, the wet squishing sounds inside her mouth. Sometimes I found her revolting.

"I pretended I wasn't going to go. They were going to be too annoying about it. You're the only one I've told."

"Really?"

"Yeah, you get things that they just don't understand."

She was looking at me closely, trying to see if her games were working.

"What do they think you're doing tonight?" I couldn't help but ask.

"Pfft, who cares? I'm sick of them. Are you staying over?"

"Maybe," I said, then took another bite of my pear. The juice squelched out of it, running over my chin and down my neck. She leaned forward and licked it up, her tiny cat tongue rasping up my throat.

"Please stay," she said, close enough so her sweet breath tickled my cheek.

I wanted to run. I couldn't bear for it to happen again, to be hurt again. But psychopaths don't get hurt; they dish out the pain. If I was really a psychopath, I would be able to stay.

So instead I shrugged and said, "You're not going to tell me that you need to practice kissing, are you?"

"Fuck off," she said, "I learned how to kiss in primary school."

Her voice was confident, but as she turned to put the core of her pear back in the bowl I saw the uncertainty flicker over her face.

"Fine. But can I borrow a T-shirt to wear to bed?" I asked. The corners of her lips twitched and I knew what she would say.

"No, you'll get it all gross and sweaty." She stared at me, waiting. Expecting a side glance, a quiver of the mouth, a question in the eyes. I wasn't going to give them to her.

"Fine," I said.

I got under the covers and pushed the notes onto the floor. I watched as she stared at them, floating like embers onto the cream carpet. They were important to her, it was clear then. But she soon looked back to me when I began to take off my clothes. I dropped piece by piece down on top of the notes, stripped right down to nothing. The feeling of my bare skin against her bedsheets was weird. I wanted to laugh. But I didn't. I just stared at her. It was her that looked rattled then, but not for long. I should have known that. She sat down on the quilt next to me.

"Let's see," she said, and pulled the quilt down. Every part of me wanted to shrink away, to cover myself, but I forced my muscles to remain rigid as she surveyed my flesh. We watched as my nipples hardened.

"Are you cold, or turned on?"

"Cold."

She raised a leg over me, like she was mounting a horse, and sat down on my hips.

"You're really beautiful, you know?"

It sounded like she'd heard it in the love scene of some bad rom-com. I tried to think of how a psychopath would respond, but my mouth had gone too dry.

"Promise me you'll come to Europe with me."

She looked down at me like I was everything, so I nodded. She took the T-shirt off then, pulled it over her head and shook her hair, swapping from the hero to the heroine in whatever movie she was performing in her head. Still, it was cool to see her naked. I only had a moment to take it in, dark nipples, tan lines, a mole just above her belly button, before she pressed her warm flesh over mine. She kissed me and the moment was exquisite. Perfect. Her skin so soft, her mouth hard and wet. She made a little sound, a girlish whimper. She was still acting. I wanted her to stop.

I pushed my fingers into her underwear and felt her body shake and twitch against me. The moan she made then wasn't for anyone; it was real. Her fingers were in my hair, her teeth bit onto my shoulder, but still in the back of my mind was tomorrow. As I moved her underwear aside and pushed my fingers in harder, right down to my knuckles, finding the right spot with my thumb and rubbing against it lightly, I thought of all the times she'd made me cry.

"Fuck, Ava," she kept whispering, "fuck."

As she copied what I was doing, pushing my thighs open, as the tremble began going through my own body, as her fingers poked and dipped and I felt something different, something bigger than I'd ever felt when I'd tried this on my own, I was still thinking of how I'd get even. As her hand clapped over my mouth to stop me from making a sound, as the pleasure crashed onto me in waves, I was imagining her reaction when she realized I had won.

36

I didn't give her a chance this time. Once we reached the end of her street the next morning, I let her walk ahead. I went toward the back entrance of the school, let her have the front. I kept my head down, my eyes glued to my feet as I walked from class to class. I kept as far away from her as possible during the soccer match on the oval in PE. Still, I knew it would happen. Like throwing a ball into the air: no matter how high it went, it was going to come back down. I was just waiting for it.

After PE ended I saw the way they were looking at me in the change room, side glances and stifled giggles. I rubbed a hand over my back, half expecting there to be a sign saying Kick Me. They were only slightly more original. I didn't notice until science class, when I went to pull out my textbook. Everything was covered in slime and bits of eggshell. They must have put eggs in my bag during PE, and as I'd walked to class they'd broken up into bits. I raised my hand and asked to go to the bathroom, where I took the contents from my bag, bit by bit, and tried to wipe the slime off with wet toilet paper. It had already soaked into the edges of the pages though. They'd stink soon enough. I went back to class and sat staring at the back of Mel's head, seething.

As I walked out of class the laughter started. At first it wasn't loud enough to make me think it was at me. But, as I walked down the corridor the laughter became stronger.

"Hey, psycho," Theodore called, and I turned, as if to my name, "you're fucking filthy."

He was grinning, so proud of himself. If he was involved I knew it must be bad.

"You actually make me want to puke, you know?"

Mel appeared, face swathed in fake concern.

"Theo!" She slapped his arm. "Don't be mean."

She walked up to me, slipped her hair over her shoulder so that the people by the lockers could see her clearly and held something out to me. It took me a moment to realize it was a tampon. She was holding it between her thumb and forefinger by the end of its string, so it dangled in front of my nose. The smile on her face was one I knew well now, the smile that said she'd won. She hadn't.

"Psycho!" someone called after me. It was meant as an insult, but the word only gave me a feeling of power.

When I got into a bathroom stall I took my skirt off. It was red pen ink, it didn't even look like blood. She must have snapped her red pen in half, then put the ink on my chair while I'd been trying to get the egg out of my bag. I sat on the toilet seat in my underwear and took out a paper and pen.

Dear Mel, I want you. Every time I watch you walking home from school, I'm waiting to make my move. I watched you last night. I was outside your window. I want to fuck you so bad, I want to make you scream. From your admiring admirer.

The next day, Mel didn't come to school. During lunchtime I sneaked around to her house and put another letter in her mailbox, just a note folded in half with her name on the front in my terrible left-handed scrawl.

Dear Mel, why won't you reply to me? I know you love me. You are torturing me, so soon I will be torturing you. I'm going to make you scream. I'm going to make you bleed. SOON.

37

By the end of the week, people were talking. Some said Mel had been talent scouted at the shops, and was now being primed for the catwalk in Milan. Others said that she had glandular fever. There was only a week until the final exams, and then all this would be over. School would end, and I would have played the last hand. I would have won.

It was in the final PE class when it finally came out. Saanvi and Cass were whispering in the corner of the change room, heads bent close together.

"Oi, slut!" Veronica Britson called to Saanvi from across the room.

"What?"

"Ha, you answered!" squealed Veronica.

"Ha ha, yeah, good one."

"Where's Mel? I've been hearing the weirdest shit about her."

Saanvi and Cass looked at each other.

"She said it was okay," said Saanvi.

"Yeah, I know, but…" Cass trailed off.

Saanvi lowered her voice, knowing full well that everyone in the room was listening. "She's being stalked."

"What?" squeaked Veronica.

"Yep. Some creepy guy is in love with her and has been sending her weird letters."

"That's awful! Poor Mel."

"He's been following her home too."

"The guy says he's got a gun! He's just waiting for his chance to kidnap her," added Cass.

"Fuck!" said Veronica.

"I know," Cass breathed.

"Don't tell anyone though, alright?" said Saanvi. Veronica nodded solemnly. Everyone else in the change room quickly looked away.

I thought that would be the end of it. The last day of classes came and went. No one gave me a hard time. Mel wasn't there. It was over. I had made it out alive.

It was on a Sunday night, the night before exam week, when my mum called me downstairs. I had been trying to study, and starting to comprehend just how behind I was in almost every class. I had my science textbook turned back to the beginning of the semester and I was desperately trying to teach myself the entire syllabus.

"Ava!" she called again. "Come down here."

Throwing down my pen, I ran down the stairs into the living room.

"What?" I said, irritated.

"Don't you know that girl?"

I looked over at the television. It was *A Current Affair*. The made-up woman in an electric-blue pantsuit was talking into the camera. Behind her, there was an image of Mel, with the headline in big bold letters: *STALKED*.

"What the fuck?"

"Ava!"

"Sorry."

"And now to Tracey Mingum with this exclusive report. And a warning, some viewers might find this content distressing."

The word *exclusive* came over the screen, and then cut to Mel, sitting in her room and staring out the window.

"At first I thought it might be a boy from school, you know? Someone who really liked me." Mel's voice sounded tinny in voice-over.

The screen cut to her walking down the empty school corridor.

"At first the letters were really nice. So I guess that's why I didn't tell my parents."

The screen cut to Mel looking straight into the camera.

"Then what happened?" a sad-sounding female voice said from behind the camera.

Mel looked down at her hands, and I peered closer, trying to figure out if she was acting.

"The notes started getting…violent. The things they said—" she sniffed "—it was horrible. I've never been so scared."

The image cut to Mel walking down her street, then turning to look over her shoulder.

"'I'm going to make you scream,'" she read aloud, her voice crackling. "'I'm going to make you bleed.'"

The video cut back to Mel looking straight into the camera, tears streaking her face.

"I used to have dreams, you know? And now I feel so lost."

"What were your dreams?"

"I was going to go to Europe, be an actress. But now I'm too afraid to even leave my house!"

I wanted to feel indignant, to tell my mum to turn it off. That's what a psychopath would probably do. Instead, I felt something clawing and gnashing inside me. Something that was getting bigger and bigger with every second.

I stared at the back of her head as she huddled over her test. I hadn't expected her to show up. I didn't think any of us had. When she entered the gym the room had gone silent. The whole of year twelve was in that room; that was three hundred desks, three hundred stressed-out, gossiping seventeen-year-olds and still... Not a sound.

It was halfway through; the tick of the clock was amplified like a clichéd nightmare. I couldn't concentrate. I couldn't stop staring at the back of her head, feeling cold. A psychopath would be glad; a psychopath would be happy to hurt her. Those words, when I wrote them they'd meant nothing. But when I heard Mel read them aloud on the show, they sounded so different. So violent and horrible. I didn't know how they could have come from me. The noxious taste was in my mouth again, spinning my stomach, clogging my throat. A whisper rumbled through the crowd. I turned to look out the big windows. Two uniformed police officers were walking with the principal through the quad.

"Silence please!" the teacher said from the front, and three hundred heads bent over three hundred tests again, except mine.

I was sure they were coming to arrest me. During the test. On my way home. As I sat in my room, staring at my textbooks but not reading even a word. I deserved it. I knew that. I was as bad as the man who had stood over my bed that night with the baseball bat in his hands. There was something deep and fundamentally wrong with me.

The next day it started all over again. The first test of the day began and I sat staring at the back of Mel's head. Had she been awake all night, scared? Worried a real psycho was after her, biding their time, wanting to hurt her. Wanting to make her bleed, make her scream.

We broke for lunch. Everyone scampered out into the sunlight and hot, real air. Mel headed for her huddle with Saanvi and Cass. I followed.

"Mel," I said to the back of her head, "can I talk to you for a sec?"

Saanvi sneered at me. "Are you seriously talking to us right now?"

Cass looked at her feet.

"Mel," I said, "it's about the notes."

"Fuck off, psycho."

But Mel turned toward me. I'd imagined a dullness in her complexion, shadows under her eyes, but there was none.

"It's fine," she said, and began to walk.

It wasn't until we were out of earshot, standing in the shade of a thick-trunked eucalypt with four wooden benches surrounding its base that she turned to me and hissed, "What? What do you want?"

I kicked at the wood chips. My confession had been right there, ready to spill out any second all night. Now I didn't know how to say it.

"I didn't want to upset you," I said lamely. "Are you okay?"

She crossed her arms and waited.

"Those letters. They…" I put a hand over my face. "It was me. I wrote them. I'm sorry. I'm really, really—"

I could have gone and on, but Mel had grabbed my arm. I forced myself to look at her, to face the anger, the yelling, the tears, whatever she was gearing up to throw at me. But her face looked exactly as it was.

"Yeah, obviously," she said. "I'm not an idiot."

"The letters," I stammered, thinking she didn't understand, "the ones about following you home and all that horrible stuff. I was trying to, I don't know, get even or something."

"Well, dah!" she said. "I knew that from the start. I was just fucking with you."

I stared at her openmouthed.

She turned on her heel and went back to the group.

38

I slept all day in the weeks before graduation. It was like the tiredness from the previous months had just been waiting in the bays and now that I could finally rest it was released, pummeling me, smothering me. Bea and my mum thought I had the flu, so I carried around tissues and complained about a sore throat, so that I could get away with staying in bed.

I only got up to go and return the brass cat that Mel had stolen to the old woman's house. I left it on their doorstep. I didn't want it in my room anymore. On my way there, I left food and some extra blankets in the house where I'd seen the boy camping out.

My results arrived in the mail, but I showed no one. I would graduate, but only barely. When I saw my score I wanted to be sick. I didn't want to go to graduation, but Mum and Bea insisted.

"It's one of those things that no one wants to do and is so bloody boring," Bea said.

"Is this meant to be convincing me?"

"Seriously though, it's an important life event. You'll regret it if you skip it."

So we went. The three of us in the car, driving the long winding route out of Lakeside together. I wished it was for good.

Mum brought her camera and sat up the back of the gym, smiling when I turned to her. Bea had brought a book.

Sitting in my assigned seat, I watched as Saanvi arrived with her parents and older brother, Cass going back and forth between her mother and father, who were sitting on opposite ends of the gym. Mel's mum and dad flanked her when she walked in, like bodyguards.

The clattering and chattering quieted as the principal took the stand.

"Well, this is it," she said. "It's over."

Looking around and ignoring the speech, I realized she was right. It all seemed so final. After today, I would never be forced into a room with these people again. I might never be called "psycho." This would all be in the past. Theodore, Saanvi, Cass, even Mel. Potentially, I'd never even see them again.

"Now, before we continue with the ceremony, I'd like to make special mention of one of our students who's had a really tough year. As I'm sure all of you are aware, Melissa Moore has been put through a terrible situation. Since the airing of *A Current Affair*, a donation account was set up to fund Melissa's dream of moving to Paris. Melissa, where are you? Do you mind standing?"

We all watched as Mel stood.

"I'm happy to report here today that, as of this morning, over ten thousand dollars has been raised for Melissa's living expenses and tuition fees."

Mel grinned, a blessed, modest smile. It was the perfect resolution of the high school movie she had envisioned for herself.

Soon, everyone was on their feet, hands clapping in a round of applause, everyone except for me.

Part 7

POOR BEHAVIORAL CONTROLS

2016

39

It should have all ended when I got back from Paris. If it had, I wouldn't be here, planning my statement, wishing things were different.

I was going to stop, I really was. In fact, for a long time, I did. For two whole years I didn't even look. I stayed well away from their online profiles; I didn't google their names. I tried not to think about anything that had happened in the past. For the first time since high school, I tried to just live.

For a while I did okay. There were a lot of changes to focus on. Nancy got lawyers involved in Celia's will. I didn't fight her. I'd never asked Celia to give me everything, despite what Nancy thought. It was hard to have someone who I cared about hate me so vehemently. So when she lost the fight and the zeros appeared in my bank account, I did try to make it right. I tried to give her money; I wanted her to have the house, at least. But she packed her car and left by the end of the week.

Evan had been right, you see. Celia did have money. A lot of money. All those photographs Celia had shown me of her on the arm of various men, the ones I'd seen again and again, I guess I never really looked closely enough. If I had, maybe I would have recognized some of them from the papers, or the history books. Although, I can't forget, you are a detective. Probably best for me not to get too deep into all that.

Living in Celia's house all alone felt a little strange at first. But

I got used to it. Slowly, I started to feel less like a shadow, more like a real person. I went for long, very slow walks with Chucky, who was now deaf and blind in one eye, sometimes to that mall that Bea had taken me to all those years ago. It had started to look a little wild, weeds creeping out from every crack in the pavement, huge silvery cobwebs, birds nesting in the drainpipes. I ran every morning. Anything to feel my pulse in my ears, sweat on my skin, anything to feel alive without creeping around in the dark. I listened to music up loud. I gave my worn-out T-shirts and trainers to the charity shop, and bought new clothes. Tailored pants, leather shoes, tops in cotton and linen and silk. Colors now, no black and gray. I went on dates, quite a few of them. But only ever first dates. I still knew my limitations. I still knew what I was.

I read a lot of books. Nonfiction mostly, often memoirs, like reading about other people's lives could give me clues on how to create my own. I did short courses online, and at the college in Greensborough. Business, finance, drawing, photography. I gave a lot of things a shot. I was trying to find my place, I guess. Trying to figure out what to do with my second chance. I liked to think that's why Celia gave everything to me. Though the other option, some misguided spite to Nancy, was probably more likely.

Evan came over often. He helped me repaint the walls into a calming pale blue. He helped pull out the cheap Perspex kitchen cabinets and replace them with pale timber. But he never stayed over, and I never asked him to.

One night I finally agreed to let him teach me to ride.

"Just think, now you can say 'It's just like riding a bike' and mean it," he kept saying. We walked his black fixed gear down to the empty lake. He pushed me around the footpath that circled it. But I just felt stupid. I wobbled every time he let go and put my feet down straightaway.

"Let's try again another night," I said, but we both knew I'd never give it another go.

I was trying desperately to construct a life, to construct a person. No wonder it failed. I'm no expert, but I don't think that's how it works.

I didn't even look, I can swear to that. I was minding my business, cooking a stir-fry for one, half watching some dumb game show on the television, canned laughter and the smell of simmering sauce filling the empty house. It was the night after the failed bike riding lesson, and I was still feeling low, embarrassed at how terrible I had been at something kids can do. My phone binged. I thought it might be Bea asking if I wanted to come over later, or my mum asking me how to work her Apple TV. *Cassandra Fischer is live right now.* I didn't even know you could do that. I pressed on it, and there she was, halfway through a story, her face pressed up against her boyfriend.

"And then he was saying, no, we can't go inside. And I was like, why not? What's up with you? And then he looked like he was panicking."

"I wasn't!"

"Yeah, you were."

Her face was glowing. Little hearts and thumbs-up signs were floating up the screen.

"And then, can you believe it? He actually got down on one knee! Yep! So anyway, just wanted to let you all know it's finally happened. See ya!"

Her finger came in front of the camera, the video paused on the blurry image of a diamond ring, and then the video disappeared. I continued staring at my phone, as the laughter continued from the television and whispers of smoke began filling the house with the smell of burned sauce.

It was amazing how quickly I slipped. It was like she was reeling me in, egging me on. She had never used social media a lot, but now she was posting constantly about wedding dresses, tasting cakes, picking flowers and color stories and tablecloths. It felt like an invitation.

40

You'd expect someone like Cass would awaken on a Monday morning with birds flying into her window, and she'd sing to them as they helped dress her into pale silks of pink and blue. No. In reality she'd wake to the grating dings of her alarm, and hit snooze again and again until eventually her fiancé would groan, "Get up, Cass."

She'd make herself a peppermint tea and drink it as she got ready. She still didn't wear makeup, so it never took long. She'd walk to her tram with her headphones in her ears, listening to a podcast, perhaps, as she would laugh every so often.

When she got to the Collingwood Arts Institute, where she worked as a student counselor, she'd lean on the desk as the school receptionist set up. They'd tell each other about what they'd done after work, which usually comprised the specifics of television shows and dinner, and then whine about how they didn't know how they ended up so boring.

"So how's it going with, you know, everything?" the woman asked, referring to a conversation they'd had over happy hour on Friday. "Feet still feeling a bit chilly?"

"Oh God," Cass said, feigning just embarrassment even though in reality it was clear she was mortified. "I guess I had one too many."

She had. She hadn't even noticed that her voice was getting

louder and louder, or that there was another woman sitting alone at the next table, listening to every word. Me.

"I don't think it's anything to worry about," the receptionist said, lowering her voice. "Honestly, one little last hurrah, just to get it out of your system. Just pick a cute stranger, someone you'll never see again, have one quick ride and you're done."

Cass assured her that, really, she'd only been joking and almost aggressively changed the subject.

When she got to her office, she'd sit quietly, sipping on a second cup of tea and filing through her iPad, taking notes on the students she was seeing that day. Sometimes the appointments would be back to back, sometimes she would spend hours in her office, just taking notes and writing emails. But, week to week, she could always rely on Oliver.

To begin with he'd come once a fortnight. Then once a week. Now it was almost every second day.

He knocked with one knuckle. "I know I don't have an appointment. Are you busy?"

"No, no. Never. This is what I'm here for," she said, bringing the microphone app onto her iPod and hitting Record. "Come in, sit down."

He took his usual spot on the couch. At a guess, I'd say Oliver was nineteen. He had dyed black hair, and a uniform of black band T-shirts and skinny jeans, which only accentuated his spindly legs.

"How are you?" he asked, always eager.

"Fine, just catching up on emails as usual. How's your new song coming along?"

His face lit up. "It's sick. Bryan thought of this new bit on the keys, and now it sounds kind of like synth-pop, but it is still really heavy and cool."

"That's really good. So you're feeling more positive about school, then?"

"Yeah, way more. I think I'm going to be fine this semester. I probably won't ace it or anything, but I'll definitely finish."

"That's great."

"Thanks." He was grinning now.

"So why did you come in today? What happened?"

"Oh." He looked down at his hands now, leaned back in the couch, away from her. "Nothing really, it's no big deal."

"Doesn't matter if it's a big deal or not." Cass leaned back in her chair too, mimicking his body language. "You can tell me anyway."

"She called me last night."

"Your mum?" Cass asked.

"Yeah." He still wasn't looking at her.

She didn't say anything. It was a technique Cass used a lot. Whether it was bullying, depression, anxiety, whatever—she'd let the students fill the silence.

"She was high," Oliver said eventually.

"That must have been difficult," was all Cass offered.

"I shouldn't have answered, should I? You said I should just cut her off. She's not good for me. This always happens."

"We agreed together, didn't we? I would never tell you to do anything. It always has to be your decision."

"Yeah, well you know what I mean. We decided that I'd cut her off. But she called me six times in a row and I was worried something was wrong. I thought now that I've moved out it would be easier. But it just feels harder. Now that I don't know she's at home safe, I'm always worried about her."

"She's the parent. Not you."

"I know. But I had to answer, didn't I? What if something had happened to her? Maybe she needed me?"

"Did she?"

"Yes. No. I don't know, no more than usual. She just wanted someone to rant to about how she was going to get better. How she was going to change, and she wasn't going to do it anymore—she didn't need it. As if I hadn't heard it a million times."

"Do you think that's really why you answered?"

"What do you mean?"

"Do you think that you answered because you thought she might need you?"

"Yeah, why else?"

"Why else do you think it might be?"

I left her to it. She knew the answer, so did Oliver, so did I. He desperately wanted his mother to love him, to ask him about himself, to seem like she cared about him. But we all knew that this woman, whoever she was, would always love booze, crack and whatever else she could shove up her nose or in her arm more. I don't know why she thought he needed to say it.

I didn't have to follow Cass to know where she'd be after work. She always went to the same place. A small cocktail bar on Brunswick Street. She told her fiancé that she finished work at six, when really she finished at five. She'd sit up at the bar and get at least two glasses of wine in before jumping down from her stool and going to wait at the tram stop, chewing on some mint gum.

I thought I had plenty of time, to find the best place, the best seat, to watch. I parked my car down a side street and tossed the book I was reading into my bag. Checking my reflection quickly in the sun visor, I slipped some stray hairs behind my ears. I locked my car and made my way past the small terrace houses to Brunswick Street. Sunlight bounced off car windshields, making me squint as I dodged my way down the street, wishing I'd remembered to put my sunglasses in my bag. You see how little I was paying attention? The time away from it all had dulled my senses, diminished my focus. A few years back, my muscles would have been quivering in anticipation, I would have been hyperaware, paying attention to everything around me while planning moves and countermoves meticulously. Instead, I was idly pondering how much the area had changed since I'd lived nearby as a teenager. Since I'd wandered drunkenly across this street with them, vodka seeping straight into my bloodstream. I was thinking how strange the last vestiges looked, the grimy Thai restaurants, the grungy music venues, sharing their walls with the pristine veneers of artisan coffee shops and designer clothing brands. That's what I was thinking about when I heard my name.

"Ava?"

I focused. Eyes clearing, pupils dilating. Among the people weaving past one another in the heavy foot traffic, a woman was standing still. She was staring straight at me, an uncertain expression in her eyes. It was Cass.

"Ava? It's you, right?"

I wanted desperately to turn and run, but Cass was moving now. She was walking toward me.

"Yeah," I said, and almost flinched when she threw her arms around me.

"How are you? It's been forever, hasn't it?"

"I'm okay."

Her face was so close to mine. I could see things I hadn't noticed from a distance. She had the beginnings of a crease between her eyebrows. Her cheeks were not so round. Up close she didn't look like the girl I had known; she looked like a real person now. An adult.

"Where are you going?" she was saying.

I didn't know how to answer that. On my left, was the door to the bar where I'd been planning on watching her. On my right was oncoming traffic.

"I was just about to go in here." She looked at the door, and I wanted to say *I know.* "I'm meeting someone, but I'm a bit early."

She never met anyone there; I didn't know why she was

lying. But I also didn't know why she was here earlier than usual.

"Cool."

Cool. I hadn't said that word in a long time, but having her here right in front of me was making me feel small. It was making me feel like I was still that same wretched idiot I had been in high school. I guess I was.

"Look," she said, "if you're not in a rush, can I buy you a drink? Just a quick one?"

There was no way I could disappear into the background now. She was looking at me, her face still way too close to mine, too expectant.

"Okay."

"Great! Would you prefer somewhere else, or is this place okay? I come here all the time."

I know, I wanted to say, but instead I just went with, "Okay."

She opened the door and headed in. The noise of the street, the glare of the sun, the scent of rubbish and food and people, was snuffed out. It was dark in there. It smelt of lemon and bleach.

"I'm going to be a bit naughty and get a cocktail. What about you? Can I tempt you?"

I shrugged. "Sure."

"Great! You get us a table."

The bar was almost empty. A couple sat near the front, talking quietly. His hand was on her knee, but she had her arms crossed. They were probably breaking up. I chose a table near the back in the shadows, more out of habit than anything else. Sitting down and putting my bag on the floor, I watched Cass. She was chatting pleasantly to the bartender as he shook up the drinks. This was how it was meant to go: she'd sit at the bar, and Evan would come to get a drink. He'd put on the charm and flirt and I'd watch and it would be easy, so easy.

But now Cass was walking toward me, smiling, sitting down

next to me. She'd gotten me something blue in a martini glass; it made a clinking sound as she put it down on the wooden table.

"God, you know for a second I'd thought you'd left! I didn't even remember this back bit was here, and I come here all the time!"

I know, I wanted to say.

"Were you at work today?" she asked.

"No," I said. "You?"

"Yeah, I'm a psychologist."

No, you're not, you're a school counselor, I wanted to say, but instead I said nothing.

She took a long sip of her drink.

"You know it's so weird that I ran into you today. It's Saanvi I'm meeting here later. Remember her?"

My hair prickled. My stomach dropped. Somehow, she must have seen the shift. She took another gulp of her drink, then sucked the liquid from her lip and looked at me.

"Ava—" her eyes were focused on mine "—I'm really glad that I ran into you. To be honest, I've been hoping I would see you for a long time."

"Why?"

"I know school was a long time ago, and you probably can't remember it, and if you do, you probably don't want to. But, look, for what it's worth, I'm really sorry."

"What do you mean?"

"For everything. I know I wasn't in that room that night." She hesitated—shit on someone's face is a hard thing to mention over cocktails. "You know, at Mel's dumb party, but still. You were my friend and I knew what happened but I didn't stick up for you. We bullied you, and it was unforgivable."

I wanted to hit her. I wanted to grab her hair and pound her forehead onto the table.

"You didn't bully me."

She shrugged. "That's the way I saw it, looking back."

"Are you still in touch with any high school people? With Mel?"

"Some. Not Mel though. To be honest, I was always terrified of her. Once she left, I realized that I didn't even really like her that much. So I never made the effort to stay in touch, although it seems like things are working out for her, not that that's any surprise. She was always the kind of person that you just knew would have an awesome life, you know what I mean?"

I didn't.

"But if you're not in touch with her, how do you know things are working out?"

"She's an actress in Paris! It sounds like a bloody fairy tale. Anyway, what about you? Are you still friends with anyone from school?"

"Not really, no."

"Yeah, it happens, doesn't it? Life just goes on and before you know it you're an entirely different person."

Cass didn't seem different to me. She still talked too much when she felt awkward.

"Yeah." I looked over her shoulder as a rectangle of bright sunlight suddenly fell across us. Evan had just walked through the door. I grabbed the drink and took a sip. My tongue puckered. It was so sour, like I'd just sucked on a lemon.

Cass was still talking, but I was barely listening anymore. "You know I always thought life would be this huge adventure. Like I would live in all these exciting places and do all these amazing things."

Evan had spotted me, and now he was staring straight at me, confused.

"I thought I'd do something really important, you know? Actually change things, make some sort of difference. But I guess not everyone can be important. It's just not possible, right? Some people have to just be regular."

He opened his palms in question, wondering if he should come over, and I shook my head as subtly as I could. He shot me a baffled smile and turned to the barman to order a drink.

"Oh God, I'm boring you, aren't I? I haven't even asked you what you're up to now."

"You're not boring me. I know exactly what you mean."

"Is the drink okay?" she asked.

"Yep," I said, and forced down another sip.

"God, look, I've already finished mine." She slurped down the last inch. Sunlight lit her up once again, and she turned to the bar and smiled. "I'll get Saanvi to get me another one."

She pointed at her empty glass and then made a thumbs-up sign over her shoulder. I turned to look. Saanvi was right there, standing at the bar. In slow motion, she leaned against the bar, watching Evan's beer being poured. Then she noticed him. She did a double take, then put a hand on his arm and smiled. Fuck. Fuck, fuck, fuck.

"Looks like she met someone," Cass said, following my stare. "He's pretty cute actually. We shouldn't interrupt. Oh, I didn't ask you? Married, single, partnered?"

"Oh," I said, still staring at Saanvi as she tipped her head back to laugh. She looked so different from the last time I'd seen her. She wasn't in her uniform of black anymore; she had on a plain white T-shirt and worn-out-looking blue jeans. But it wasn't just that; there was something changed in the way she held herself.

"Or divorced," Cass was saying. "God, it's possible now, right? I'm actually getting married in two weeks. Isn't that nuts? Sometimes the idea of it still seems incredible. You know? Being here with you right now, honestly I could be seventeen again."

"I'm not with anyone," I said, still watching Evan and Saanvi speak. "Dating a bit, but you know. Not really interested in something serious."

"Really? That's so great. All my friends are kind of obsessed with settling down all of a sudden. It's like a virus. One person got married and now all everyone wants to talk about is moving in with someone, or thinking about children. Not that I'm complaining, God… Imagine if my fiancé could hear me talking like this? Comparing marriage to a virus."

Saanvi and Evan were making their way over now. Him with a beer in his hand, her with two glasses of white wine.

"Sorry, didn't get you another cocktail. I'm afraid it's house white only for me at the moment."

"That's fine," Cass said, slurping down some as soon as the glass was in her hand. Saanvi and Evan squeezed in around our small table.

"This is Evan," Saanvi said. "We went to uni together."

He nodded politely at Cass, and then looked at me.

"I'm Cass—" Cass extended her hand to shake his "—and this is Ava."

"Nice to meet you." Evan grinned at me.

That's when Saanvi looked at me. Her smile slid away.

"Ava?"

"Yep!" Cass said to her. "How crazy is it? I bumped into her right outside here. It's like a high school reunion."

"You guys went to high school together?" Evan was looking at me with real confusion now. I'd told him Cass was my friend's girlfriend. I'd told him that she kept cheating on him and then lying about it and I didn't think it was fair. I'd dared him to help me catch her out and he'd laughed and called himself a femme fatale.

"Yeah," Saanvi said, "we were all friends for a while in year twelve."

She looked down at her hands and then back up at me. "How are you, Ava?"

"I'm fine," I said.

"You look really great." She eyed my new clothes, my expensive bag.

I didn't reply. She was uncomfortable, stewing in uncertainty about why I was there. Why I wasn't yelling at her, or ignoring her or telling her to fuck off. I let her stew.

"We were just catching up." Cass never liked a silence. "I was saying how it feels like forever ago, but it also doesn't feel like that long ago either, you know?"

"It seems like another lifetime to me," Saanvi said. "I can barely even remember it."

"Did you know Veronica?" Cass asked me. "I heard she's in Germany now, teaching economics. I always thought she was such a ditz too. And do you remember Miranda? I actually bumped into her the other day and didn't even recognize her. The girl looked like G.I. Jane. She was in the army for ages, I think, and now I think she's a cop. God, I was afraid she would arrest me on the spot for what a bitch I used to be to her. And do you remember Theo?"

I looked at Evan, but he didn't react. I don't think I'd ever mentioned Theodore's name, thank God.

"I'd say she probably does," Saanvi butted in.

"Oh yeah. Right." Cass's eyes flickered between us, but then settled back on me. "Apparently he got kicked out of uni and now he's moved to Thailand. Apparently he's training to be a monk or something. I always thought he was a bit of a jerk-off to be honest, although I guess everyone was a dickhead in high school."

"I definitely was," Saanvi said.

"What are you up to now?" I asked her.

"Yeah, are you still doing architecture?" Evan added, and Saanvi's face fell. He had no idea he'd put his foot in it but I wanted to kiss him.

"No, I decided it wasn't for me."

"Really? I thought you had a good job and stuff?"

"Yeah. I didn't like the lifestyle."

"So what are you doing now?"

"I'm working a few days a week in a bookstore and doing some freelance design on the side. Honestly—" she smiled at him, a real smile "—I prefer it. The pace of my life is so different now. Leaving that firm was the best thing I did."

Liar.

"Which firm did you work for?" I can't help it.

"King & Dinisen. Just for a few years."

"Oh." I cocked my head at her. "Aren't they the ones who got in all that trouble a few years back? It was in the papers, wasn't it? Something to do with plagiarism?"

She barely blinks. "Not sure. I'd left by then."

I kept looking at her, but she turned to Evan.

"What about you?" she asked him. "Are you still working in architecture?"

He looked from her to me. "Yep," he said.

"God, I think only about five people that I know from then actually still have architecture jobs. Which firm are you at?"

He took a sip of his beer. His Adam's apple jiggled. When he swallowed, his composure had returned. He tapped his nose. "I'm on a project at the moment, but I can't really talk about it. It's all hush-hush."

"Really? Oh, is it the Women's Hospital? Or the new RMIT building? God, you can't keep me in suspense like that."

She laughed and leaned forward, touching his knee.

"I should go," I said. "I'm going to be late."

"What are you late for?" Evan asked. Saanvi's hand slid slowly from his knee, all four of us watching it.

"I was on my way to meet someone when I bumped into Cass. I should get going."

"Hey, have we met before?" Cass said suddenly. She was looking at Evan quizzically.

"Don't think so."

"Are you sure?"

Fuck. They had, I remembered. They both met him that night they slept over at my house. If Cass can put it together, she'd know something's up. She'd know Evan was my neighbor.

"I just have one of those faces," he said. "You know, one of those faces that look like lots of other people's faces. People say that to me all the time. I bet I must have at least ten doppelgängers out there."

"Weird," said Cass, but she was still surveying him carefully.

"I should probably head off too," Evan said. "I just popped in for a quick one. Me and Ava here seem to have gate-crashed your catch-up."

"It's fine!" Saanvi exclaimed. "You can't leave yet—you haven't even finished your beer."

She was right; his pint glass was still half-full.

"Well, I've got to go," I said, and stood. I couldn't bear to be so close to these people anymore. I needed fresh air, light. The lemony bleach smell was making me queasy.

Cass stood too. She hugged me again and my body went stiff as a board. "It's been so good seeing you."

Releasing me, she leaned down and got her phone out of her bag. "I know it's late notice and all, but if you give me your email address I'd love to send you an invite to my wedding."

"Really?"

"I thought you'd already put together the seating plans," Saanvi said, fixing Cass with a dubious look.

"It's fine. I'd love for you to be there, Ava." She passed me her phone.

My fingers left sweaty smears on the screen as I keyed my email address in. I gave it back to her and, surreptitiously, she wiped it on her pants.

Outside, the sky was bright, the cars were loud. There was heat on my skin and real air in my lungs. People banged into me as they passed but I didn't care. My heartbeat was slowing, my hands were starting to steady.

I was almost back to normal by the time Evan caught up to me.

"You were making friends in there," I laughed tautly. "Did you get her number?"

He didn't smile. In fact, he was glaring at me.

"What the fuck is going on, Ava?"

41

When I parked back in the driveway, I sat in the car for a while. It was pitch-black outside now. I couldn't stop thinking of it. The way Evan had looked at me. Not just with anger and annoyance. Also, confusion and something else, maybe pity. He was looking at me in the way I was always afraid he would. Like there was something wrong with me. So I'd just turned and walked away. What else was there to do? I got into my car and drove. I didn't put on the radio, or music. I let the car be silent as I made my way back to Lakeside. My phone rang—Evan—but I ignored it. There was nothing I could say to explain it away.

I kept seeing his face as I sat there in the dark car, my own breathing sounding loud in the silence. I knew I should get out and go inside, put the lights on, turn up the stereo, cook dinner, read a book. But now, it all seemed so pointless. All of these interests I was trying to force onto myself, all this construction I was trying to do. It wasn't going to work. I already knew who I was, what I was. There was nothing to be done.

Unclicking my seat belt, I found myself walking away from my dark house. Instead I walked up the hill. The windows of Bea's house were glowing. As I walked toward the front door I saw into her kitchen window, what had once been Evan's kitchen window. Bea was standing in front of the stove, her orb-like stomach pressing against the knobs. My mother was sitting at the table, sipping on a cup of tea. They were chatting casually, Bea throwing words over her shoulder, my mother laughing and putting the cup down and sinking back into her chair. I almost turned around and left, but then my mum looked up. Her eyes went wide, half a second of fear crossed her face, and then she smiled and got up. The front door opened.

"Honey, you bloody scared me! Thought there was some peeper out there for a sec."

She held the door open, and I passed her and went to sit down at the table.

"Oh hey," said Bea, "that's good timing, I was just about to text you. Have you eaten?"

"Nope," I said.

"Good."

I went to the cupboards and began setting the table. I didn't think I'd be able to eat; my insides were churning and toxic. That taste was back in my mouth, the noxious taste I'd thought I'd left behind in high school.

"How are you going?" my mother asked. "Made your mind up yet on what you are going to do with poor old Celia's money?"

"Still deciding." I hadn't thought about it in a long time. "Everything feels like a big commitment."

"Well, you have to do something. Buy some shares or put it in a long-term deposit. You're losing money as it is, just with depreciation."

She'd told me this before. I knew I should care, but I didn't. Once this was over, once all of this was in my past, then I'd figure it out. Until then, I just wished she'd stop asking. I heard the jingle of keys and the door opened to Aiden. For a horrible moment, I thought he might have talked to Evan, but he didn't look at me any differently.

"Hi." He smiled vaguely at the two of us, then went over to Bea and put his arms around her, rubbed her belly. "How was your day?"

"Okay. Didn't get as much work done as I hoped—still jumping up every ten minutes to pee."

He laughed, his face in her hair. I looked at Mum, to see if she was also getting a little tired of all the constant displays of affection, but she was looking down into her tea. A small smile on her lips.

"Smells great." He grabbed a beer out of the fridge and flicked off the top.

"I was just telling Ava she really should invest that money, don't you think?"

"I guess." He took a chug and sat down at the table next to Mum. "You know what I'd do? I'd buy this place."

"What, your house?" I asked. "Don't you already own it?"

"No, I mean Lakeside. It's been with the liquidators for, what, almost ten years now? I bet you'd get it for a steal."

"Shit." Bea turned around to look at me.

"What?" I stared down at her belly. "Are you okay?"

"Yeah—" she waved a hand "—I just think that's such a great idea. You should do it!"

"Maybe." I got up and nudged Bea out of the way so she would sit down.

"Watch out," she said. "There's a rogue bay leaf in there somewhere."

I dished out the steaming food that was making my mouth fill with saliva and my stomach swirl in opposition.

In my pocket, I felt my phone buzz. Putting the four bowls on the table, I let them start a conversation about something else, and pulled it out to have a look. There it was. The invitation to Cass's wedding. I slid my phone back in, and forced myself to take a mouthful of my food.

My phone felt hot against my thigh, like a weapon, like something dangerous, like something set to explode. Whether it would be me or Cass that would be destroyed I wasn't sure, but at that moment, I didn't even care.

42

Over the next two weeks, I watched Cass almost constantly. It was a lot harder now; there was no more sinking into the background. Even from a distance, she would probably notice me. Evan was calling again and again, and once, while Cass was making her peppermint tea early one morning, she looked up and out the window. I think she heard the sound of my phone vibrating against my thigh.

The weather was changing, turning from warm to hot. Flowers were wilting under the sun's fervor. The backs of my arms turned pink and tender from crouching in the full sun to watch her. Cass floated around in her floral dresses, almost flashing her underwear when she toppled over on the way out of the bar one evening. I didn't go in anymore. Sweating in the grimy outdoor seating of the café across the road, I caught glimpses of her up at her usual stool when the door swung open for people coming and going. I didn't need to be inside to know she was drinking more and staying longer. Anyone could see she was stressed, ready to snap, hitting the breaking point.

I was starting to get worried. I'd bought a dress online, I'd gotten myself ready. There'd be lots people from school there, but my skin felt hard again, like armor. If I'd learned anything since school, it was that everyone does bad things when they think no one's watching. You don't need to set someone up, to plan and plot against them. You just need to be there to catch the moment when they reveal themselves. Still, time was running out. Cass's life wasn't perfect. I could clearly see that. But she hadn't done anything bad yet; there was nothing I could use against her.

It was a Friday, Cass's last day of work. She was tying up loose ends, tidying her office between students. She was hungover that day, turning up ashen-faced and running to the bathroom twice to be sick. It was almost five o'clock when Oliver turned up.

He sat down on the couch and started chatting about his band straightaway.

"We've got a gig on Saturday—you should come!"

"That's great," she said. "Are you excited?"

"It's just a support gig, a half an hour set, so it should be fine. Hopefully people don't think we suck."

I'd tracked down his band on SoundCloud. They were actually pretty good, in a messy, clumsy sort of way.

"As long as you like your music, that's all that matters."

I'll give Cass a bit of credit. She was hungover and stressed out and I bet that office was the last place she wanted to be, but still, she listened to every word the students said. Even that morning, when a guy spoke for a full hour about the video game he was obsessed with in minute detail, Cass was focused on every word.

Now she carefully asked, "Have you been in touch with your mum?"

I stole a peek inside in time to see Oliver crumple, like she knew he would. Cass had put her finger on something that I'd only half noticed. When things were bad with Oliver, he would come in smiling. He would be overly cheerful and focused on something good.

"I know I wasn't meant to talk to her anymore, but it's hard. I know that makes me sound pathetic. I'm too old for this shit."

"No one is ever too old to care about their family."

He was leaning into the corner of the couch, like he was

trying to make himself as small as possible. Like he was trying to disappear. I pulled away, relied again on just my ears.

"She wants me to move back in."

"Do you want to do that?"

"Fuck no," he said, "but she needs me. Fuck! This is so ridiculous. I'm such an idiot."

"You're not an idiot."

"I am. I'm a fuckup. You know, I'm so sure I'm going to mess up this gig on the weekend. That's why I want you to be there. You always make me feel calmer."

"Why do you think you're going to mess it up?"

"You know why. I'm worried it'll happen again, like at the end-of-year performance last year."

"You think you'll have another panic attack?"

"Yeah, something like that. It's fucking stupid, I know. I just freak myself out and I get so worried what people are going to think. You're probably going to say it's all linked to my mum and my fear of disappointing people or something, right? I don't want to be like this. It was meant to be fun. But now I'm kind of dreading it—isn't that stupid?"

There was only silence in response.

"Okay," Cass said finally. I heard the squeak of her chair. She must have been standing. "Let's try something different."

I sneaked another look. She had crossed the room. Oliver straightened up and looked at her as she settled next to him on the couch. I saw it there, in his eyes, what I should have noticed weeks ago. The way he looked at the buttons of her cotton floral dress, like he was dying to rip them open.

"Sit forward," she said, "and push your feet onto the ground."

He did as she said, watching her movements carefully. He was at least a head taller than her, and his legs were far longer, but he tried to get to the same position as she was in: both feet firmly on the floor, back straight, hands in the lap.

"Great, now close your eyes and listen to my voice."

I couldn't help but grin. With their eyes closed, I could keep watching them and they would never know.

"Okay."

"Take one long, deep breath in, then slowly let it go."

Their ribs lifted and fell in unison.

"Now, feel your feet on the floor. Squeeze the muscles of them tight. Tight as you can, every muscle. Your toes, your arches, your ankles. Now release."

She went on like this, through their legs, their stomachs, their shoulders and their arms.

Finally, she said, "Open your eyes."

He looked at her. "Wow."

I couldn't look away. I knew how dangerous it was, how likely that one of them would turn, see me, but it didn't matter. I was spellbound. Something was going to happen. Even from the window, I could feel the tension crackling in the air.

"Did that help?" She smiled back at him, in an almost-embarrassed sort of way.

"Yeah." His eyes were fixed on hers.

"You can do that on your own before your gig. It'll be like I'm there."

"Thanks," he said, "you've really helped me so much. Without you, I don't know where I would be right now. Honestly, it's like you've saved me."

He held her gaze, then smiled and looked down to his lap. "Sorry. Corny."

"It's fine. I'm glad to hear it," she said, and leaned back into the couch cushions. "You know I think that helped me too. I feel more chilled then I have in ages."

"Really?" He leaned back next to her, shifting slightly closer as he did.

"Yeah, being old is crap. I never thought there would be so much to worry about all the time."

He nudged her with his shoulder. "You're not that much older than me."

"I am."

"No way." He was staring at her again, then said, "We're basically the same age. We're both millennials, right?"

"Mmm."

"Plus—" he did it then, he actually did it, he leaned forward and touched her face "—you don't look old. You're beautiful."

"Oliver." Her voice was low with warning, her eyes on his hand.

"I know," he said, but didn't move it, "but you're just so pretty. It's hard. I've never met anyone like you."

His thumb brushed her cheek softly. She closed her eyes.

"Honestly, you make me feel amazing. It's like you're magic. Like you are this amazing, glowing person."

I was sure she'd jump up, pull away, something. But she didn't. She kept completely still, eyes still closed, and he leaned in and kissed her softly.

"I've been wanting to do that for so long."

Then she did move. Very slowly, her knees began to part. Oliver looked from her face down to her lap; even he was surprised, but he didn't waste the moment. He took his hand from her cheek and reached beneath her skirt. She lifted her hips and his hand slid into her underwear. He stared at her face as he moved his fingers, but it remained passive. He kept going, and eventually she couldn't keep her composure. Her face contorted, her mouth opened and a soft groan escaped her lips.

43

I wore black to the wedding. It felt appropriate.

It was taking place at a small winery on the Mornington Peninsula. I made the long drive leisurely, my heeled shoe resting on the accelerator, sunglasses on, the sea stretching out next to the road. It was a great day—Cass would be happy about that. The sun was warm on the bare skin of my forearm as I rested it on the rim of the open window. The sky was clear and blue. It was perfect.

It took a while to find a parking spot. There were cars everywhere on the estate, parked in clusters and zigzags on all available grass. Usually, this would have frustrated me, but not that day. I was too excited.

I know what you're going to be thinking, that I'd snapped a picture of Cass and Oliver. Oh no, it was so much better than that. On my phone I had an audio file; I just had to find the right time to play it. Would the sound of Cass's moans be a good accompaniment to her walk down the aisle? Or maybe even better, the first dance. After it was done, nerves gone, champagne popped, and they could just hold each other as man and wife. Would that be a good time for the sound of Cass's groan? Or for the *Wait, Oliver, no. Stop. You're my patient* that followed almost immediately afterward? I could imagine it perfectly, the laughs at first, the smiling faces of people sure it was a joke. Would he still have his arms around her when they got to, *I'm getting married this weekend! I'm so sorry, this is so wrong!*? Probably not. Would someone have found it and shut it off before it got to the part where Oliver started to cry?

I know what you'll probably ask me now. You'll want to know how I came to have that file on my phone. You'll ask me if I waited for the moment Cass left. If I walked right into the building, no one even asking if I was a student, or what I was doing there. You'll ask if my heart was beating when I went up to the receptionist as she was packing up her things and told her that there was a call waiting for her in the staff room. If I told her that it was her father, if I said that I didn't know what it was about, but that it was urgent.

You'll want to know if Cass's iPad was right there on the desk, whether it was easy to email myself the recording of her last session.

You might ask me a lot of things. But I won't answer those questions. I am here to confess, but not for that.

The venue was beautiful. A modern construction built entirely of large glass panels and honey-colored wood surrounded by acres of vineyards. They'd decorated everything in crisp white and glinting gold. There was a collection of round tables, all with starched tablecloths and centerpieces of red and pink flowers surrounding thick candles, set up on the grass under the branches of a huge old oak tree. Inside, were rows of chairs and, down the middle, an aisle.

People milled around outside. Couples sipped champagne. A group of men in tuxes stood together with cans of beer, laughing at Cass's fiancé, who was pricking himself as he tried to pin in his lapel flower.

A woman in pink emerged with an air of self-importance. It took me a moment to realize it was Cass's mother. Her hair was now snow-white.

"If you'd like to take your seats," she announced, "the service is about to begin."

The men downed their beers and clapped the groom on the back, and he made a pale-faced beeline to the front. I took a seat in the last row, and had a good look around. There was music playing from the built-in speakers in the walls, but I saw no DJ. This was good; it was exactly what I was hoping for. There must have been a stereo somewhere; I just had to find it. The room was large, but with so many people pushing in and bustling around, it was hard to see into every corner. My eyes glided across the long table against one wall, where platters of cheese and fruit and cold meats were being eyed by the guests close by. There was a long bar toward the back, where waiters in white bow ties were setting up lines of empty champagne glasses.

A woman and her husband plonked down next to me and began talking loudly.

"This is pretty, isn't it?"

"Glad it ain't me. I remember standing up waiting for you at ours. I was shitting bricks."

"Why do you always have to do that?"

I almost didn't notice Saanvi, but caught sight of her as she took her seat near the front with her date. I'd never seen her look so stunning. The dress she had on was made from a gray-blue silk; it looked almost like shimmering water. I couldn't see the front, but the back draped low, exposing the flawless skin of her back. I wanted to keep watching, see who her date was, see if there was anything I could do. But no. Saanvi had her turn. We were even now. I was here for Cass.

Then, the music changed. It turned to the low romantic tones of an acoustic guitar. I whipped my head around again, and saw it. There, behind the bar, was a man who I'd thought was one of the waiters. But on second glance his suit was slightly different, and he wasn't wearing the requisite bow tie. He was looking down at something in his hand, something I would bet anything was an iPod. The music grew louder and he looked up and gave someone out the door a thumbs-up.

For a moment I thought about trying to squeeze out, to push past the woman and her husband who were hemming me in, and trying to replace this song with my own soundtrack for the evening. But it was too late; everyone was already standing. It would have to wait until later. Until the first dance.

The guitar tune changed, becoming familiar. I almost cracked, really, almost erupted with laughter when I realized what it was. Will you be able to guess? No, it was too ridiculous, too ill chosen for anyone to think of. It was the Jeff Buckley version of that Leonard Cohen song, *Hallelujah*. A song that is so sad, so bitter and sour and tragic, it could actually make you cry if it wasn't so overused. But Cass was beaming, cheeks pink, a crown of flowers on her head, as she walked down toward the man she would very soon be getting an annulment from. I didn't laugh though. No. Because as everyone turned to look, I saw who it was that was standing next to Saanvi. He wasn't looking at Cass, but at me.

Saanvi's date, in a suit jacket but no tie, was Evan.

44

Yes, Evan. The Evan. My Evan. He and Saanvi were there together. As Cass walked, Saanvi leaned back and whispered something in his ear, her hand resting casually on his shoulder.

We must have sat down, I guess. I can't really remember the ceremony, all the words about true love and commitment, about sickness and health and death do us part didn't reach me. My head was spinning. My fists were clenched, knuckles white. Anger pounded hard in my ears. He'd probably told her all about me. They probably swapped stories, tit for tat. They probably whispered about it after they fucked, naked and sweating and limbs entangled, *No, we shouldn't laugh, poor pathetic Ava, so glad I'm not her, so glad I'm not with her.*

Then Cass and her new husband were kissing and people were clapping and standing again. I stared at the back of Evan's neck. The press of his flesh against his collar. And my anger threatened to turn to tears, but no, I wouldn't let it.

The happy couple sat down at the table and began looking through the paperwork, and the bow-tied men began filling the empty champagne glasses. I pushed past the woman and her dumb ugly husband and went toward them.

"To cheer the newlyweds," the waiter instructed.

"Sure." I downed the glass, the tiny bubbles itching my esophagus, put it back and took a fresh one.

I went to stand outside. The sun was low and glary. It

bounced off the bleached white tablecloths, right into my eyes. I looked at the dirt instead.

A chorus of voices sounded from inside, "To the bride and groom!"

I took a gulp myself, *to the bride and groom.* I couldn't forget why I was here. I would focus, do this, get this done, then I'd be free. It would be over, once and for all. Mel would always win—I knew that. Theodore, Saanvi and now Cass. That was enough. That could be the end of it. I could leave, go anywhere. Go where I would never see any of them, Evan included, ever again. I just had to get through tonight.

I could imagine Mel here now. Laughing at me. *What? You wanted to show them all how hot and rich you are now? As if anyone even cares enough to notice you. You're nothing, remember? It's pathetic.*

Two scuffed male dress shoes stepped in front of me.

"Ava?" And there he was, standing too close, touching my elbow, looking into my eyes.

"Hi," I said, showing him all my teeth as I smiled. "We met at the bar the other day, right? Nice to see you again."

"Don't."

"You should get back to your date. So nice that things are working out for you. Don't let her get too close when Cass throws the bouquet—you two might be next."

"Are you finished?"

"Yes."

I knocked his shoulder only lightly as I passed him.

For the next hour, people mingled. They sipped their drinks and stood in circles and said, *Didn't she look beautiful?* or, *It's such a perfect day,* or, *How early do you think I can get away with leaving?*

I mingled with Steve, the guy I mistook for a waiter, and eyed-off the mechanics of the stereo. Turned out, he was Cass's half brother on her dad's side. He was almost the exact same age as Cass, which I didn't ask questions about. He was also in charge of the music. Steve leaned on the bar and chatted to me about bands he liked and how you had to be tacky but still tasteful for a wedding—his job was all about finding the balance.

I could have done it then. I could have leaned forward and grinned at him and said I had a secret special song to play for Cass and was it at all possible to put it on. He would have agreed. But with the clatters from the kitchen and the rumble of conversation, it wouldn't have had a great effect. Most people probably would only barely have heard it.

I know what you will be thinking: Cass doesn't deserve this. She didn't smear shit on my face, true. And yes, she did apologize, I know. But do you think that is really enough? I don't. I believe that standing by and letting something happen makes you guilty. If you have the power to stop something, to change the course of what's going on so that someone doesn't bleed or cry or whatever it is, but you don't, then you are complicit. Just because you are too spineless to do anything, or it's too hard, or you are too comfortable, doesn't make you innocent. You might not agree with me, but that's what I believe. A drunken *whoops sorry* almost a decade later won't change that.

The candles on each table were lit now. The fairy lights in the oak tree glittered against the gray sky. Steve was going on about how the new Justin Bieber album was actually really good and that no one really understood Sia, when I noticed that people were hesitating before taking their seats. In front of each place was a rectangular white card with a name written with computerized calligraphy. I pushed away from the bar and approached my table. I didn't have to wander from place to place; I just knew that I'd be at the table where Evan and Saanvi were taking their seats. It would be just the sort of misguided thing Cass would do, to think I would be most happy with someone I knew, like we could just wash the past away.

I slid out my chair.

"Hi, Ava." Saanvi's smile was forced and polite. There was

nothing about the way she looked at me that hinted at resentment or anger. I couldn't help but let my eyes slide over to meet Evan's. He hadn't told her anything, that was clear.

"Hi." I took my seat.

"You look really pretty," she said.

"Didn't anyone tell you you're not meant to wear black at weddings?" Evan said. "It's bad luck."

"Evan!" Saanvi turned to him, truly annoyed. "That's so fucking rude."

"Yes, I've heard that," I said.

The woman sitting next to me turned and smiled. I'd barely noticed her when I'd approached. She was about my age, wearing a bright blue silk top and cigarette pants. I returned her smile stiffly.

"You don't remember me, do you?" she said.

"No." There was no point pretending. Although she did look sort of familiar.

"Fair enough, we weren't friends. Veronica Britson. I think we might have had one class together, maybe PE."

I nodded, I vaguely remembered that she'd been sort of ditzy but Cass said she did economics now.

"It's like a proper high school reunion at this table," I said.

"Yeah—" she shot me a wry smile "—hope they keep the booze flowing."

"The flowers are beautiful, aren't they?" Saanvi offered.

"The most brilliant flowers I've ever had the luxury of viewing," Evan replied. Saanvi shook her head at him.

Veronica grinned at Saanvi. "Is he new?"

"Very," Saanvi responded.

"You guys make a cute couple," I said. "Is it serious?"

Saanvi looked at me, at a loss for words. "We've only gone out once."

"I guess you'll have to wait and see. Although if you guys both did architecture you must have heaps in common."

I looked at Evan, but he wasn't biting. "We do."

"Hey, guys! How are you going?" Cass came up to the table. "Sorry I haven't even spoken to most of you yet. This day has been insane."

Up close, you could see that her makeup was caked on. It made her skin look heavy and thick.

"It's fine." Veronica smiled. "You look fucking amazing. Have you been having fun?"

"Yeah, it's been perfect. Really fantastic. Everything has been going perfectly."

"That's great," Saanvi said.

"Perfect," I said.

"Ava!" Cass said. "I'm so glad you could come. Honestly, having you here makes me feel so good."

That did it. I stood up.

"Thanks so much for inviting me—it means a lot."

I put my arms out, and she leaned in to hug me.

"Hope you are feeling alright about Oliver," I whispered into her ear.

She pulled away slowly. Her face was now white underneath her makeup. It made her look like she was wearing a flesh-colored mask on top of her real face.

"What?" she breathed.

"There you are." Cass's mother came to stand next to us. "Now I'm going to have to steal you away, Cassie. Auntie Julie says she hasn't even had a hello from you all day. Come on."

Cass let herself be led away.

"Are you alright?" I heard her mother say.

Back at the table, the night stretched on. Veronica's partner came to sit down and began a passionate conversation with Saanvi and Evan. Eventually the food arrived, showy and tepid, and I attempted to eat.

Cass was at her table now, sitting next to her husband and

not talking to anyone. I caught her eye and grinned at her, giving her a little wave.

"There's no way," Evan was saying. "It just won't happen."

"That's what they said about Brexit," Veronica said.

"I'm with Evan," Saanvi interjected, sure she was right as always. "I didn't think he would get this far, but there's no way he'll win. He was on reality television for God's sake. He's like a clichéd villain in a superhero movie. I mean, who votes for someone like him?"

"A lot of people," Veronica's partner, Jen, said. "We can't really understand, being so far away."

"I'm still allowed an opinion."

Cass caught my eye again. Next to her, her husband stood and dinged his spoon against his champagne glass. The microphone squeaked as he turned it on.

"Hi, everyone." His brow was shiny. "Cass and I just wanted to give a big thank-you to you all for coming today. I'm going to keep this short, then my best man, Shaun, is going to say a few words."

"Shauno! Shauno!" chanted men with beer cans.

"He swore nothing embarrassing, right, Shauno?"

"Yeah, mate, promise I won't mention that time in Thailand with the lady boy."

A mild laugh rippled around me.

I slid my chair back. This could be the time. Right now, while the groom was vowing love and singing Cass's praise. Veronica noticed my movement.

"Just running to the loo," I whispered.

I kept my head down as I walked back toward the building. No one noticed me; all eyes were on the groom.

"Cass is the ray of sunshine in my life," he was saying.

It was almost empty inside now. Just two of the men in bow ties stacking up the chairs and clearing them out of the room. I guess the dance floor was going to be in here later. There was no one behind the bar. No one near the stereo.

"I'd be so lost without her." He was starting to get choked up. I had to be quick.

I went around the bar. The stereo was right there, with a black cord attached to the iPod. I slipped my phone out of my handbag, unlocked it.

"What are you doing?"

I looked up. Evan was on the other side of the room, walking toward me.

"Nothing."

I found the track. Unplugging the iPod, I clicked the black cable into my phone instead.

"I know you've got some plan here." Evan leaned against the bar and stared at me. "I'm not going to stop you."

"Good."

"But I want you to just think, just for a second, if this is really what you want. Do you really think that whatever you're about to do, whatever your plan is to ruin this wedding, is it really going to make you feel any better?"

So I thought about it. Really thought hard.

"Yes," I said, and pressed Play.

Nothing happened. I turned the volume up. Nothing.

"Saanvi told me."

"What?" I looked up at him.

"She told me what happened to you back in high school. About the bullying, and what she and the others did to you at that party. I had to get her drunk, but she told me everything."

He knew. He knew it all. I stared at the stereo, turned some knobs, tried to work out why I wasn't hearing Oliver's voice come through the speakers.

"I've figured it out. I know that that guy with the roofies was Theodore. I know you've been stalking these people, that you've been trying to get payback."

My hands started shaking, fumbling on the knobs that I'd

already tried but was trying again. I'd never thought of it like that before. That word. *Stalking.* It sounded so nasty.

"Ava," he said, "look at me."

I couldn't. Instead, I looked up at the speakers, where the best man's voice should have been amplified. But it wasn't. Of course. I hadn't thought. I'd fucked it up again. They had switched to a different system for outside. Looking past Evan I could see it. The best man's mic cord snaking to a small PA desk and a large black speaker. It had been behind me when I was sitting at the table. I hadn't even noticed it. The sound was being broadcast through there.

"Come on," he said, "talk to me."

But I couldn't. I pulled the cord out from my phone and grabbed my bag. Then started to run. I had to get away from him. I didn't want to see his eyes. I didn't want to know how differently he'd be looking at me now, now that he knew what a freak I was. Now that he knew I was so pathetic, so nasty, such a psycho. He was right. I was a stalker. I could go to jail for what I'd been doing.

I ran out the back way, out to the vineyards. I'd let him go back, find Saanvi. They'd have a nice night, a nice life, and I'd slip away into the dark.

The lines of vineyards stretched endlessly in front of me, a grid fading slowly to black the farther I got away from the lights of the wedding. The scent of overripe fruit was cloying and sweet.

"Ava!"

He was chasing me now. I could hear him behind me. His breath, his footfalls. I whirled around.

"What?" I yelled. "What do you want?"

He reached me and leaned forward, hands on his knees, breathing heavily. "God, when did you get so quick?"

"Why are you here? Why are you following me?"

"Um, Auntie Ava," he puffed, looking up at me, "I don't think you're one to say anything when it comes to following people."

He was smiling, trying to joke.

"Go back to the party. I won't do anything. I'll go. Just leave me alone."

"Can't, I'm afraid."

"Why?"

"Well, obviously I'm in love with you," he said, and I was about to scream, yell at him for making fun of me again, right now of all times, but he straightened up, looked at me seriously.

"Really. I love you. I've tried to stop, but I can't help it."

I waited for his chin to quiver, for the laugh to come, for the *got you*. It didn't happen.

"I see you, Ava. I see what you are, what you've done, what's been done to you, and I still love you."

His face was solemn. I'd never seen it like that before. His skin was pale in this light, with the huge starry sky pressing down around him. He looked so vulnerable. I could barely stand it. He didn't mean it. There was no way. It wasn't possible for someone to love me, not when they knew the truth.

"No, you don't."

"I do. All that love and forever crap, I want that to be with you. I want you to be the person I argue with about grocery shopping. It's you I want to slowly live to resent. I want to get fat and bald and out of touch with you, Auntie Ava."

"You don't!" I yelled. "I'm all messed up. I'm a leech. A parasite, a disgusting psycho—can't you see? Anyway, I'd be so wrong for you. I don't even know if I like girls or guys."

"Who cares?" He shrugged one shoulder. "You don't have to get everything sorted out at once. We'll figure it out as we go along."

He meant it. He actually genuinely meant it, I could tell. This wasn't a joke or a trick. I could see it there in his eyes as he stared at me. Warmth. Love. I don't know how I'd missed it for so long. I couldn't deal with it. The way his eyes were fixed onto mine, imploring me to come to him, to touch him. I broke away, looked to the ground. My arms were still shaking in the heat.

"Look, I know love isn't going to save you from all this shit. But this hate you're harboring isn't either. You can't live just for hate—there's too much in the world already. I can't bear to see you keep on going like this."

He didn't understand. "I can't let them win."

"Win what? If this is a game, you're the only one playing."

I didn't reply.

"If you want me to fuck off, I will. I promise."

It was like time slowed down all around us. A slow inhale, a mild breeze brushing my hair across my cheek. If I told him to go, that would be it. He would be out of my life, for good this time. No going back. No second chances.

I watched my foot step forward, then the other, wobbling on the heel. They were sore, I noticed, blistered from the run. I reached out gently, touched his shoulder with my hand, felt the coarse material of his suit jacket with the pads of my fingers. His eyes were so unguarded, his face so vulnerable. He reached out and wrapped his arms around me. Folding me into his chest until the shakes began to stop. Music floated down the hill toward us. The first dance had started. It took me a moment to realize what it was. Ed Sheeran "Thinking Out Loud." I could feel his laugh jiggle through his body.

"So obvious," I murmured.

"So bloody tacky."

"There won't be a dry eye in the place," I said, but my own voice was cracking.

I pulled him closer, his belly pressed softly against mine, and we began to sway to the music. His arms were gentle; I could feel his breath on my bare shoulder, feel his heartbeat beating against my chest. The music rose and he took my hand and made me spin, I laughed, spinning around in a circle, then took his hand and let him spin. I could have stayed there forever, dancing with him to that cheesy song. Being alive in that moment and not having to think about what all this would mean, about what would come next.

Soon enough, the song ended and Evan took a step back, still holding one of my hands in his.

"What do you say we blow this joint?"

I nodded.

"I'm going to go tell Saanvi I'm leaving. She's going to think I'm an absolute dickhead, and she'll be right. Although, she'll really be glad. I think I've started to annoy her."

"You, annoying?"

"Yeah, crazy, right? I'll be back in one minute." He reached forward and kissed me lightly, but even that made my insides fizz with nerves. "Don't go anywhere."

He dropped my hand and walked back up toward the light.

I'm not going to say in that moment I felt better. That I felt fixed, whole again. I didn't. I was hollowed out, exposed. I was wearing my guts on the outside and it was terrifying. But, standing there in the gray light, in the vines stretching out all around me, there was something different niggling at me. It might have been hope.

It's hard for me to think about that moment, considering where I am now. What I've done since.

Part 8

CUNNING

2018

45

The door opens. I flinch, though it hasn't been loud or sudden. I've gotten used to this space. I've gotten comfortable.

A young man in a blue-and-white police uniform looks in on me. He smiles, and obediently I smile back.

"Sorry to have left you in here for so long," he says.

Is this you? The person to whom I am to give my confession? This man is not what I expected, not what I pictured at all.

"The detective got held up," he's saying now. So it isn't him. I still have time. The relief is exquisite. "It should only be another ten minutes or so."

"Great."

"Do you want anything, a water or cup of tea? Sorry, someone really should have asked you before?"

I shake my head on reflex, although my mouth is parched and my throat dry. I want to tell him that I have been asked before, but I can't bring myself to speak. He nods and closes the door, returning me to the solitude I've gotten used to.

Ten minutes. It's not long. I need to focus. My mind has been doing loops and cartwheels this whole time, jumping from topic to topic, time to time. I need to get my thoughts in order if I'm ever going to explain all this to someone else.

Mel. That's what you'll really want to ask me about. You might let me talk about the other stuff, sure. You might even write down some of the worst of it, pass it on, check if it's all valid. It is. I promise. But really, I'm sitting here in this small concrete room for one reason. Mel. It always comes back to Mel. Well, it always did for me anyway.

It started up again with an envelope. A cheap, white envelope with my name and address printed neatly on the front in blue ballpoint, nothing on the back.

I didn't open it for a few days; I'd been getting a lot more mail recently and it piled up quickly. Things had been very different since the wedding. I'd tried, really tried this time, to stop. I deleted all my social media accounts; I couldn't trust myself with them. Still, my fingers had itched to look, just look. I'd caught myself thinking of excuses to go to the suburb Cass lived in, or to walk past the bar on Brunswick Street, but I'd stopped myself. It was an obsession, an addiction, and I knew how easy it would be to slip.

I still sometimes dreamed of escape, thought about Paris or Léa, or being free, but I tried my best to swallow that away as well. To just be normal. To be what everyone expected of me. Everything we'd spoken about that night at Cass's wedding quickly became something that Evan and I didn't talk about. Maybe that was part of the problem.

Perhaps if I'd told him everything, whispered my truths within the comfort of bed and darkness and warm arms around me, then I wouldn't be here right now. But I can't blame anyone but myself. Apart from that—the unspoken "it" that existed between us—things with Evan were good. Unimaginably good.

So, like a rubber band around my wrist, every time I thought of them, I forced myself to focus on work. On building instead of destroying. When I woke up sweating, thinking of Cass's broken expression as she stared at me from across her wedding party, I called a property lawyer. When I thought of Saanvi, sitting alone as the power came on and off in her apartment, I booked in a meeting at the liquidation firm. You see, Aiden had been right. Lakeside Estate was a steal. The liquidators were gagging to get rid of it. Buying it was easy. It had taken longer, and cost more than I'd ever anticipated to fix the place. But bit by bit, I did. Those short courses I'd done in business and finance started to feel relevant. I employed builders, carpenters and electricians. The community center got a roof. One at a time, the houses were finished and people started moving in.

Things were getting better. I felt like I was going to be okay. That all of it was finally behind me.

46

It was less than a month ago, but it feels like longer. Evan pulled me closer, squeezed me into his bare skin and sleepy sweaty smell. The rain pattered against the window outside, the gray morning light trickled in.

"I wish we could just stay here, watch movies all day," he whispered. "People shouldn't have to go to work when it's raining."

"Yeah, or just stay in bed all day." I kissed his jawbone.

"I like that idea."

"Nope." I pushed myself up and shook my hair in his face. "I've got loads to do. And you're going to be late."

"You're hot when you're commanding."

I got out of bed, the cold air prickling my skin, and headed for the shower. As I stood under the stream of hot water, as it poured down my neck and warmed my skin, I imagine now that I thought of how serene I felt. How everything, finally, was in place. But I'm sure I didn't. I'm sure I was just running through lists in my head of what I had to get done that day, thinking how the rain would hold back construction and the best method to accommodate that.

After Evan left for work, I made myself a strong black coffee. I pulled on a thick woolen sweater and turned the heater on and sat at my kitchen table, which had become my desk. It was littered with bills and agreements and contracts. There was a pile of mail waiting to be answered, and a pile of mail that hadn't been opened. I'd sipped my coffee and stared at the Bureau of Meteorology website on my laptop, hoping, somehow that the rain it forecast would disappear as I stared. But the blue shapes kept sliding across the map. It was autumn after all, but I'd hoped we had another few weeks before the rain started. I was waiting on a truckload of asphalt to arrive for the limning of the lake. The original diggers hadn't gone deep enough, so instead of hitting clay they'd just left it with mud. Hiring a new crew of diggers was too expensive, so unless I wanted a swamp instead of a lake I had to line the basin with asphalt. If the asphalt was down now, the early rain would be filling the lake and saving me on a water pump. Instead it was just creating more mud. Sitting there, I imagined it. That, and the sodden orange leaves that were streaming into gutters and clogging down pipes.

I closed my laptop lid and looked over the papers for a distraction. I'd pulled the unopened letters toward me, thinking it would be the easiest job. I'd flicked through them, stacking the bills to go to my accountant, throwing the junk mail into a pile for recycling. Finally I reached a letter with handwriting on the front. My name and address printed neatly in blue ink. A stamp with a picture of a butterfly on it. I flipped it over; there was no return address. Tearing the envelope open I pulled out the last thing I expected: a black-and-white playbill.

Delusions of the Damned, it was called. The heading in bold font above an image of figures blurred in movement. I turned the page, and there she was. Mel. The black-and-white headshot, the same one they are using on the missing posters now, would you believe.

I sat at my table, beginning to sweat under my woolen sweater as the heater whirred hotter and hotter. Mel had sent it to me. I knew that. It was an invitation. An attempt to lure me back in, to make me keep playing.

The production was on all week at a small warehouse theater just outside the city. I'd never been there, but I knew the place; it was squashed between a student pub and a car park. Immediately, without any conscious decision, I started planning. I could tell Evan it was a work meeting that had run late, that I'd gotten stuck in rush hour traffic, decided to have dinner alone somewhere, bumped into an old friend. I could sit right at the back where she wouldn't notice me, I could see where she went afterward, where she was living now, if she was dating anyone. I hadn't even known she was back in town; she could have been back for weeks or months or even longer. I had no idea. All thoughts of asphalts and clogged drainpipes became irrelevant. I opened my laptop and typed in the address for Facebook and my stomach clenched and my fingers trembled. Then my phone rang.

"Hello?"

"Hey, it's me." It was Beatrice. "Are you home?"

"Yeah."

"Listen, do you mind looking after Layla for a few hours? I know you're crazy busy but I've got this insane headache and—"

"That's fine."

"Sure?"

"Yeah, it's no problem."

Within a few minutes, I opened my door for them. Bea looked tired and stressed. Layla was in her arms in her thick red coat. She was grabbing Bea's sweater tightly. The cold air was nice on my face; it smelled of damp leaves and wet grass.

"Thanks heaps." Bea pulled the wool out of Layla's hands and passed her over to me. "This one has a been a little terror this morning, haven't you, Layla?"

"Yes," Layla said sheepishly.

"I think I can handle her." I rearranged her weight on my

hip; she was almost getting too heavy to carry this way. "You alright?"

Bea rubbed her face. "I'm fine. I just need a long sleep I think."

"Take as long as you need."

Bea left and I arranged Layla on the rug and pillows that I kept for her visits. I rubbed her head. She had hair now, about four inches of it, and it was so fine and soft that I could never be close to her without touching it.

"Are you hungry?"

She shook her head and smiled sweetly at me. "Kitty?"

"Alright, but remember to be careful this time, okay?"

She nodded solemnly. Layla loved the brass cat that used to belong to Celia, the one that Mel had stolen. It was one of the few things of Celia's that Nancy had left behind, so I'd kept it, even though it made me think of Mel as well. The last time I had let Layla play with it, she'd swung it at the wall and left a dent. I took it from up off the shelf and put it on the floor in front of her.

"Thank you, Auntie Ava," she managed, then in a whisper to the statue, "Hello."

Auntie Ava. It made me think of Evan. I thought of that morning, and it was like I could still feel the warmth of his body pressed into mine, as I sat back at my computer. The familiar blue and white colors filled the screen and in black letters: *Would you like to reactivate your account?* It all seemed unnecessary and juvenile all of a sudden, when I had so much to lose. Not just that, but maybe I didn't need to know. Maybe I didn't even care. Somehow, Evan's belief that I could be my best self made me want to prove him right. I wanted to live up to his expectation. Be that real, solid, good person he saw in me. So I closed the window, ripped the playbill in half and put it with the rest of the recycling. That was it—I'd taken control, made the choice. I was done. It was over.

Of course, I was forgetting that Mel knew me too. Mel knew the other me, my shadow self, and that was just as real. I don't know, I still haven't decided, but maybe the bonds of trauma and darkness are stronger than those of love.

A week later she called me.

"Hey, bitch," she said, "how are you going? It's been forever!"

"Mel?" I don't know why I asked. I knew straightaway it was her. Her voice was an echo from a nightmare. One that had woken you up screaming, but you thought you'd forgotten.

"I can't believe you didn't come to my play," she went on. "It wasn't the same without you."

"What do you want?" I tried my best to sound exasperated, whereas really I desperately wanted to know the answer.

"Listen—" her tone changed, she sounded sincere, but maybe she'd just got better at acting "—I feel like you and I have unfinished business. We were such good friends, remember? I think you owe me a chance to explain."

47

The door opens once more. I'm ready for it this time, I don't startle. The moment feels stretched out, the sound of the door gliding ajar until it bangs softly onto the wall. I don't look up. I can feel you there, standing in the doorway, a shape blocking the light. I know you are looking straight at me, expecting my head to rise, for me to say hello, meet your eyes. But I can't. My muscles are quivering, my hands shaking. It's happening. Right now. Everything, my whole life, all that I've done and that has been done to me, has led me to this moment.

The light changes as the shadow shifts, the door swings back across and clicks shut. Then I hear something I was never expecting. The clack of women's shoes as you walk toward the table. So, you are a woman. I wouldn't have thought it, but now it makes sense. It's perfect.

"Sorry it's taken me so long," you say. "I thought you'd have just left to be honest, but thanks for sticking around."

Your voice is calm and even. It's firm, but not unkind. Self-assured. You'd have to be in order to be a detective, I guess. You'd have to be more than ready to deal with any bullshit thrown at you. I want to look up at you. I'm desperate to see your face. But I can't. The quivering has taken over now. Even my kneecaps seem to shuddering. I thought I'd be confident; I thought this would feel good somehow, to get it all off my chest. It doesn't feel good. I'm terrified.

Your shoes come into my field of vision. They are black leather, practical, but still with a square of heel. The chair across from me slides out, the metal squealing against the cement floor. You sit down on it, and pull it back in under the table. I look across the desk. You have a notepad in your hand, which you open to an empty page. You unclick the lid of your pen and push it onto the end. Your fingernails are short and pink, unpainted. They are clipped sensibly short but not bitten.

"So, the desk sergeant said you had some information for me. About the Melissa Moore case."

I understand then. Your dismissive tone, why I've been waiting so long. The relief pours through me, relieving the quivers, making me want to laugh. Giggle inappropriately like that stupid teenage girl I once was. It's so obvious now. You don't realize I'm here to confess. You think I'm another one of those bored losers who want a piece of the glamour. You think I don't have anything important to say, that I'm just wasting your time.

"So, what did you want to tell me?"

Your tone is becoming irritated. You want me to look at you, that's clear. You are flicking the pen against the pad. I've been staring at your hands too long; you think I'm acting strangely. But I can't look up. If I see your face, meet your eye, I don't know if I'll be able to do it. The urge to laugh is dead now. Knowing that you don't know what I am makes it feel even harder, somehow. I don't know where to start. After all this thinking, it's all gotten muddled up. I'm starting to sweat. I take my jacket off, biding time. The air feels cold against my wet underarms.

There's a squeak. You've leaned back in your chair; you're getting impatient. I have to do it. Now. Now is that time to seal my fate.

"It all started so long ago." My voice sounds hoarse. I swallow, wet my tongue, start again. "Mel and I were friends when we were… Well, no. Not friends exactly."

I stop. This is all coming out wrong. I had planned this whole thing, I can do it. I have to. I take a breath. Remember what I'd planned. I have to start at the beginning.

"It started in high school. It started in the change room—"

"Ava?"

There's familiarity in your voice. I wasn't expecting that. The surprise makes me look up. Finally, I see you. Your face is unknown to me, the short haircut, the lines on the forehead. But your eyes, I know your eyes. They are exactly as they were.

"Miranda?"

"Yeah. God, I should have recognized your name, made the connection. How are you?"

I don't answer, but it doesn't seem to matter. She continues, "What a blast from the past this whole case is turning out to be."

I try to laugh. It sounds strangled.

"I didn't know you were a cop now," I say, but then that's not quite true. I vaguely remember Cass mentioning it when we drank cocktails at that bar.

"Yeah, well I don't blame you." She smiles at me. "I was hardly the athletic type. God, it seems like a different lifetime, doesn't it? There can't be anything worse than being a fat girl in high school, fuck. I joined the army when I finished—they sorted me out fast."

"It's amazing how people change." The cliché slips from my mouth. This isn't the conversation we are meant to be having. It isn't the time for chitchat, for catch-up sessions and nostalgia. I'm trying to confess to a crime.

"Some people do, sure. Don't think Mel Moore did though, looking at her life now. Borrowed money from everyone she could you know—after all this time she was still a user. Still expected to get everything for nothing. Although I guess I shouldn't be repeating that."

She looks me up and down. "You look good you know, Ava. I'm glad we both managed to get out of that hellhole alive."

I shrug stiffly. "So you're the head of the investigation?"

"Nah. I'm just part of the team." She smiles warmly, like we are on the same side. "You know, I've imagined telling my teenage self about this, that I'm in the investigation to find the girl that made my life hell. It's the ultimate poetic justice, don't you think? God, I remember the crap she used to do to you as well. All that 'psycho' stuff—it was horrible."

If I let her keep going I'll never do it.

"I came here to tell you something," I force out, "about Mel. About what happened to her. About what I did."

We stare at each other, a little bit of the warmth drips from her face. It's replaced by weariness. A crinkle between her eyebrows. I open my mouth to continue, to finally spill it all, get it out, find some sort of release, but she cuts me off.

"Ava, stop." She leans forward, the table creaks, she talks low. "Let's be honest here. We all know, whatever did happen, that bitch got what she deserved."

It doesn't feel real to be leaving the police station, getting into my car, starting the ignition. The sky is deep and black now and the rain has stopped. The clock on my dashboard says 09:18. I've been in that station a very long time. I should feel free, the weight on my shoulders, the sickening clench of my stomach should be gone. I can't forget, Mel made me feel this way once before. I'd felt this guilt those days of the exams back at school, and it had only made her laugh. Maybe, now, if she knew how I was feeling she'd only scoff, roll her eyes, sneer.

I take the long way home, through the suburbs. There is construction all around the city, roads being widened, a new train station being built, apartment complexes shooting up everywhere. Outside my car, lights flash past as I drive toward home. People watching television together in houses, drink-

ing glasses of wine in bars, rushing down aisles before the supermarket closes. I'm tempted to go past the café where Mel
and I met. It's not too far from here. But I don't. I can't. I force
myself to keep going straight.

She was late, of course. Even though it was her idea, even
though she'd been the one who'd practically begged me to
come. I'd waited for her at a sticky table in the corner, sipping
at my coffee and wishing I had ordered tea instead because the
caffeine had made my heart beat too fast. The place was busy;
there were people waiting out in the cold. I had just decided
that I'd leave when she walked through the door, a gust of
freezing cold wind blowing in with her.

She looked over at me and grinned. Still, after all this time,
she had that magical edge to her. That gleam. She came over,
pulled me to her and kissed each of my cheeks, like we were
still in Paris.

"Ava! It's so great to see you. Sorry I'm a bit late." She sat
down across from me. "God, you look so good. Exactly the
same as high school, you lucky thing. I'm getting wrinkles."

I knew what I was meant to say, but she was right. The
lines that went from her nose to the edges of her mouth were
deeper than before; the skin around her eyes looked fragile,
like scrunched-up tissue paper.

"I guess all that lurking in the shadows is good for your complexion," she said, and held my eyes for just a moment. Then,
"Anyway, let's order. I'm dying for a coffee."

She caught the attention of the waitress, who barely looked
at her as she jotted down her order.

I had planned this conversation in my head the whole way
there, but already it was swerving way off the script. I wasn't
there to keep playing, to try to mess with her life or to follow her home afterward. I really was done with all that. I was
there because I wanted to ask her why. Now it doesn't seem
important. It seems almost laughable in fact. But in that mo-

ment, I thought that if I had an answer, if I knew why all that time ago she'd suddenly turned on me so maliciously, then my whole life might make a bit more sense.

"Anyway…" She'd turned back to me from the waitress and grabbed both of my hands in hers. I'd forgotten how small and soft her fingers were. "You know what I've been doing. I want to know about you. Tell me everything, every little detail."

A car horn shrieks through the night. I jolt back to reality. I'm drifting into the other lane. I correct my steering and flash my lights in apology. The car speeds up next to me, the middle-aged man driving glares at me through the passenger window, shakes his head. I look back to the road, ignore him. I need to focus, get home.

I drive perfectly the rest of the way. Signaling well in advance, sticking religiously to the speed limits. Finally, I turn off the road toward the gates. I press the intercom and a voice crackles out of the speaker. There's someone there now; I've hired security. Maybe I shouldn't have. If I've learned anything in my life, it's that what is locked inside is far worse than the unknown. What is in the light is more dangerous than what is lurking in the dark.

My car climbs the hill. There's a few people awake. The woman who has moved in with a newborn baby has her light on. The teenage son who is living with his parents leans out of his window, smoking a cigarette. There's a flickering light, maybe a candle, showing the curtains of the bathroom window of the newlyweds' place.

Finally, at last, there is my driveway; there is the welcoming yellow porch light. I pull in, put the car into Park, turn off the ignition. I take a breath, then get out of the car, lock it and go up toward the front door. I feel movement, look up. The man across the road, the one who we'd joked had killed his family, is standing in his window looking at me. I know what he is remembering. He'd seen me last week. He'd seen my tearstained cheeks and muddy clothes. It was dark, way past midnight, and I'd thought everyone was asleep. I'd made it all the way back to my house when I'd heard the sound. He was right there, a plastic bag full of rubbish in his hand as he stood next to his bin. But he was staring at me. I'd scurried away. Now I put up a hand to wave at him. He closes his curtains.

Evan has left a lamp on for me next to the door. I put my coat on the hook, leave my bag in the corner and switch the lamp off.

Upstairs, he is curled up, asleep in bed. I take my clothes off, all of them. They stink of anxious, fearful sweat. I get under the covers and wrap myself around him, push my flesh against his, try to absorb his warmth.

"I'm meant to be big spoon," he croaks.

I nuzzle into his neck.

"Your meeting went late, everything okay?"

"Yeah," I say.

"Good." He resettles into the pillow and within moments his breath has become deep and even again.

48

I didn't think I'd be able to sleep. But I did. I slept like the dead.

I wake slowly; the sun has only just risen. Evan is a rock of weight next to me. I try not to think of her. This is over. I don't need to think of her anymore. But I can't help it. I can't help but think how it could have been so different.

Closing my eyes I try to return to unconsciousness, but it's too late. She is there, on the back of my eyelids, laughing with her head thrown back as I almost reverse into a parked car.

"God, how'd you get your license?"

"Did you ever get yours?"

"Nah."

"Then shut up. I'm a great driver."

"I can see that." She grinned at me, her dark hair fluffing up against the headrest. Despite everything, I couldn't help but smile back. I put the car in Drive and swerved out of the parking lot.

"How long a road trip is this going to be?" she asked.

"You've been there before."

"Oh yeah, that's right. It took ages. We'll need some tunes, then." She leaned over and began fiddling with the knob of the radio.

This was the last thing I had planned. I thought we'd have a very short and civil conversation over our coffee, then I would leave and never see her again. But she'd asked me question after question about the development and I'd ended up telling her all about it. I told her about what I hoped it could be, and how stressful I was finding it, how the mountain of work never seemed to stop. She said she wanted to see it. It was strange how quickly it felt normal to be around her again. How everything that had happened in the last ten years seemed to fade away and I felt like we were both just silly teenage girls again, like nothing really mattered and the day was long with possibility. For one strange floating hour, we were friends.

The radio whirred from hip-hop to pop but she kept on swapping it round.

"Don't you think music just sucks these days? I swear it's just the same old crap being regurgitated again and again."

"Alright, Grandma."

"Oh fuck off, Ava. You're the one who has become some kind of developer millionairess with your fancy car and handbag and shit. You look like you are trying to pretend you're forty."

"Millionairess, are you joking?"

"No way. It's crazy, you know, that you're already so successful that you've forgotten about little old me." She looked up at me from the radio with overexaggerated doe eyes.

I laughed at her again and turned onto the main road. She finally settled on a station and leans back.

"Oh here we go, this one's not so bad."

Miley Cyrus's new song echoes upstairs and I wake with a jolt. I've overslept. I'm alone and naked in our bed. Downstairs, Evan is singing along. I can hear the clang of him cooking, smell the scent of freshly percolated coffee drifting up the stairs.

I get up, shower, put on clean clothes. I go downstairs and wrap my arms around him from behind, kiss his neck.

"Morning."

"Good morning, yourself. You're in a good mood."

"Why wouldn't I be? A handsome man is making me breakfast on a Saturday morning."

He turns, pulls me to him. "It's nice to see you smiling. You've seemed a bit off lately, like there was something on your mind."

I shake my head, kiss him lightly on the lips. "Just work stuff. It's exciting to see it all coming together, but kind of stressful too. Just logistics. I feel better today because it's the last of it all."

"Glad to hear it," he says, turning back to the stove. "Finally we won't be lying when we say the name of this place."

"Yeah, exactly."

The houses, the convenience store, the community center. They were all more or less finished. Today the lake is finally being filled. We are going down there after breakfast with Bea, Aiden and Layla to watch the final finishing touch.

Sitting down to breakfast, I smile at Evan over my eggs. Miranda has given me absolution. This is my second chance.

After we've finished eating, I take Evan's hand and pull him upstairs. We make love, and it's as slow and tender as the first time. A new beginning. As we lie, naked and tangled together, him softly stroking my hair, there's a knock at the door.

"I'll get it," he says.

"You're not going to have another shower?"

"No way."

"That's gross, Evan."

"It's not. I like smelling of you," he says.

I have my second shower of the morning, and when I turn the water off, I hear crying. I dress quickly, rush downstairs.

It's Layla who is crying, her blotchy face pushed against Bea's neck. Evan is standing on a chair looking in the top cupboards. Even Aiden looks frazzled.

"What's happened?" I ask.

"Kitty!" Layla screams.

"She wants that ugly statue of Celia's, but I can't find it," Evan is saying. "Do you know where it is?"

Right where I am standing, one week ago, Mel was in this kitchen. I can see her now, holding the bronze cat in her hands. "Oh my God! I remember this! I can't believe you've held on to it all this time. That's wild."

I didn't want her to be there; I was wishing I hadn't invited her. Wishing she would leave. She'd gotten bored in the car, irritable. As we drove up the hill, she'd looked around with her face all puckered up.

"God, how depressing that you've been living here this whole time. I can't even imagine it."

We'd parked outside my house and I'd hesitated in the driver's seat, trying to think of something to say, feeling stupid and embarrassed by everything I'd talked so excitedly about an hour before.

She pulled open her door and stepped out. I followed, hating her and hating myself even more.

"If you own this whole place why'd you choose such an ugly house? Although I guess they're all sort of ugly. I guess I imagined you'd have built some really swanky place since you're so rich and successful now."

"I'm not rich." I'd already told her that in the car; I didn't know why she kept saying it. I pulled out my keys. "I'll be barely striking even until all the houses are filled."

She walked in ahead of me once the door was open. Surveying everything, giving her opinion. I was barely listening, just wishing I'd never let her back in, feeling myself sinking, feeling the pressure on my skull grow and grow. The toxic taste I'd long forgotten was clawing back into my throat.

By the time she was standing in the kitchen, Celia's brass cat in her hand, I knew it was time for her to leave. But I hadn't had the guts to ask her yet, and I had to do it. Otherwise it would all have been for nothing.

"Actually," I told her, reaching out for the statue, "I knew the woman who owned it. She was—"

"God, that night was so dumb, wasn't it? Breaking into people's houses. I would never do that now."

I took a step toward her and pulled the statue out of her hands. I didn't want her touching it.

"Okay." She looked at me as if I'd done something strange. "Don't worry, I wasn't going to try to steal it again."

It was now or never, I'd told myself. If I was ever going to get an answer, I had to ask the question.

"I want to ask you something."

"Shoot," she said, leaning back on the bench. Cold light beamed through the kitchen window. I wished we could be having this conversation in the dark.

"Why?" It had come out sounding choked. "I know it shouldn't matter anymore, but I have to know. Why did you do it, that night at your party. What did I do wrong?"

I braced myself, waiting for it. Waiting for the confession of an abusive home life, or of shame over Mr. Bitto, for passing on humiliation, or acting out because of an eating disorder, losing control of herself. I braced myself for tears, and pleas for forgiveness, for trying to work out what was true and what were lies, for what was just Mel acting again. But none of that came. She just shrugged.

"Why not? It was pretty funny."

I didn't say anything. I couldn't even look at her. But I could still hear her voice, that mocking voice that had followed me around for so long.

"God, look at your face. I did it because it was funny, and you were so pathetic and obsessed with me. I wanted to see what you'd do. Never thought you'd go full psycho—that was a surprise."

"I think you should leave now."

"Fuck, Ava. You want me to go so you can have a little cry? Oh no, the mean girls put poo-poo on my face ten years ago. God, you are still such a loser, it's embarrassing."

Then there was a loud crack, and the statue was wet in my hand and Mel was looking up at me from the floor. She was looking at me the way I must have looked at the intruder who'd stood above my bed all those years ago, when I was still just a normal seventeen-year-old girl.

It took a moment for the blood to start oozing down her face.

"Ava?" Bea asks. "You alright?"

I blink, look over at her and Layla, refocus.

"Sorry." I kneel on the tiles next to her. "I thought it was getting too dangerous having her play with something so heavy. You could probably really hurt yourself with that thing."

I stroke Layla's hair. "I'm going to buy my very own real-life cat, okay? And you get to help me pick. How does that sound?"

"We are?" asks Evan, stepping down from the chair.

"Why not? It'd be nice to have a bit more life around here."

Layla looks between Bea and me, then grins. "Today?"

"How about tomorrow?"

"You don't have to do that," Aiden says, wiping his daughter's cheeks dry with his fingers. She sniffs and smiles up at him.

"Nah, it's okay. I want to. Anyway, we should probably head down."

We pull on our coats and begin walking down the hill. Evan and Aiden walk together, pushing Layla along in her stroller. Bea and I dawdle behind them.

"You alright?" she asks. "You went really pale in the kitchen. I thought you might be about to faint."

"No, it's fine. Just felt a little weird for a second."

"God, you're not pregnant, are you?"

"No way."

"Hey, there was another news report on that Mel girl last

night," Bea says, and I'm not sure if I imagine it but her voice sounds different. Strained, as though she's practiced this before in her head. She's never mentioned the disappearance before.

"Any news?"

"No new leads, they said. Have you seen her at all since high school finished?"

"Nah," I say.

She doesn't speak for a moment. We walk in silence. I look up at the sky; there are rain clouds forming. I hope they'll hold off for another hour, just until this is done.

"You know, I can see your house pretty well from my drawing desk," she says.

I stop moving. But no. It's not possible.

"You're watching all my visitors coming and going?"

"Coming," she says, not looking me in the eye, "not always going."

I force out a laugh. "Are you worried I'm cheating on Evan? Having good-looking brunettes arrive, and then creep out the back way?"

She doesn't laugh, but her shoulders aren't as braced as before. We keep walking down to the lake in silence.

We stand together to watch, collars pulled up against the biting wind, hands squeezed into pockets or underarms, as the workman turns on the pump. We watch the water erupt out of it, and pool in the asphalted basin. I stand where I was last week, when they put the asphalt down over the mud. I'd watched them, heart in mouth, waiting for a yell of shock that never came.

It takes a long time to begin to fill. Bea and Aiden take Layla home after ten minutes—she's getting cold. But Evan stands with me and watches the waterline rise. It's over. Finally, it's all finished.

Evan's fingers lace with mine. Still, somehow, they're warm.

"Should we go home?"

I nod.

Together we walk back up the hill. From now on, I will do everything with love. I will give my heart to Evan completely. I will be the perfect partner, the perfect sister, the perfect aunt. I will seem like the most normal woman alive, be exactly what people expect of me.

I can't help but turn, and look back down to the lake. At its gleaming surface, reflecting the silver sky. The man has turned the pump off. The water is beginning to still.

No one will find her now.

★ ★ ★ ★ ★

ACKNOWLEDGMENTS

Over the years, *The Spite Game* has had many titles: *Ava*, *Grey-fields*, *Lakeside Estate*, *Tough*. It has also taken many forms: a short film, a short story, a feature screenplay, a novella. This story was my white whale. It surfaced on long, dark bus rides, in early-morning showers, in the restless hours of sleeplessness. Finally, I can release it out into the world. So many people have helped me over the years to get to this point.

Ten years ago, it was a short story. I was twenty and had worked a casual job at a half-built gated community constructed in the middle of Australian bushland. At the time, I was infatuated with Australian Gothic and Bluebeard, and this seemed like the perfect setting for my own interpretation. The story was my final assignment at university and the first piece of writing that I was actually proud of.

Then it was a short film about a teenage girl toying with the idea of psychopathy. Thank you to Jemimah Widdicombe, Lara Gissing and Mathew Chuang as well as every festival that screened *Tough*.

Next it was a screenplay. I was twenty-five by then and sure the Australian film industry would be an easy nut to crack. Huge thanks to Joe Osborn for his intelligent insight and to Ian Pringle for her continuous support.

So what do you do when you write a screenplay and have absolutely no idea what to do with it? Thank you eternally to my sister, Amy, my mum, Liz, and my dad, Ruurd, for not only suggesting trying my hand as an author but also being my first readers and my first editors. You gave me the confidence to believe it was even possible to be an author. Thanks for listening to me obsess over this story for so long.

Turns out, thirty thousand words is not technically a novel, but writing the novella of this story cut my teeth as an author. It gave me the passion to start fresh and begin a new project about a missing girl and her replacement.

Thank you forever to MacKenzie Fraser Bub—literary agent, vibrant woman and friend. Thank you to my editor, Kerri Buckley, who really understood this work and helped it to be ten times better. Thank you to Nicole Brebner, Natika Palka and Sue Brockhoff for believing in me as a writer.

Although I had written this story many times, I knew the only approach to facing my white whale was to face the blank page. Thanks to a Varuna fellowship, I was able to finally get this story out of my head right. Amid misty mountain walks and quiet time curled up next to the heater, *The Spite Game* poured out of me. Thank you so much to Carol Major, who helped me realize that sometimes the scariest things happen in the light. Thank you to brilliant writers Laura Elvery, Catherine Hainstock, Suzanne McCourt and Courtney Collins for all our fireplace chats on storytelling and Peeping Tinas.

Thank you so much to everyone who helped me with those final touches. To my writers group, Rebecca Miller, Claire Stone and Jemma van Loenen. To Phoebe, who, on a long dog walk, helped me remember the wonder and recklessness of traveling overseas alone for the first time. Thank you to Tegan, Isobel and Martina for reading early drafts. To Hans and Lucy Roleff for the German translation and to Genevieve for the French. Thanks to Edwina for letting me borrow your shower story.

Thank you to everyone who has ever bought a copy of one

of my books. You are the reason I get to have this job and I am forever grateful.

And of course, thank you to Ryan. For being there through all of it.